THE
MISSING

Shiloh Walker

B

BERKLEY SENSATION, NEW YORK

THE BERKLEY PUBLISHING GROUP
Published by the Penguin Group
Penguin Group (USA) Inc.
375 Hudson Street, New York, New York 10014, USA
Penguin Group (Canada), 90 Eglinton Avenue East, Suite 700, Toronto, Ontario M4P 2Y3, Canada
(a division of Pearson Penguin Canada Inc.)
Penguin Books Ltd., 80 Strand, London WC2R 0RL, England
Penguin Group Ireland, 25 St. Stephen's Green, Dublin 2, Ireland (a division of Penguin Books Ltd.)
Penguin Group (Australia), 250 Camberwell Road, Camberwell, Victoria 3124, Australia
(a division of Pearson Australia Group Pty. Ltd.)
Penguin Books India Pvt. Ltd., 11 Community Centre, Panchsheel Park, New Delhi—110 017, India
Penguin Group (NZ), 67 Apollo Drive, Rosedale, North Shore 0632, New Zealand
(a division of Pearson New Zealand Ltd.)
Penguin Books (South Africa) (Pty.) Ltd., 24 Sturdee Avenue, Rosebank, Johannesburg 2196,
South Africa

Penguin Books Ltd., Registered Offices: 80 Strand, London WC2R 0RL, England

This book is an original publication of The Berkley Publishing Group.

This is a work of fiction. Names, characters, places, and incidents either are the product of the author's imagination or are used fictitiously, and any resemblance to actual persons, living or dead, business establishments, events, or locales is entirely coincidental. The publisher does not have any control over and does not assume any responsibility for author or third-party websites or their content.

PRINTING HISTORY
Berkley Sensation trade paperback edition / November 2008

Library of Congress Cataloging-in-Publication Data

Walker, Shiloh.
  The missing / Shiloh Walker. —Berkley Sensation trade pbk. ed.
    p. cm.
  ISBN 978-0-425-22438-0
  1. Kidnapping—Fiction. 2. Women—Psychic ability—Fiction. I. Title.
PS3623. A35958M57 2008
813′.6—dc22   2008030845

PRINTED IN THE UNITED STATES OF AMERICA

10 9 8 7 6 5 4 3 2 1

To my husband and kids...always. I love you.

To my readers, with all my thanks.

And to Sherry-Sherry, it's not exactly blue.
Do you remember?

PART ONE

ONE

Summer 1992

"SHE'S a local."

Cullen Morgan glanced toward Kip Wallace. Kip—who in the hell wanted to be called Kip? Then he shifted his attention back to her. Damn. She was something else. He'd seen her from a distance over the past three days, and she looked every bit as perfect up close as she did from far off. Her skin gleamed a warm, mellow gold, but judging by the thick curls and the exotic slant of her eyes, Cullen had a feeling the glowing color didn't come from days spent on a beach slathering her skin with suntan oil. Although that was a picture.

She passed by him, and he smiled at her, but she never once looked in his direction. He continued to watch her as she walked down the beach. Her butt looked just about perfect in the cutoffs she wore. She wore a swimsuit, faded and serviceable, and Cullen decided that plain tank suit looked better on her than the bikinis he'd seen on more than half of the girls since he'd arrived at the Dunes.

The resort was nestled on a pristine stretch of white sand just a little west of the Florida-Alabama state line. Half of his friends were spending the summer in Cancun or in Europe, but Cullen's parents were on a "togetherness" kick. They wanted a nice family vacation, so for the next two months they were staying in a little condo on the beach.

Wasn't too bad. He had to do something with his parents two or three nights a week, and once a week his dad insisted he go fishing with him, but there were worse ways to spend the summer. Although if he didn't have to deal with guys like Kip, he'd enjoy it more. Cullen's parents had money, but it was a fairly recent thing. His dad was an accountant who'd made a couple of smart buys in the stock market, and he had a knack for turning ten dollars into a hundred. By the time Cullen was twelve, his parents had taken him out of public schools and sent him to private ones. Their summer vacations went from long weekends in Gatlinburg to month-long trips to England or an Alaskan cruise. Now his parents were talking about buying one of the condos going up along the beach.

"—to her first."

Kip nudged him in the side, distracting Cullen from his study of the girl's very nice ass. Scowling, Cullen glanced over at Kip. "What are you talking about?" Kip, with his perfectly cut blond hair, looked like he belonged on the beach. He looked like half of a whole, made to go with any one of the bleach blonde Barbies who strolled around. Cullen wished he'd go find one of the little Barbie dolls and leave him alone, so he could watch the babe in peace and quiet.

"I was asking you if you thought that I could get her phone number before you do."

Cullen laughed. "You're kidding, right?"

Kip grinned. "Hell, no. Come on. Who can get her number first? You or me? Loser has to rummage up a six-pack for the bonfire Friday."

Shaking his head, Cullen stood up and dusted the sand off the back of his swim trunks. "I don't bet on girls. My mom would kill me. And I'm not going to try scoring some beer, either. My dad would kill me."

Kip's sneer had Cullen itching to knock it off his tanned, perfect face. "You always worry about what your parents would think?"

"No more than you always wonder what your friends think," Cullen replied. He looked down the beach and wondered if he'd look like a loser if he went chasing her down the beach. But before he could make up his mind, he heard a familiar voice calling his name. Glancing back, he saw his dad standing on the boardwalk, tackle box and fishing reels in hand.

He looked back at the mystery girl, but she was nearly out of sight now. Shit.

* * *

TAIGE Branch could feel the weight of the boy's eyes drilling into her back. Normally, she paid about as much attention to the tourists as she paid to the sand that got in her shoes. Something that was everywhere, something that was annoying, but nothing she was going to think about beyond that.

In turn, they could be obnoxious, rude, or friendly as could be. None of those traits appealed to Taige. She didn't want friends, and she didn't want some rich frat boy trying to cop a feel. But if she had to take her choice, she'd take the frat boy. Some boy feeling her up was a lot easier to deal with than friendliness. She had very little experience with friends. Wandering eyes and hands, she'd been dealing with those since she was fourteen. She handled it now in the same manner she'd used then, a quick stomp on the foot, a knee to his balls, or a jab in the throat.

The bleach blond was the typical kind she'd dealt with before, a privileged little brat with loaded parents, the kind of jerk who thought he could have anything he wanted, including some hot and heavy action with a local girl. He'd made a few passes at her since he'd arrived on the beach with his parents two weeks earlier, and she'd done what she always did: ignore him.

But the guy on the left, the one she had felt staring at her, she hadn't quite been able to dismiss in the same way. She'd seen him around, out fishing with his dad a few times, in the wildlife refuge a few miles down the road, and in a couple of the oyster houses in town. This was the first time she'd seen him up close, though.

Taige had passed within a few feet of him, close enough to see the faint tan line on his shoulders and neck where he'd been wearing a tank top like the one he'd worn the other night while he was out fishing with his dad. Close enough to see that his hair wasn't black like she'd thought but a deep, rich brown. The sun had brought out some gold highlights, and she imagined if he was down here long enough, his hair would lighten even more.

And she'd been close enough to see his eyes.

His eyes were the most amazing color, nearly the same shade of turquoise as the Gulf. She loved that color. Taige could spend hours out on the water, staring at the ever-changing waves, and she had the unsettling feeling that she could spend hours staring into his eyes, too.

Those sorts of mushy feelings were the kind she was unfamiliar with. Warm, soft feelings had little place in Taige's life since her mom and dad had died, leaving her alone. Her uncle had taken her in, but Taige wished they hadn't been able to find Leon Carson. She would have ended up in foster care, because they hadn't been able to find any of her father's people. But it would have been better than where she had ended up.

Hell would have been better.

Hell . . .

Like an insidious whisper, Leon's voice echoed inside her head: *"You got the devil inside you, girl. You going to hell, and there's nothing you can do to change it."*

How many times had she heard him tell her that? Hundreds. Thousands. Almost every day, sometimes more, for the past eight years. Ever since the social worker had brought her to the church were Leon had been preparing his sermon for the coming Sunday. She'd left Taige alone with the man, and Taige had stared at him, into the gray eyes that looked so much like her own, like her mother's. He had pale blond hair like Taige's mama, and he had a beautiful voice. She had thought he sounded like an angel when he sang.

But he was no angel. And though he often walked around the house singing hymns in a rich baritone, his voice sounded more and more like a Hollywood monster than a minister from Gulf Shores, Alabama. He was as close to the devil as anything walking on the world, and Taige had the scars to prove it. Most of them were faint, and almost all of them were a couple of years old or more. The last time he had hit her had been nearly a year ago, and she had hit back. Then he'd slapped her with an open hand, knocking her to the floor, and when Taige had climbed to her feet, she had grabbed a dirty knife from the sink and brandished it at him.

"You're evil, just like your mama was evil. Just like your

daddy was evil—lying with that whore and making another demon child," Leon had said.

"Touch me ever again, and this demon child will send you straight to hell where you belong." And she had meant every last word. Apparently Leon figured it out, because he didn't ever touch her again. Days passed when they never even saw each other, although Taige wasn't stupid enough to think he had actually realized the error of his ways.

He'd go inside her room when she wasn't there. She could sense his presence and knew that he spent hours going through her things, as though he hoped to find some sort of proof that she was the demon he accused her of being. There wasn't much for him to find. Anything important, like the few pictures she had of her parents and her books, she'd long since started hiding outside of the small house. Those things she kept tucked away in the storeroom at Ernie's.

The little oyster house just outside of town was the closest thing to a home that Taige knew. She spent hours and hours there in the small office helping the owner with paperwork, reading, or listening to music. The cool air of the office was like a glimpse into paradise. Leon didn't believe in a lot of modern conveniences like air-conditioning.

It was little wonder she was more comfortable there than at her home. Ernie, whoever he was, had long since gone on to bigger and better things, and the little restaurant was owned by Rose Henderson and her son, Dante.

Rose had known Taige's mother and her father; Taige could spend hours just listening to the stories about her parents. Dante had taught her how to swim and how to fish. Taige worked for the two of them, either helping out in the kitchen, or with the paperwork, or on rare occasions in the dining room. Sometimes she went out with Dante on the boat, and they'd stay out on the water until they had caught enough fish to feed thousands. Or at least it seemed that way, but food didn't last long at Ernie's. It was one of the best places to eat in the area, but it was set back from the road and was unpretentious, at best. An honest person would probably call it a dive, and Taige had to admit the place wasn't much to look at.

But the food was good and fresh, the people were friendly, and Taige felt safe there. Safe and accepted, or about as accepted as she'd ever be.

By the time she got to Ernie's, the lunch crowd was thinning out. It was the middle of the week, and for the next couple of hours, there would be only a few stragglers here and there. Mostly quiet this time of day, unlike what happened around five o'clock, when the place would be hopping until midnight or later. She entered the kitchen, the familiar scents of seafood cooking filling the air. Rose stood by the stove, and if Taige was right, then Rose was making jambalaya.

She glanced back at Taige and smiled. "There you are, baby. Where you been?"

Taige shrugged. "What are you making over there, Rose?"

Rose grinned, her smile gleaming white against the darkness of her skin. "You know what I'm making. I can tell by the drool all over your chin."

"I'm not drooling." Yet. Her belly rumbled demandingly, and she dug a bowl out of the industrial dishwasher. Rose laughed and ladled out a heaping serving for Taige.

The first taste, spicy and savory, exploded on her tongue, and she didn't bother waiting for the food to cool as she quickly devoured half of it.

"You didn't sleep last night."

Rose's voice was quiet and devoid of emotion, but nonetheless, Taige heard the worry in it. She shrugged. "I slept a little."

"A little—how little? What did you get, maybe two hours?"

"Probably," Taige muttered. She shoveled another spoonful of food into her mouth, but she knew better than to think Rose would let it go at that.

"Those dreams again?"

Taige nodded haltingly.

"Was he there?"

He being her uncle. Leon Carson had been sleeping in his bed when Taige finally fell asleep, but when she woke up from the dream, he had been standing over her bed. "You had another one of those devil dreams," he'd said, shaking his head in that sad, mournful way of his, like she'd done something to let him down.

He always seemed to know when one of the dreams came. The dreams were just as hard to control as the visions that came to her during the day. Vision, prophecy, it didn't matter what she called them. They happened, and they had for as long as she could remember. Taige had been eight years old when she had the dream where her parents died—and they'd died that very night.

"Yeah. He was there."

"Did he . . . ?" Rose glanced around, knowing how much Taige hated anybody to know what her uncle did.

Taige shook her head. Nobody was standing close enough to hear. "No, Rose. He didn't do anything. He won't, either."

Rose shook her head. She had a scarf wrapped around her head, completely covering the wealth of dark hair. The scarf was white, and Taige knew that somehow, when Rose left, it would be as white then as it was now. Taige couldn't work in the kitchen without covering herself with stains. She didn't know how Rose managed it.

"You can't know that, girl. He done it before. He gets mad enough, he'll do it again."

"No. He won't." Because Taige knew he had believed her when she told him she'd kill him if he ever touched her. Leon was a lot of things, but he wasn't stupid. Self-preservation was high on his list of priorities. He couldn't do his preaching on Sunday, telling the damned that they must repent if they didn't want to burn in the lake of eternal fire, not if he was dead.

Taige looked down at her bowl, still half full. The food she had eaten weighed in her belly like lead, and she blew out a breath. She turned to dump the jambalaya and caught Rose looking at her with mournful eyes. "I'm sorry, girl," Rose murmured. "Come on, we don't need to talk about it if you don't want to."

Guilt churned in Taige's stomach as she looked into Rose's dark eyes. She hated making Rose feel bad, inadvertent as it was. "I know you worry. And I know it's because you love me."

Rose smiled and pressed her hand against Taige's cheek. "You look so much like your mama. You've got so much of her inside of you. Not just your gift, either." Her voice dropped. "It is a gift, Taige. You're going to do great things with your life. Just like your mama did. But you got your daddy's strength. You've had to, to live the life you have. Lord, but I wish he had some family left around here that you could have gone to. You would have been so much happier if you had family instead of that crazy uncle."

Taige covered Rose's hand with hers and smiled. "I got a family, Rose. I got you." It was nothing more than the truth. Taige had lost her parents, and the crazed bastard they put her with would have liked nothing more than to beat the "evil" out of her, but Taige hadn't been alone because of Rose and because of her son. Rose and Dante were the family that Taige hadn't thought she would have.

Rose had been there when Taige got her period. Rose had been there when Taige came face-to-face with bigots, and Rose had been there as the years passed and Taige's weird gift became stronger and stronger. *It's a hard road you've got to walk, Taige, half-white, half-black, and different from just about everybody else. You're different in ways most people couldn't understand, because you got the sight.*

But you're strong. You can do it. And I'll always be here, Rose had murmured to her, time and time again. True to her word, Rose always had been there, and Taige loved her dearly.

"Oh, baby." Rose pulled Taige in close, holding her tight. Taige breathed in the familiar scents of lotion and spice and fought the burn of tears in her eyes. She pulled back when Rose's arms loosened and opened her mouth to say something.

But the skin on her spine rippled. A cold chill danced along her flesh.

Rose recognized the look, although Taige knew that her friend didn't truly understand. As much as Rose meant to her, Taige wished desperately for her mother, for somebody who would understand the odd, disturbing dreams, the random visions, and the pressing need to act. It was imperative, as important to her as breathing, and although she might well pay dearly, she had to act.

"I've got to go," Taige said unnecessarily.

She pushed the bowl into Rose's hands and was out the door before Rose even managed to call out, "Be careful."

The door banged shut behind her, and Rose lifted her gaze to the heavens. "Lord, take care of that girl."

* * *

THE currents were strong.

Cullen rode the boogie board through the waves, a grin splitting his face and exhilaration pulsing through him. He wasn't ready to hit some of the big waves, but he could see why it would be such a thrill.

There was nothing like the feel of it, the water moving around him, under him, almost like it was alive. He hit the shallows and immediately turned to head back out when something caught his attention: the little yellow inflatable boat, bobbing up and down in the waves, drifting farther and farther from the shore. A couple had brought it down with them, and they'd let their little boy play in it on the sand, and for a while, the dad had pulled the boy around in it in the shallow water.

The sun shone down brightly, sparkling on the water, and Cullen squinted against the light as he stared at the yellow boat. The boy was there, and even at a distance, Cullen could see the stark terror on his face as the kid realized how far he was from the shore.

"Hey!"

He saw the boy about the same time the kid's parents did, and all three of them hit the water. But the waves were rough and getting rougher. Cullen swam toward the raft, outdistancing the parents. He was a strong swimmer, but he was used to the pool at the Y, not the rough waters of the Gulf.

In slow motion, he saw it as the wave came up, smacking the little boat the same way a kid might play with a tub toy. There was a high-pitched scream that ended abruptly as the boy went over into the water. Cullen was still too far away. He swam faster, pushing his body harder than he'd ever done before. He ducked under, trying to see the boy. Salt water stung his eyes. Nothing. He was aware that more people had joined him. He kept looking and looking until his lungs burned and he had to surface. He dove again and again. But the third time he came up, he knew he'd been too late. Others continued to dive, and he heard their voices, heard somebody crying, and knew it was the boy's mom.

"Shit." Cullen didn't know who had said it, but he echoed it wholeheartedly. His heart felt like a leaden weight, and he took a deep breath, prepared to go under again.

She burst out of the water looking like a mermaid. Water dripped from her hair, her nose, her cheeks—and from the boy she held in her arms. The mermaid legend seemed even more apt as she looped an arm around the boy's upper body and started to swim for shore.

*   *   *

Too many people, Taige thought. She didn't fight the water, just let it carry her and the still child closer and closer to shore until she could put her feet down and walk through the sand. It dragged at her, slowing her down, when she knew she had to hurry.

Hurry.

Hurry.

A distant echo in her mind, Taige knew the kid was fading away, that she almost hadn't made it. Still might not. She dropped to the ground, the boy hitting the sand harder than she'd meant. Immediately, she bent over him and pinched his nose. She blew into his mouth. Stopped, checked to see if he was breathing. His pulse was there, but it was faint, and she administered rescue breathing again.

Behind her, she heard somebody crying, felt somebody trying to grab her. "My baby, let me have my baby!"

Taige turned her head and snarled. "Can I get him breathing first?" Then she focused back on the boy. Focused on the feel of him—not physical, but him, the ethereal part of a person that remained long after death. The soul. All she had to do was keep the soul inside him until she could make him breathe on his own.

She felt it, that tiny spark, as his breathing kicked in, and she shoved him onto his side and stroked his back as he vomited up salt water.

He was crying and choking by the time he was done, but he was breathing. He was going to be fine. Taige whispered a prayer of thanks, and then she stood.

If she could just get out of sight before she collapsed, she'd be okay.

* * *

As the boy wrapped his arms around his mom's neck, crying and whimpering, everybody around them breathed out one huge, collective sigh of relief. Cullen turned to look for her, the girl who had saved the boy's life.

"Miss, there is no way . . ." The father turned to look for her about the same time that Cullen did.

But she was already gone. Down the beach, where the land curved inward, he could see her, walking with long, fast strides. Quietly, Cullen separated himself from the mass of people and started jogging down the beach. His legs felt damned heavy, and the fine, sugary sand seemed to turn into quicksand, pulling at his exhausted legs, but he kept going.

There was no way he wasn't going to talk to her this time, not after that.

He hadn't even realized she had been on the beach, and he had been looking. How could he not have noticed her? He'd been waiting for another glimpse of her since he'd seen her that first time three days earlier. He wasn't going to sit around hoping for another one.

He caught up with her just as she reached the boardwalk. "Hey, wait a minute."

She barely paused. "Go away."

She didn't even look at him, just kept walking along the sand with her head down and her arms crossed over her belly. She looked sort of sick, her dusky skin a little gray. She was walking fast, but now that he was close to her, he could see she was wobbling a little. She stumbled, and he reached out to try to steady her, but she jerked away. She tossed her wet hair back from her face and gave him a hard, cold glare. "I said go away," she snarled again.

Didn't seem possible, but her voice was every bit as sexy as the rest of her, even as hot and angry as it was. He stared into her eyes, hardly even aware of what she had said. Gray eyes, a pale, almost surreal silvery gray that glowed against the soft caramel color of her skin. Her lashes were long, thick, and curly.

Cullen was still staring at her, almost dumbfounded, when she snorted. "You got a hearing problem? I told you to go away." She shook her head, mumbled under her breath, and turned on her heel, stalking away from him.

"Hey, I just wanted . . ." His voice trailed off. Wanted to

what? Tell her that he had dreamed about her? Tell her that what she had just done was amazing? Ask her out? All of the above? But she just kept walking on, her body stiff.

Over her shoulder she called out, "Yeah, I know what you want."

He heard the innuendo in her voice as clear as day, and oddly, it stung. Yeah, that sort of thing had crossed his mind. How could he look at a girl who looked like that and not think about it?

But it wasn't just that. There was more to it.

Considering the way she kept moving away from him, like she couldn't stand to be on the same stretch of beach, Cullen suspected he wasn't going to get a chance to find out what it was.

* * *

"You damned that boy."

Wearily, Taige opened her eyes and saw her uncle standing in the doorway. "I saved him from drowning, Uncle."

"God wanted him, and you stole that child from His arms with that evil inside of you."

Baldly, Taige responded, "If God wanted the boy, then He would have taken the boy." She wanted to roll over and go to sleep. Her entire body ached, and she couldn't get warm. It was like that anytime she did this, reaching out to another person using her mind. It was a hell of a lot easier to pull a drowning person to shore than it was to pull a fading soul back into life, and saving a drowning person wasn't all that easy.

If you'd been faster, he wouldn't have been so far gone, part of her whispered. *That boy almost died because of you.*

"That boy was meant to die! He cheated death, and now all his life, evil will follow him. Just like it follows you."

Taige smirked. "Only thing following me is you, Uncle. Does that mean you're evil?"

Leon Carson, unlike most of the locals, was pale as death. He spent his days inside his office or inside the little ramshackle church off of Highway 20. He rarely went outside, and it showed in his pale, almost pasty skin. Now that pale skin flushed an angry red. "Evil. You insult the Almighty when you insult one of His servants."

"I insulted you, Uncle. Not one of God's followers." Knowing he wasn't going to leave her alone anytime soon, Taige forced her aching body upright. She still wore the tank suit and shorts she'd had on earlier, and the shorts had dried stiff and felt scratchy on her body. Her teeth felt all fuzzy, and she had a feeling she stank to high heaven. She wanted a shower, but she wasn't taking one here.

When her uncle was in one of these moods, the only safe place to be was far, far away.

She pushed her aching, stiff body out of bed and slid her feet into a worn pair of tennis shoes. Leon continued to rant at her, punching at the air with his fists, threatening her with fire and brimstone. He took up most of the doorway, and rather than risk brushing past him, she opened the window over her bed. She heard him moving closer, and she shot him a warning look.

He fell silent, and she smirked, knowing that he was remembering her promise. "Someday you will have to pay for all your sins, girl," he whispered. He shook his head and even managed to give her a mournful look, as though the thought hurt him.

"At least I know my list of sins will be shorter than yours, Uncle dear," Taige muttered as she ducked out of the window. It was a good drop. Like most of the houses this close to the water, Leon's house was set on stilts. The ground was probably a good twenty feet down, and she hit hard, the jolt rattling her entire body. Still, it was better than staying in that house one more second.

Behind her, she heard Leon railing on about the sins of being a demon child. Tuning him out, she headed off in the direction of Rose's. It was a good three miles on foot. If Taige hadn't left her bike at the beach, she could have made it in less than thirty minutes. But on foot, it was probably going to take a good hour. At least she was away from Leon. Her legs were heavy and leaden. Each step felt like she was slogging away through mud instead of walking along the roadside.

When the headlights splashed on the road beside her, Taige felt a chill dance up her spine. The car went on by at a snail's pace, and Taige refused to look toward the driver or the passenger. It kept on down the road, and Taige started to run. Adrenaline burned away some of the exhaustion, and she fell into a quick, easy pace. She saw a car come around the curve, and she knew it was the same car. As it started toward her, she darted off the road into the grass and ran through, heading for the Paradise Dunes, one of the privately owned resorts. The lights shone brightly, but it was a good half mile away, and behind her, she heard a couple of car doors slam, followed by an obnoxious male laugh.

One quick glimpse into their minds told her they were drunk, and as one of them called to the other, she recognized the voice and the name: Joey Rosenberg and Lee. She couldn't remember Lee's last name, but she knew them. They were trouble.

Worse, they were fast. Taige still felt half-dead, and she wasn't moving very fast at all. She put on an extra burst of speed just as one of them tried to grab her. She felt the rush of air on her neck and heard him swear as he missed.

Just a little closer. The resort probably had a security guard, and he would be along the entrance road just ahead. If she could just—Joey tackled her, and Taige's shriek was muffled against the grass. He shoved a knee into her back and fisted a hand in her hair, keeping her pinned.

Oh, no. This is not going to happen—

Rage and fear mixed inside her as he struggled to pull her cutoffs away. Taige hissed and tried to flip over. "Grab her, Lee," Joey panted. "Strong little bitch."

Just as she started to get some leverage, Lee grabbed her wrists and jerked her flat. She felt Joey's hands, sweaty and slick, as he managed to jerk her shorts down. He used his weight to pin her legs, his knees digging into her thighs while he fumbled with his own shorts.

Nonononono! Taige could hear the scream building in her head. Building in her throat. Rage burned red inside her, chasing away the fear, and it was like she had taken a step outside of her body. She could see the ugly, violent scene unfolding like she was watching some movie playing out before her, instead of having it happen. She could hear her harsh, strangled breaths; she could see how Lee knelt in front of her, holding her wrists in one of his hands and using the other to keep her face pressed into the sandy earth. She gagged on it. She could feel the grit and the sand in her mouth as clearly as she could feel Joey's hungry, excited pants as he bent back over her. She could see his bony white butt, too, as he bent low and fought to spread her thighs, struggling with her swimsuit.

Everything inside of her stilled. Everything stopped and then slowly, like some slumbering monster, she felt it wake inside her: something powerful and potent surging, and life resumed its normal pace. But she didn't feel Joey on top of her anymore. He was no longer trying to pry her thighs apart, and he was no longer laughing. Instead, he toppled off of her, his hands digging at his throat.

She could feel his throat, almost like she had her hands wrapped around it, and she felt his hands like he was trying to claw her away. Except they were no longer touching. The only hands on hers were Lee's. Lee was too drunk to realize something was wrong. All he knew was that she was there half-naked, and he was horny. He pounced on her as Taige shoved up onto her hands and knees, choking on the sand and half-numb with shock. Confused, numb, and terrified, she felt that power in her. It was almost like somebody else had control, and that somebody else was trying to choke the life from Joey.

Tighter and tighter, the power wrapped itself around Joey's throat. His pulse started to stutter, and his eyes rolled back in his head.

Lee pressed his wet mouth to her shoulder, and the power snapped, rushing back to her, ready to seek out another target. Off to the side, Joey sucked air, and he snarled, "Little whore!" Something hit her in the head, and pain bloomed red like a flower inside her skull. Everything grayed, and Taige sagged to the ground.

"Get the fuck off, Lee. First time's mine." Once more, life took on that surreal quality. She could hear them speaking, feel hands shoving and pulling at her, but she couldn't move to fight them off, couldn't even find the energy to care.

They flipped her over. Hot hands touched her breasts, pinched and squeezed. A heavy weight crushed into her again, pressing her into the ground. She could feel them jerking at her swimsuit, hear them swearing.

She groaned and tried to lift her arms, tried to shove them

away. Joey pulled back his hand and punched her, hard and fast. "Stupid cunt," he muttered. "Shut up and be still."

At that point, Taige didn't have much choice. Little black dots swarmed in on her, and as she tripped into the darkness, she was even a little happy he'd hit her. She didn't want to be awake when they—

The weight pressing her into the ground disappeared. Just suddenly gone. Voices rose and fell. She heard something crack, then a scream, followed by a weird, whimpering grunt. Angry voices. She tried to sit up, tried to get to her feet and run. She rolled to her side, tried to push her weight up, but couldn't. Her body felt like leaden weights, and her legs felt watery. Try as she might, Taige just couldn't move.

She lay there, hardly able to breathe, as somebody came near. She flinched, and to her shock, she whimpered. Then hands closed around her arms, and she was still unable to move, although all she wanted to do was fight, kick, and scream.

But the hands just rolled her over, one arm sliding behind her shoulders, and then a gentle hand brushed her hair back. She heard a voice, deep and soothing, speaking to her. Taige forced her eyes to open. In the faint moonlight, she saw a face, vaguely familiar. His lips moved, forming words, but she didn't hear a word he said as the gray cloud swarming at the edges of her brain finally moved in, and everything went black.

* * *

WHEN she closed those strange, misty gray eyes, Cullen had one brief moment of panic. Terror, fury, and helplessness had him shaking as he tapped her cheek and tried to wake her up.

Her head lolled to the side, and she lay in his arms as limp as a dishrag. Her chest rose and fell with slow, shallow breaths, but he was still terrified. Even pressing his fingers to the strong, steady beat of her pulse didn't reassure him much. There was a little bit of blood trickling from her left nostril, and she had a thin layer of grit obscuring her features. He gently brushed away as much of the dust as he could. Under his fingers, her skin felt soft as silk and warm.

She had a pretty mouth. Very pretty. The kind of mouth that would make a guy's brain empty of all blood as it flowed south. The bastard who had been on top of her had fisted his hand in her hair, and now most of it had fallen free from the braid she'd confined it in.

A soft, weak moan fell from her lips, and the sound of it sent a fresh wave of fury hurtling through him. He shot a vicious look at the punk who was still lying on the ground, moaning and clutching his right leg. The drunk asshole had sobbed like a baby when Cullen took his knee out. The other guy had taken off running, and a few minutes later, Cullen heard an engine roar. As he picked the girl up, he glanced at the sobbing guy on the ground and said, "If you don't want me to do the left one, you'll shut the hell up."

Cullen was pretty sure that if Master Bruhns knew what he'd done and why, the man would understand. He'd been taking karate since he was eight. He'd competed in competitions at the national level, but this was the first real fight he'd ever been in.

First time out, and he'd taken somebody's knee out. Cullen hoped to hell he didn't ever have to do that again. The bone had made a sickening, wet crunching sound that even the boy's pitiful scream couldn't quite mask. If he wasn't so hot with fury, he thought it might have made him sick.

But he'd seen what those two were going to do, and if he needed to, he would have done a lot more than bust a kneecap.

The stink of booze had clung to both of them, and it reinforced what Cullen had figured out on his own, without all the assemblies at school and without the awkward, well-meaning talks from his parents. Alcohol screwed up the brain, especially if the brain's owner wasn't all that impressive to begin with. Give a couple of dumb jocks who thought they were God's gift some booze, and you could have a problem.

She moaned again, and the sound was louder. Gently, he tapped her cheek and said, "Hey. It's okay. You're safe."

The girl went from unconscious to wide awake in the space of one heartbeat. Her lashes lifted, and he found himself staring into the wide, misty depths of her eyes. Her pupils flared, and she tensed. If she could have retreated into the hard dirt at her back, she would have. Cullen eased back. "It's okay." He shifted to the side so she could see the kid lying on his back. He still clutched as his knee, and he wouldn't look at Cullen or the girl.

"He's not going to touch you," Cullen promised. He shot the bastard a dirty look and raised his voice so that he knew the kid heard him. "He touches you again, I'm going to rip his balls off."

Her voice was clear and steady when she responded, "Oh, I'm not going to wait to do that. I'm going to do it right now."

She rolled to her feet, moving with a liquid grace that reminded Cullen of the way she'd looked when she cut through the water earlier, saving that boy's life. *Still a mermaid,* he thought whimsically.

Cullen was perilously close to being a serious geek, and he knew it. He played basketball, took karate, and had even spent a couple years on the swim team at school, but still, he pushed real close to the line of geekdom. He loved to read. He loved to write. Since he was twelve years old, he'd been writing his own stories and, to the delight of his parents and his own self-conscious pride, he had even written two different short stories that had been published by a fantasy magazine.

His room had its share of typical teenaged kid stuff—video games, a computer, a ball that he'd caught when he went a game with his dad at Yankee Stadium—and bookshelves. Tons of books, most of them either fantasy, science fiction, or books on Greek and Roman mythology.

Mermaids hadn't ever been his favorite figures from mythology; he was more into the Amazons or Herculean myths. But this girl could definitely change his mind. She still reminded him of a mermaid, although she wasn't the kind who would lie around on a bed of rock while she combed her hair and used her voice to lure men to their deaths.

She'd be a fighter. If Neptune really existed, he would have had an army of mermaids serving under him, and they'd all look like this girl. Then Cullen shook himself out of that fantasy, tucking it away so he could remember it later—might be a story there.

* * *

It hurt to breathe. Taige stood there, shaking with rage and fear and confusion. She felt weak, and her head felt muffled, like it did after a particularly intense dream. But so much worse.

Something had happened. Taige wasn't sure what, but something had happened. Whatever weird ability let her see events before they happened was mutating. Going from a weird tool of sorts to a weapon.

Just frickin' great. She stood staring down at Joey, and she could feel it forming inside her head again. That odd awareness, almost like a physical presence. It wanted to hurt Joey, hurt him worse than he already was. Joey lay on his side, clutching his right knee and whimpering like a baby. He had a series of mottled bruises around his throat. It almost looked like fingerprints. But she hadn't actually touched him.

Yes, you did. She could remember the feel of his throat, but not under her hands. She'd touched him, somehow, and left those bruises on his neck, choking him as he tried to rape her.

Then the hottie had shown up and taken Joey's knee out. Joey didn't look like he knew who scared him more: Taige or the tourist. She crouched down beside him just long enough to punch him in the nose, a short, straight-armed jab. She heard bone crunch, heard Joey's scream, and she watched as blood fountained. "You ever touch me again, I'll cut your dick off. We clear?"

She didn't wait for an answer. Instead, she stood and looked at the other guy. He looked familiar, and she ran faces through her mind until she placed where she'd seen him. On the beach in front of the Dunes, and later. She just barely remembered it, but he had followed her away from the crowd at the beach after she'd pulled boy out of the water.

The white sands, the turquoise green waters, and the endless stretches of beach drew tourists all year around, but in the summer, Gulf Shores, Alabama, often had more tourists in residence than locals. She had seen this one a few times, and he had stood out in her mind because he was so damn cute.

Cute and decent. Decent enough to help out a girl he didn't know.

"Thank you." She wished she could think of something else to say, but the ache in her head was getting worse, and her belly was knotting. She had to get to Rose's and lie down before she fell down. She turned away, but she only made it a few feet before he was at her side.

"Where are you going? You need to call the cops."

Taige shook her head. *Oh, no. No cops.* She didn't even want to think about the trouble she'd get if they took her to the station and called her uncle. And they would, too. She was a minor out late, and she'd nearly been raped. If she looked half as rough as she felt, then she'd be lucky if they didn't try to cart her off to the hospital.

But she didn't need the attention from that on top of what she'd done earlier. No, absolutely no cops. "Sorry, but I'm not calling the cops."

"Are you nuts?" The question slipped out of him before he even seemed to realize what he'd said, but he didn't take it back. "You got any idea what they were going to do?"

She stopped and looked at him. Yes. She knew exactly. She probably knew better than he did. The ability that had let her save that boy earlier had also led her to girls who had been grabbed off the highway and raped until they bled. When she was twelve, it had led her to the partially decomposed corpse of a nine-year-old boy who'd seen his mother's boyfriend selling cocaine.

"Yeah, I know," she said, unable to curtail her sarcasm. "I figured it out when he was trying to rip my shorts off. But I'm not going to the cops. And I think he's probably going to think twice before he grabs another girl like that."

"They were going to rape you. They need to pay for it."

Taige grinned then. "Then go take care of it. I'll let you handle the bill. Hell, I'll even tell you where to find the other son of a bitch." She would, too, and the thought of what Sir Galahad might do was enough to have her grin widen. Then it faded. "But I'm not calling the cops. I need to go."

The ache in her head was getting worse, and Taige had a bad feeling she might puke. The thought of walking a good two miles still was enough to make her want to cry, and she hadn't cried in years.

He didn't want to let her leave. She knew he was frustrated. She could see it in his eyes. But Taige didn't bother trying to explain. She just turned away and started to walk.

One foot in front of the other. She could do this.

But ten steps later, she wasn't so sure. Everything started to spin kind of like she was stuck on a Tilt-A-Whirl, and she knew she wasn't going to stay upright. Just when she felt her knees start to buckle, a hand came around her arm. Automatically she shied away; Taige didn't like being touched, especially by people she didn't know. All the mental baggage waited just under the surface, and one touch was enough to open a bridge between their minds.

But there was nothing. Strange, too, because the frustration and anger she saw in his eyes should have surrounded her, stinging her skin like angry fire ants. Yet it was like staring into waters of the Gulf right after a storm; she could see the water, but she couldn't see beyond it.

It was—bliss. And she probably would have enjoyed it even more completely if her legs hadn't decided to give out at that moment. But they did give out. Fortunately, the hand on her arm kept her from falling to the ground. Instead, she tumbled forward against his chest. His other hand came up, and he murmured softly, "Hey, easy there."

He brushed his thumb over her cheek, scowling. "You still don't want me to call the police? Maybe I should drive you into town at least. There's a hospital around here somewhere, right?"

Oh, no. No hospitals. She wasn't doing no damn hospital. Taige shook her head and tried to pull away, but her legs were still wobbly, her head was still spinning, and Galahad was staring at her with dark, concerned eyes. He was wearing a faded button-down shirt with a wild Hawaiian print. It hung open over his chest, and Taige could feel the warmth of his skin and the slow, steady beat of his heart.

Her own heart skipped a beat, and the only thing she could think was *Damn*. She blinked and looked away as blood rushed to her cheeks. His hands tightened a little, and his voice sounded strange enough that she looked back up at him as he said, "Yeah, I'm taking you to the hospital."

He stared at her with dark eyes, worried eyes, his hands holding her close to keep her from falling, and Taige felt herself fall just a little bit in love. It took a few minutes for his words to work through the fog that had wrapped itself around her brain, and by that time, he'd managed to guide her halfway to the resort's parking lot. She stopped walking and jerked against his hand, even though she really wanted to keep contact with him. There was something very nice about being touched without having a flood of thoughts and images swamping her.

Still, if he kept touching her, he was going to get her into that car and take her into Foley to the fricking hospital. "I'm fine . . . Hey, what's your name?" Taige really wanted to know, because she had a feeling she was going to spend a lot of time daydreaming about him.

"Cullen. Yours?"

"It's Taige. Cullen, I appreciate the help, but I am fine. I just want to go to bed."

"I bet you do," he muttered, shaking his head. "Taige, you aren't fine. Where's the hospital?" He tugged on her arm again, and Taige didn't feel steady enough to fight him, so she fell into step beside him. He led her to a rusted-out, patched-up vintage Mustang, and Taige had to smile.

It was parked in the middle of Porsches, BMWs, and Volvos, all of them gleaming and polished and perfect. His car looked like a mutt sitting in the middle of a pedigree dog show. "Nice car," she murmured.

He slid her a narrow look as though he knew exactly what she was thinking. But he didn't say a word about the car. Cullen cocked a brow at her and repeated, "Hospital?"

She folded her arms across her chest and shook her head. "No. I'm not going to no damn hospital."

"You can't just go home."

She didn't have any intention of going home, either, but she wasn't going to tell him that. Her knees buckled, and she knew she had to sit down. "Look, how about you take me to a friend's house? Her son is an EMT. He can look me over, and if he thinks I ought to go to the hospital, I'll go."

But Dante wouldn't insist on that, not unless she was in serious need of a doctor, and she knew she wasn't. He could check her over, and Rose could fuss over her, and she'd be fine.

Cullen stared at her as though he seemed to realize just how unsteady she felt, and he guided her around the car so that she could lean against his rusted-out Mustang. It was mottled between some indeterminate shade of blue, that ugly primer gray, and rust. But it could have been covered with slime, and she wouldn't care. It took some of her weight, and she finally stopped feeling like she might hit the ground.

"What about your folks?" he asked softly. "They'll be scared. Won't they want you to get looked over?"

She looked away. "My parents are dead. I live with an uncle and he—" She just barely managed to stop herself from saying, *If those boys had killed me, Leon would have offered up his praise to God.* She finally forced herself to say, "He won't care. Look, just take me to my friends. I feel like hell."

* * *

THE door opened to reveal a skinny black lady. The top of her head might have barely reached Cullen's shoulder. The guy behind her looked like a damned giant. He probably stood a good head taller than Cullen, and he probably weighed the same as Cullen and the lady together. Cullen topped out right at six feet, but he felt like a midget standing there. The man's eyes narrowed on Taige's battered, bruised face, and then they slid up to Cullen's, like he was imagining how Cullen would look after a close encounter or ten with a big, blunt object.

The woman, though, was focused on Taige. "Oh, baby," she murmured, reaching out to touch Taige's face. She immediately stepped aside and shoved on the big guy's chest until he did the same. "Out of the way, Dante. Go get me the first aid kit."

Dante—great name, Cullen thought. He could see hell burning in the big guy's eyes, and even though he hadn't done a damn thing, he wasn't all that happy to be standing in front of the man. Dante didn't move, and the woman spun around and slammed the heel of her hand into his chest. "Boy, I told you to get out of the way. Come on, now, honey, let's look at you."

Taige gave the woman a wan smile. "I'm okay, Rose. I just need to get some rest."

"Okay," Rose muttered. She shook her head and then repeated it again, like she couldn't quite believe what Taige had said. "You're okay?"

Cullen said, "I tried to get her to let me take her to the hospital, but she wouldn't go. Said somebody here's a paramedic . . . ?"

Rose jerked her chin toward the man who still hulked in the shadows like he was ready to rip Cullen's arm off and beat him to death with it. "Yeah. My boy, Dante, does emergency rescues. He can look her over well enough—if he'd get his butt moving."

Dante's lip curled in a snarl, and without saying a word, he turned and stomped off down a dark hallway. The woman reached up and patted Cullen's arm. "Don't you worry about him. He's just protective of Taige. We both are."

Rose shouldered Cullen aside, tucking her small body up against Taige's and leading her through an arched doorway. "Get that light on the wall for me—what's your name?"

"It's Cullen."

"Get the light on for me, Cullen, and then you sit right down there and tell me what happened." She eased Taige's body onto the couch and gave her the same look Cullen had gotten from his mother a time or two before. "Because I know this girl, and she ain't going to tell me a damn thing."

Dante slid into the room, moving quieter than a man that big ought to be able to move. In his arms he held a box that looked more like a tackle box than any first aid kit Cullen had ever seen. But he didn't turn it over to his mother; instead, he crouched down by Taige's head and started looking her over. Cullen knew the man was listening to every word Cullen said, but Dante didn't say anything until Cullen had finished speaking. "You should have taken her on into the emergency room, no matter what she said," Dante said. He had a deep, gruff voice, and when he glanced at Cullen over a big shoulder, Cullen saw the fury simmering there.

Fortunately, it didn't seem like it was directed at Cullen now, and he breathed a little easier. "I tried to. But I don't know where it is, and she wasn't too interested in telling me. She said she'd have you look her over, and if you insisted, she'd go."

That made Dante laugh. Then he looked at Taige, shaking his head. "Yeah, like she's ever done a damn thing just cuz I told her she ought to." Dante sighed and opened the box at his side. "Let's get you cleaned up. And Taige, if I tell you that you need a doctor, you're going, even if I have to throw your skinny ass over my shoulder."

Rose smacked Dante lightly on the arm. "You watch how you talk to her, boy. And don't worry. You say she needs a doctor, she's going to a doctor, and there isn't a damn thing she can do about it, either."

* * *

"So did she make you go to the hospital?"

The shadow fell over Taige, and she opened her eyes, squinting up at Cullen. The sun was at his back, and she couldn't make out his face very well, but she recognized his voice. He crouched down beside her, and she lifted her sunglasses onto her head, meeting his eyes. He winced and touched his fingers to her swollen left eye. "Ouch."

The touch was gentle. It didn't hurt at all. But Taige wished it would have. Hurt would have been a little better than her reaction. Heat. Just that gentle touch had her heart pounding in her chest. Taige had always snorted when she read things like that, how just some guy's touch could do that, but until now, she hadn't ever had it happen, hadn't ever believed it could happen.

But with her heart racing away in her chest, she had little choice but to believe just that. "It's just bruised. Dante tried to make me go, said there could have been scratches on my cornea or something." Then she shrugged. "I waited until the doctors' offices opened and went to the clinic. Dante's got a friend that works there, and he took a look at me. Made Rose happy, and it got Dante off my back."

"They family?"

Taige shook her head. "No, at least not by blood. Rose knew my mom and dad, though. I've known her since I was a baby." She grimaced and added, "And the way Rose acts, you'd think I still was a baby."

"She was worried. Can't blame her for that."

He dropped down on the blanket next to her. His leg brushed against hers, totally by accident, she was sure. She just hoped he couldn't see the look on her face. Nonchalant as possible, she shifted away. Not because she didn't want him touching her, but if she wanted to actually carry on a conversation with him, he couldn't be touching her. She'd start mumbling and stammering and acting like some stupid . . . girl. How embarrassing.

"Since you didn't go to the hospital, I guess you didn't call the police, either," Cullen was saying.

"No reason to," she said, shrugging. "I wasn't hurt, not really." Then she grinned, a mean, nasty grin. "Dante came home the next day, and his mama had to play doctor on his hands. He looked like he went a few rounds with a brick wall, the way his hands were torn up."

Cullen laughed. "Well, that would explain it. I ran into one of those guys at the store. He saw me and took off in the other direction, but not before I saw his face. He looks like he got hit by a brick wall. A few times."

A breeze drifted by, and she caught her hair in her hand, holding it out of her face as she stole a glance at him. "I don't know if I remembered to say thank you."

He reached out, caught a thick curl, and tucked it behind her ear. "Nothing to say thanks for. Anybody—"

She shook her head. "No. Not anybody would have done it." Sadly, she knew that not even half of anybody would have gotten involved. Sucked knowing the things she knew sometimes.

"Yeah, well . . ." He shrugged it off, and she grinned a little as she realized he was uncomfortable. His cheeks were tanned, but not tanned enough to hide the dull rush of color as he blushed. He focused his gaze out over the blue green waters of the Gulf. "I'm glad I saw you out here. We're heading back home day after tomorrow, and I've been worried. Didn't know how to find you, except going back out to your friend's house. And I tried that. Got lost."

Taige grinned, hiding the rush of pleasure at the thought of him looking for her. Then she felt like an idiot. He was a nice guy. After what he'd done, she knew just how much of a nice guy he was. So he'd been worried. No reason to read anything else into it.

But she knew it wasn't going to keep her from thinking about him after he'd gone. She realized she was still staring at him and grinning like a fool, and she shifted her gaze back out to the beach. "So where is home?"

"Georgia. Small town about an hour north of Atlanta, close to the Tennessee state line." From the corner of her eye, she could see that he was staring out at the Gulf, smiling faintly. "Going to miss the beach. Easy to get used to it."

Taige had to agree. "I can't imagine living anywhere else."

"My dad bought one of the condos, so we'll be back. Not sure when." He paused for a minute, and Taige glanced over at him to realize that now he was the one staring. At her. "Maybe I'll see you when we come back."

Her heart skipped a beat. She almost blurted out something totally lame, like *Oh, I'd love that*. But she managed, just barely, to keep her voice even and her comment to a simple, "I'm pretty much always around."

An awkward silence fell. He cleared his throat, and Taige busied her hands by combing through her mass of hair and separating it into sections so she could braid it. From the corner of her eye, she could see him watching her, and she fumbled a little and had to start over. "Can I ask you something?" Cullen asked softly.

She tensed. She had a feeling she knew what he was going to ask—or at least some variation of it. "What?" she asked warily. She didn't really consider herself touchy when people asked her, but it did make her a little uncomfortable and irritated her that people could be so damn nosy. She hadn't thought that Cullen would be the kind to meddle like that.

But to her surprise, he didn't ask her if she was black, or mixed, or any other polite variation of a rather nosy question. What he did ask, though, wasn't any easier.

"I was just wondering what happened to your parents."

Her gut reflex was, *I killed them.* She'd said it before. It wasn't a new thought. She'd woken up late that last night—the night they'd died—and she'd been screaming for Mama and Daddy, but they were gone. They'd gone out to get some dinner, see a movie, and they'd left her with the teenager who lived across the street from them in the small Mobile suburb. Taige couldn't even remember the girl's name now—just the look on her face as she stared down at Taige, screaming in the bed and calling for help.

The girl had freaked out and called her own mother. Taige didn't remember that woman's name, either, though she remembered how she'd smelled. Like lotion and Ici. To this day, anything that even resembled the way that discount perfume had smelled was enough to make Taige sick. The woman had held her and tried to calm her down, murmuring some nonsense about nightmares and bad dreams.

All the way up until the knock on the door, nearly three hours later. Taige could remember the cops standing in the door, and the grim look on their faces. They'd made her leave the room, but she didn't need to hear to know what happened. Her mama and daddy were dead.

Her voice was hoarse and rough as she answered, "They were killed by a drunk driver when I was little." She swallowed, cleared her throat to try to ease the pressure there. "We lived in Mobile. They'd gone out. Date night, Mama called it. Somebody hit them on their way to the movies, killed them instantly."

She kept her face averted as she wiped the tears away. It still hurt. Eight years later, it still hurt. "Mama grew up here. They found my mama's older brother, Leon, and sent me to live with him. They never could find any of my dad's folks." Taige had long since stopped hoping for that to happen, although there had been years when she had been convinced that if she prayed hard enough, if she was good enough, somebody would come and get her. Somebody who loved her.

"That's got to suck," he said. "Mom and Dad drive me nuts, but I can't imagine losing them like that. Being sent off to live with somebody else. Even family. They might love you, but it can't be the same."

"He doesn't love me." The words slipped out of her before she even realized it. She hadn't meant to say that, not in front of him, but there was no taking the words back, and she didn't want to, either. She hated pretending that her life with Leon Carson was fine, that he took care of her, that he even gave a damn about her. "He hates me. Hates having me there."

Then she shoved to her feet, grabbed her stuff, grabbed the

tote lying on its side in the sand. She shoved everything inside it, her bottled water, the book she'd been trying to read, her sunglasses. But Cullen was still sitting on the beach blanket, and she didn't want to wait for him to get up, so she just left it. "I've got to get home."

"Hey . . ."

She strode away, sand flying beneath her feet. The sand muffled the sound of his footsteps until he was right behind her. Before he could touch her, she turned around and stared at him. She lifted her chin insolently and demanded, "What?"

"I didn't mean . . . I'm . . ." Cullen seemed to fumble for the words. He reached up, scratched his head, squinted at her. "I'm sorry. I didn't mean to pry or piss you off or whatever got you so mad."

She wasn't mad. She was humiliated. She tucked her chin against her chest and turned away. "It's no big deal. I just got to get home."

"Why?" he asked bluntly.

Taige glanced up at him. "Because I want to?"

"If he really hates you, why would you want to go home?"

And to that, Taige really didn't have an answer. She stood there with a scowl on her face. He reached out and caught her bag. She tried to hold on to the straps for a few seconds, but he wasn't letting go, either, and she wasn't going to stand there and fight him over who got to carry it. Then he held out his other hand, wordlessly.

Slowly, Taige put her hand in his, and he led her away. It never even occurred to her to ask him where they were going. Taige didn't care.

It was probably the most perfect night she could ever remember having. Or at least the most perfect night in years. They went into town, and they rode go-carts. They played in the arcade. They ate pizza and ice cream. And when he took her home, well past dark, he walked her to the door, and before he left her on the porch, he dipped his head to kiss her.

Light and fast, just a butterfly touch. As he straightened up, Taige felt blood rush to her cheeks. She would have been more embarrassed, except she realized he was blushing a little, too.

He walked off, and Taige turned around with a happy sigh. That lingering happy feeling stayed with her even as she opened the door and walked inside to hear one of her uncle's recorded sermons booming from the living room. It stayed with her even as she showered and well into the night.

TWO

Summer 1994

"IT happened again, didn't it?"

Taige stiffened involuntarily, only to relax when Cullen reached up, his hands resting on her shoulders as his thumbs dug into the knotted muscles of her neck. "What happened?" she said, hoping she could play dumb. She hated for him to know about her issues. She hated for him to know that she was such a damn freak.

"Don't give me that." His hands tightened just a little, and she suspected he would have liked to shake her. He didn't, though. Cullen never touched her like that. "I hate it when you lie to me."

"I'm not lying," Taige hedged.

"The hell you aren't. You know what I'm talking about. You had another one of those weird dreams."

Cullen had found out about her dreams last summer. He'd been there with her late one night out on the beach when she fell asleep. She'd woken up choking for air. It had come on her hard and fast, and she had no time to worry about Cullen as she ran for the pool. It was past midnight, and the pools were closed, but it hadn't kept the curious five-year-old from climbing over the gate so he could go swimming. His parents hadn't even heard him leave, and that late, nobody had seen the little boy walking down the hallway all by himself.

She hadn't been able to hide it from Cullen any longer when the paper ran the story the next day on the front page, along with a headline, "Local Psychic Saves Another Child." It had listed several of the other times when she had either helped save some kid from drowning or found them when they wandered off and got lost. Worse, it had listed some of the more grisly things that Taige would rather nobody know. The times when she found the bodies of murder victims, three different times, three people she hadn't been able to help. Those were the ones that really made her feel like a useless freak.

After he found out, Taige had been ready for him to either laugh at her or just walk away, although they'd spent most of that summer together. But he hadn't walked off. He hadn't laughed. And when he showed up at her house the next day, he'd walked in when Leon was having one of his outbursts, yelling at Taige and calling her devil spawn. Cullen had punched Leon, knocking the older man into the wall and then grabbing him and slamming him back so hard that the back of Leon's head knocked a hole in the drywall. "I hear you talking to her like that again, and I'll make you damn sorry," Cullen had shouted while Taige bodily separated them.

"She's seduced you. The devil's harlot. You'll burn in hell with her if you don't repent! God will see to it—He will pass His judgment over you, and you will burn in hell."

Cullen had sneered at Leon and said, "If God is going to send anybody straight to hell, it's going to be you."

Then he had taken Taige's hand and led her out of the house, to his car, but instead of climbing inside, he had leaned against it and pulled her against him.

Taige had already had a bad feeling that she loved him, but after that night, she knew it was true. She'd fallen in love with some rich white boy from Atlanta—and she couldn't have been happier about it.

"You in there?" he murmured, leaning forward to kiss her shoulder. Exhausted, she'd ended up falling asleep instead of fishing with Cullen and his dad. The sun's rays were white hot, but the touch of his mouth on her made her burn even more.

"Hmmm." She lowered her head briefly, pressing her face against his neck. His arm came up and curved around her shoulder, and Taige sighed, relaxing into the hard length of his body.

"You want to tell me about it?" he asked softly.

She slid his dad a nervous look, but the older man was standing out hip-deep in the waves, too far to hear them or really even see them. Her voice was soft, almost hesitant when she finally replied, "There's not much to tell. I didn't see much. Just a girl's face. She's lost. Or she will be." It would be so much easier to deal with her bizarre ability if it operated with any kind of sense. Sometimes she saw what had already happened. Sometimes things as they happened, and then sometimes, days, months, or weeks before it happened. Not always in time to change things and not always in time to help.

"Is she okay?" Cullen's hand was warm on her neck, and he rubbed the tight muscles there. He did that a lot, sometimes without even realizing that he did it, Taige thought. He liked to touch her, and it wasn't always just because he was trying to cop a feel. Although Taige had no problems when he was doing that, none at all. Unlike the guys who had tried to get her in a similar situation, she liked it when Cullen touched her. She liked it a lot. His touch did something strange to her deep inside. Logically, she knew what it was. He turned her on, but that in and of itself was odd for her. He was the only guy who could touch her and not make her want to cringe away. He was—restful. As lame as that sounded, it was the only way she could describe it. Even when he was kissing her, touching her through her clothes, or when she was touching him, even when she was so damned hot from all those touches that she couldn't stand it, it was restful.

It never came with the bad vibes or whatever worries and thoughts he had going on inside. When he touched her, she didn't have to worry she was going to pick up some random emotion or a memory flash, and that let her relax and just enjoy it. She leaned into his hands and tried to pull something else out of that short blip of a dream. Something besides the girl's face, but there was nothing. "I don't know, Cullen."

"Isn't it usually clearer than this?"

She gave him a wry glance. "Not always. Doesn't come with an owner's manual or a remote where I can rewind and watch through it again." She pulled away from him, hoping that maybe if she wasn't touching him, her brain might function a little better.

He was quiet for a minute. He slid a hand down her arm and linked her fingers with his. "Are you going to be able to help?"

Taige shook her head. "I don't know. If I'm supposed to help . . ." Her voice trailed off. It was hard to explain, and Cullen was the first person she'd ever attempted to explain it to. The first person she'd ever cared enough about to try to explain it so he could understand. But she didn't really have the words to explain that she would just know. She'd be walking to the restaurant to help Rose and Dante, or she'd be swimming or riding her bike along Fort Morgan Highway, and she would just know. She would feel it. Whether she would be in time, that part would have to play itself out. "I'll just know. It's almost like there is some kind of magnet, and it will pull me in."

Cullen pulled her up against him, and she cuddled in close. His calm, simple acceptance was nothing short of amazing, and Taige didn't know if she'd ever get used to it. She didn't know if it would last or not, either. She worried about it sometimes, late at night when she was thinking about him or over the past winter while he was back in Georgia. They wrote, and he called her a lot, always over at Rose's or at the restaurant. Never at home. Taige had all but moved in with Rose as it was, spending only one or two nights a week in the small, depressing bedroom in the house where her uncle lived. Rose had offered her Dante's room after he had moved in with a girlfriend, and Taige knew as soon as she turned eighteen, she would do it.

Not yet, though. Not until her uncle had no more legal hold over her. He was mean enough to try to make Rose's life a living hell just to hurt Taige. Once she was eighteen, the bastard couldn't do anything. Another couple months. She still had her senior year to get through in high school, but she could do that just as well living with Rose.

"You thought any more about college?"

"Nothing to think about," she said softly. She wasn't going. She didn't have the money, and although she knew she could get a grant, maybe even a scholarship or two, she wasn't cut out for college.

"You just going to keep working at the restaurant the rest of your life?" He shifted around, facing her.

She met his gaze levelly. Taige knew he didn't get it. Knew he didn't understand. Working at the little restaurant might not be the best-paying job, and it wasn't anything special, but she didn't need special. She didn't need glamorous, and she didn't give a damn about pulling in a six-figure income.

What she wanted was quiet and solitude. Here, at home, she got that, to an extent, anyway. People here knew her. Some of the locals still treated her like some sort of freak show, but she couldn't imagine going to someplace where nobody knew her. She'd really look like the bearded lady then. Or a charlatan.

Taige could handle people not believing in what she could do, but too often that interfered with doing it, and she didn't want to risk that.

"The restaurant's all I need, Cullen."

He reached up and fisted a hand in her hair. "Maybe, but you deserve more." He leaned in, and she held still as he kissed her, soft and slow. He touched her so gently, so carefully. It seemed reverent, somehow, and it never failed to melt her heart. His tongue touched her lips, and she opened to him, groaning in her throat as he tugged her closer.

"You know, when I was a kid, that wasn't called fishing."

Cullen jerked away as the sound of his dad's voice intruded. Blood rushed to Taige's face, and she covered her face with her hands. She glanced through her fingers to see Robert Morgan watching with a stern look on his face, but his eyes were smiling. "Sorry, Dad," Cullen said. His voice didn't sound sorry at all, and Robert just shook his head and grinned.

"Can't say I blame you, but if your mama knew I was letting you two carry on like that, she'd have both our heads on a platter." Then he winked at Taige. "And she'd feel the motherly duty of giving you a talking-to, Taige. So you two just save us all that, okay? Wait until I'm gone."

Summer 1996

The sun had set and with it went the heat.

Taige lay on the beach blanket, staring up at the stars overhead and trying not to panic. Cullen was crouched over the small campfire they had built, and she wanted to roll over onto her side so she could watch him. That man certainly looked good in the firelight, the yellow orange flames deepening his already tanned skin, casting dancing shadows all over the long, rangy muscles in his body.

He'd been seriously cute that first summer, but now . . . saliva pooled in her mouth just looking at him. That man was definitely drool worthy. Over the past four years, his lanky body had filled out, his shoulders had broadened, and his face had gone from good-looking all-American teenaged male to pure male perfection. Without a doubt, the man was a work of human art and definitely worth staring at.

But if she stared at him for too long, Taige might start thinking about what she was planning to do once he joined her on the beach blanket. They'd been seeing each other for nearly three years now. Only during the summers, and neither of them talked about how serious they were. Taige wasn't really even sure if they were serious. Sometimes, especially after he left to go back home, she had to wonder how serious they could be. They were able to spend eight weeks together during the summer. A few days over Christmas break, and this past spring, Cullen had come down on his own.

She'd almost done this then. But then Taige had a bad one. Real bad. They had been lying on the couch in his parents' condo, and it had come on her like a heart attack, a girl's screams ringing in her ears. She had shoved Cullen away and rolled to the floor, crouching there like some wild animal. She could hear the girl's screaming, and she could feel the girl's terror, and when Cullen touched her, it had terrified her.

He had jerked her close against him and shook her gently, murmuring her name over and over until she finally saw him and not the men crowding around the girl. They hadn't had any time. It was happening then, and they rushed out of the condo so fast that neither of them even bothered putting their shoes on. They were halfway to the car when Taige realized her shirt was hanging open, but her hands shook too badly to button it. Cullen had done it.

He had stopped, turned around, and buttoned enough of the buttons to keep her shirt closed and then he had kissed her, soft and gentle. "Calm down. It will be okay."

Taige knew then. Not right that second, but later on. She knew he was it for her. Nineteen years old, and she had found the man she wanted for the rest of her life. He knew about the weird dreams, knew about how she saw things that normal people didn't see—things that people probably weren't supposed to see—but it didn't freak him out.

How that was possible, she didn't know. The only thing that made sense was that he was the one. The one meant for her, just like she was meant for him. That was why he didn't freak out when these things hit her, and that was why she could touch him without picking up on all those weird blips and images that happened when she usually touched people.

That time, the attack of fear had been brought on by a couple of college boys intent on getting a piece of ass. One of them had brought a girl with him, a girl who had thought she was going to a party; she didn't realize she was the party. The beach house had been back off the road.

Neither Cullen nor Taige had seen the house, or the drive that was a little overgrown, but they hadn't needed to see it. Taige had known where it was, and when she pointed to the roadside, Cullen slowed down without her having to say anything. They'd pulled up in front of the house, and they had both heard the screams. Cullen used his cell phone to call the police, and he had wasted five seconds trying to convince Taige to stay in the car.

When he figured out she wasn't listening, he had opened the trunk and grabbed two clubs from the golf bag. It was the first and only time Taige had ever held a golf club, and she was damn thankful she hadn't had to use it.

"Hey."

Jerked back to the present, Taige rolled her head toward him and smiled.

"You were out in orbit again," he teased as he stretched his body out beside her on the blanket. He dipped his head low and skimmed his lips along her shoulder.

Taige rolled toward him and smiled. "Daydreaming."

He grinned. "Really? About what?"

She covered his grinning mouth with her own and murmured, "You."

He rolled onto his back and wrapped his arms around her, pulling her with him so that she ended up on top of him. She shifted, planting a knee on either side of his hips and bracing her elbows on his chest so that she could grin down at him. His brilliant turquoise eyes glinted up at her. "So what am I doing in these daydreams?"

Now or never . . .

Taige pushed up. As she straightened up over him, she felt him between her legs. She'd touched him before, knew that his skin was strangely smooth, like silk, and under the silk, he felt hard. Right now, he was damn hard, and Taige shivered a little. It had nothing to do with the cool breeze blowing off the Gulf and everything to do with the look in his eyes as she reached behind her neck and undid the tie to her bikini.

His eyes slowly drifted down. She felt the blush creeping up her cheeks, but she didn't stop. She reached behind her for the tie at her back, and the swimsuit top fell off, landing on his belly. His belly was left bare by the faded Hawaiian-print shirt. Taige pushed the bikini top off and leaned forward. "It was something like this," she murmured, and then she kissed him.

Taige loved kissing Cullen. Flat-out loved it. She'd gone more than half of her life avoiding the touch of most people, so it was bizarre that she now craved it. But not just from anybody. She wanted Cullen's hands on her, loved the way he touched her, so gentle and slow, loved the way he made her feel so cherished.

His hands tightened on her waist, and he arched under her. For one hot, brief minute, he was pressed against her, hard and close, and Taige whimpered as a slow, hollow ache spread low through her belly. But then he shifted, bringing his knees up and slowly edging her forward so that she wasn't pressed right against him. Taige pushed back as far as the tight grip of his hands would allow.

She lifted her head up and licked his lower lip. Taige wanted to say something to him. She wanted to tell him that she was ready, but the words seemed to knot inside her throat, and she knew if she tried to say anything, all she'd manage was a squeak.

That wasn't the image she was going for. Taige would have liked to manage something sexy and mature.

Wanna do it? wasn't quite what she was going for.

She figured she could manage that, or maybe just some terrified, incoherent babbling, but she didn't want to do either of those. So instead, she pushed to her feet and shifted so that she was standing at his side instead of over him. Taige waited until he looked up at her, and then she hooked her thumbs in the waistband of her shorts and pushed them down, taking the bottom half of her swimsuit with it.

When she straightened up, she was naked. Naked and terrified; her heart felt like it was banging away inside her throat instead of her chest, and she was clenching her fists so tight, her nails bit into the flesh of her palms.

"Taige . . ." His voice sounded tight and choked. He also seemed to have trouble lifting his gaze any higher than her boobs. Slowly, she sank down beside him, throwing one leg over his hips, once more straddling him. She still couldn't talk, and just then, Cullen was still staring at her and looking a little dazed. She reached for her discarded shorts and reached into the pocket.

His eyes met hers as she held up the foil-wrapped condom.

"Taige . . ."

She forced herself to smile. Her voice shook a little, and she said, "You said that already."

He reached up and took the condom from her, closing his fingers around it. "You sure?" he asked hoarsely.

Her lips curved up in a slow smile. That smile alone would have been enough to fuel every hot, desperate dream Cullen had for the next month. Of course, there was the very hot, very real dream of Taige sitting buck naked on top of him. He had fantasized about this so many times. But the reality of it . . . whoa.

Her breasts, full and round, were a soft, pale creamy brown, topped with nipples that made him think of chocolate. In the flickering light from the fire, he could see the tight, dark curls between her thighs, and Cullen was pretty sure he could feel the heat of her burning him through his shorts.

She bent low and pressed her lips to his, her breasts flattening against his chest. His breath hitched a little as she slid her tongue into his mouth. He wrapped his arms around her. Then he slid his hands down her sides, cupped her butt, and pulled her close. She felt so good. Cullen rocked against her, rubbing against the hot, wet vee of her thighs. He was going to come in his shorts if he didn't slow down, though.

That wasn't how he wanted her first time. He definitely wanted her first time to be better than his had been, some hot and sweaty fumble in the backseat of a car with a girl he barely knew. Taige was rocking against him, wiggling and moaning deep in her throat. If she kept moving like that, it was going to be over before he even managed to get his zipper undone.

Cullen tightened his arms around her waist and rolled until she was pinned beneath him. It wasn't much better; now he was pressed against her heat, and he couldn't stop the involuntary rhythm of his hips. He stiffened his arms so that he wasn't pressed so tightly against her, but Taige slid her hands down his sides to his hips, trying to pull him closer.

Her misty gray eyes had gone dark. She said his name, and her voice was so throaty and hoarse, if he hadn't already been hard, that sound would have done it. Her nails bit demandingly into his sides. Gently, Cullen pressed his lips to hers. "Why are you rushing?" he murmured.

Then he moved down, pressed a kiss to her shoulder. He

cupped her big, warm breasts in his hands and watched, fascinated. Her skin was shades darker than his tanned hands. He pinched her nipples gently, and she moaned, a sexy little sound low in her throat. Cullen lifted his gaze, stared at her as he did it again, rolling her nipples between his fingers. Then he dipped his head and kissed one, taking the hard flesh into his mouth and sucking on her. Beneath him, Taige bucked. She brought her hands up, fisted them in his hair. His name escaped her lips in a shaky sigh.

Wanting to feel her bare body against his own, he shrugged out of his shirt. He loved the way she tasted, salty and sweet. He could hear the rough catch of her breathing, and when he slid a hand down her side, over her hip and between her legs, for a second, she stopped breathing altogether.

This was new. This was different. As often as he'd touched her, kissed her, this was different. Cullen hadn't ever had her completely naked before him. The curls that covered her sex were darker, tighter. He shifted to his side and lifted up so he could watch as he touched her. She was wet. Silky wet and hot when he pushed one finger inside her.

She tensed up, and Cullen might have pulled away, but then she reached down and wrapped her fingers around his wrist, holding his hand still as she rocked up, riding his finger. Her lids drooped closed, a soft sheen of sweat gleaming on her skin. He almost came right then, as she rocked up and down against him, whimpering under her breath.

He added a second finger, pushing it and then drawing it out, staring first at her face to make sure he wasn't hurting her and then, because he couldn't not watch, he stared between her legs, watching as he touched, staring at the pink, wet folds, watching as she rocked against him like she wanted him to touch her as badly as he needed to touch her. She whimpered, tugged on his wrist, reached for him.

The sight of that, her slender arms lifting up for him, was too much. Cullen pulled away from her long enough to tear open his shorts and shove them down. His hands shook as he tore the rubber open, and they shook when he put it on. He stared at her the entire time, shifting his gaze from the wet heat between her thighs to her pretty, flushed face, and back again. He couldn't decide what he wanted to see more of, and if his dick didn't hurt so much, he might have just kept on staring at her.

But he did hurt. He settled between her thighs and looked up. "I don't want to hurt you," he said softly.

Taige smiled. "I don't care if you do." Then she reached for him, and he went into her arms and kissed her.

Her body went stiff under his as he pushed inside. He knew he was hurting her. Tears formed in her eyes, and he tried to slow down, but she was so hot, so wet and tight. "Want me to stop?" he gritted out through his teeth.

"Don't you dare." She slid her hands down his back and cupped his butt, pulling him closer, and Cullen lost it.

He shoved inside her, hard and fast and he couldn't stop himself from doing it again and again, even though he knew it was hurting her, knew she wasn't feeling the same thing he was feeling, but he couldn't stop. "I'm sorry, I'm sorry," he muttered against her lips. He kissed her, and he could taste the salt from her tears, and he hated himself, but he still couldn't stop.

It ended too soon for him. He came hard and fast, and when he sank down against her shuddering body, he knew he had totally fucked it up. "God, Taige, I'm so sorry," he whispered, feeling sick inside. He lifted up, almost afraid to look at her.

She had a shaky smile on her lips. A smile. "Sorry for what?" she asked.

"I . . . I hurt you." Blood rushed to his cheeks and he stumbled a little as he said, "I didn't—I couldn't . . . You didn't like it, did you?"

Taige shrugged. "I didn't not like it." She bit her lip, something she did when she was nervous, and the sight of it eased just a little bit of his own anxiety. "I knew it would hurt. It gets better, right?"

You are so amazing. He had thought that about her for so long, but he hadn't ever said it to her. She'd think he was a total loser, gushing like that, right? But she really was amazing. Beautiful. Funny. Mysterious even, with this weird psychic thing she had going on. She didn't act a damn thing like any of the girls Cullen knew at school. She was oddly more adult, without even trying. At college, he was surrounded by girls who were still just confused, scared kids trying to fit into the grown-up world, the same way he felt most of the time.

But Taige didn't have any of that. She had no pretenses, she didn't try to change to fit what others thought she should be. When a lot of the girls he knew had been having sex just to be cool or get guys to like them, she hadn't. She had waited until she was ready—and she'd chosen him. "You're amazing," he whispered, finally voicing the words that had lived inside him for so long. He leaned forward, kissing her gently. He kept his weight off of her and tried to be gentle when he pulled out. He pulled the condom off, grabbing the wrapper and tossing them into the small plastic bag they had brought for garbage. When he looked back at Taige, she was reaching for her shorts.

But he grabbed them and tossed them to the other side of the blanket. "It gets better," he whispered. Then he lay between her legs and kissed her. She bucked against him, a soft, strangled shriek escaping her. "You just need to tell me what makes you feel good."

* * *

OUTSIDE, it was pouring rain.

Inside the screened-in porch, Taige and Cullen lay on a worn quilt, wrapped in each other's arms and not talking at all.

Rose had left for a weekend in Biloxi with some friends, and Taige had asked Cullen to come for dinner Friday night. That had been two days ago. They hadn't left the house even to go swimming. Cullen's dad had called him Saturday morning, and Cullen had said he'd be home in time to pack.

Taige wondered what his dad had thought of that, wondered what Robert Morgan thought of his son spending the weekend with some local girl, but she really didn't have enough experience to even guess what the guy might think. He was genuinely nice and treated her like she was somebody worth knowing, somebody worthy of his son. Both of Cullen's parents were like that.

She tried to picture herself with a kid, wondered how'd she feel if her kid brought somebody to meet her, somebody who mattered. Taige decided she'd feel a little embarrassed. A little out of place. She wouldn't want to think of her kids having sex, but kids grew up, didn't they? Cullen was twenty years old.

A little ribbon of jealousy worked through her, and before she even realized the question was in her mind, she blurted out, "How many girls have you been with?"

He stiffened, turned his head, and looked at her. A dull rush of color flooded his cheeks as he stared at her. He swallowed nervously, and she could see his Adam's apple moving under his skin.

"Uh . . ."

She wasn't going to take the question back though. She did want to know. What he'd done to her on the beach last weekend, after they'd done it that first time, it didn't seem like something that a guy with little or no experience might try. And he'd been good at it, too. Good enough that she hadn't waited more than two days before she talked him into another late-night beach trip. This time, she'd done it to him first, and after he came, she had rolled onto her back and urged him back between her thighs. He'd gone down on her again, and she'd ended up screaming his name and pulling his hair as she came.

It still hurt some when he was inside her, but it had slowly gotten better, and last night, he'd made her come that way, just from moving inside her. He'd touched her clit while he moved inside her, and it had lit her up like fireworks on the Fourth of July, coming so hard, she'd ended up scratching his back and shoulders all up before she was done.

"Don't tell me you haven't been with any girls," she warned him, sitting up and pulling her legs to her chest. "I just want to know."

"Why? Are we going to get in a fight over it?" he asked warily.

"Only if you lie to me." She swallowed the knot in her throat and tucked her chin against her chest. "When you leave for school, we haven't ever talked about not seeing other people. If you've been with some girl at school, it's not like I never said I didn't—"

His hand came up, cupped her chin. He eased her face up until she met his gaze, and then he answered, "Two girls. One before I met you. Then another girl that I dated off and on my senior year and my freshman year at college. She moved out of state at the end of that year and . . ." His voice trailed off, and he was quiet for a minute. He brushed her hair back from her face, caught a long curl in his hand, and wrapped it around his finger.

Cullen did love to play with her hair. For some reason, seeing him doing it now, while he tried to talk about this, made a fist clench around her heart. No, they hadn't ever talked about it just being the two of them. Hadn't really seemed fair, or reasonable, even, with him living a state away. Twenty years old, drop-dead gorgeous, he'd have a bunch of pretty college girls tagging after him. But she didn't want him with anybody else. Period.

"She moved out of state," Taige prompted. "Why not anybody since her? That was more than a year ago."

His gaze locked with hers. "Nobody since her because the one girl I really wanted to be with has been on a beach in Alabama," he said.

"Me?" she asked and then she felt like an idiot. How many other girls on a beach in Alabama was he seeing?

He grinned at her and leaned forward. "Yeah, you." He kissed her and rolled to his knees in front of her, watching her face as he lifted his hands, placed them on the inside of her knees, and gently pushed her thighs apart. "I've been dreaming about touching you, having you like this, since the first time I saw you." His voice dropped to a low, rough whisper that sent shivers down her spine. "Been going out of my mind wanting you. When you really want just one thing, nothing else but that one thing will really do it for you, Taige."

He lay down between her thighs and pressed his mouth against her sex, sliding his hands behind her and gripping her waist to keep her still. He licked her clit, and then he looked up at her. "You're the one thing I've been craving, so I wasn't going to waste my time with anybody else. Not when all I wanted was you."

His voice deepened and he rasped, "Lie down. Spread your legs for me."

Her back had no sooner touched the ground than he pushed her legs apart, too impatient to wait. "I don't need to ask if you've been with another guy," he muttered against her. He licked her clit again, stiffened his tongue and pushed it inside, in and out, until she was rocking against his mouth, and she could feel herself hovering, right on the brink. But just when she thought she was going to go flying off into the stratosphere, Cullen stopped. He lifted his head, rested his chin low on her belly, and stared at her. "But I don't want there to be another guy. I don't want to think about you letting somebody else touch you like this."

He lowered his head, licked her again, teased her right back to the edge again. Then he stopped. Again. He kissed her thigh and then shoved up onto his hands and knees, crawled up the length of her body, and lay down atop her, his cock pressed up against her belly. "Tell me there won't be another guy."

"So long as you promise me there won't be any more girls," she countered. "And so long as you stop teasing me . . . right now."

He smiled at her, slanted his mouth across her, and pushed inside. "No more girls."

"No other guy," she promised.

He thrust deep inside her, and Taige, already so primed and ready, came just like that. He didn't have to kiss her, didn't have to touch her anywhere else. She came hard and fast, and when it was over, he was still moving inside, staring down at her, his turquoise gaze rapt on her face, his hands fisted in her hair.

Her lids drooped closed, and he tightened his grip. "Look at me, Taige," he whispered. She was so damn pretty, so soft and sleek and hot. She lifted her lids and gave him that smile of hers, that teasing, sexy smile that made his dick get hard and twisted his heart and stomach into knots. Everything about her hit him so hard: the way she looked, the way she smiled, the way she laughed, the way she cuddled up against him after one of her dreams, and the way she trusted him to hold her while she slept. She was so perfect—perfect for him.

Only him.

"Look at me," he murmured again when her lids drooped low. He wanted to tell her. He'd been waiting two years to do it, and when he said it, he wanted to see her face when he did. He slowed the rhythm of his thrusts until he was barely rocking inside her.

She reached up, cupped his face in her hands. "I am looking. I see you, baby," she whispered, her voice soft and sweet.

"I love you, Taige."

Her eyes widened. Then her hands went around his neck, and her arms tightened. Willing, Cullen sank down against her and hugged her tight. Her lips brushed against his ear, and she murmured, "I love you."

They held each other like that, tight and close, Cullen rocking against her with those slow, easy thrusts. They came together, and it was so damned perfect, when it was done, Cullen could feel tears burning his eyes. But he didn't want her to see them, so he kept his face buried in her hair until he felt level again.

When he pulled out of her a few minutes later, he realized he hadn't put a rubber on. Taige pushed up onto her elbows, staring at his penis, still half erect and wet. "Shit," he muttered. A rueful grin curved his lips. "We sort of forgot something."

"Yeah, I'll say." Taige could feel him, wet on her thighs. She studied his face, tried to figure out what he might be thinking. He didn't seem mad or really even worried.

He blew out a breath and dropped down to sit with his legs drawn up. They stared at each other, and finally he asked, "Think you can get pregnant?"

Taige rolled her eyes. "I'm a girl, aren't I?"

"I meant . . ." He waved a hand toward the tangled quilt on the floor. "From this. Today."

She shook her head. "Probably not." Then Taige narrowed her eyes. "But what if I did?"

He reached out and snagged her wrist, jerking her into his lap. "We'd deal with it." He rested a hand on her belly, frowning a little. "Don't think I'm ready to be a parent. But we'd deal with it." Then he looped his arms around her and just held her.

You're the amazing one, Taige thought silently. He'd said that to her on the beach last weekend, but he'd been wrong. She wasn't amazing. A bit of a freak, for certain, but not amazing.

Cullen, though, was. He had his whole life ahead of him, and it was the kind of life she hadn't ever dared to dream about. Rich, smart, and capable, he could have anything he wanted. The thought of an unplanned baby thrown into the mix ought to terrify him.

We'd deal with it.

"Yeah," she murmured against his neck. "Yeah, we would."

* * *

"It's the same girl." Taige met Cullen's eyes over the thick mug of tea he had made for her. "I keep dreaming about her. Pretty little thing, black hair, green eyes, has these Shirley Temple curls. She was sitting in an airport this time."

"How many times now?" Cullen asked, puzzled.

She shook her head. "Too many. For nearly two years now.

Always the same thing. She's sitting there. Then she's gone. Just . . . missing."

He started to respond, and then his phone rang. He looked at it and swore. "Shit. It's my dad."

Taige looked up at the clock hanging over the sink. It was red with little roosters in place of numbers. She'd bought it for Rose years ago, and it had been hanging on that wall ever since. Right now, the hour hand was on rooster number ten. Almost ten o'clock. Cullen had told her last night he had to get home by nine thirty so he could pack his stuff.

They were leaving today. It left a cold knot in her chest. His leaving always hurt, but this time was harder.

He spoke to his dad, promised he'd be there soon, apologized. Then he hung up the phone and looked at Taige. "I have to go," he murmured.

She forced herself to smile. He came to the chair and crouched down beside her, resting his head in her lap. "I don't want to leave yet," he murmured. Then he turned and kissed her belly.

"You have to." She wouldn't let herself cry. "Don't worry. I'll be fine. Just need a few minutes to settle."

He lifted his head and stared at her. "It's not just that." One big, warm hand rested on her thigh, and he squeezed gently. "And it's not just this, either. Leaving you gets harder and harder every time."

"I hate it, too." Then she grinned weakly. "But knowing it sucks for you, too, makes it a little easier."

"Will you come to Georgia? Come for Christmas."

He'd asked her before. She'd always said no. But this time . . . She leaned in and kissed him. "Maybe."

Grabbing her in his arms, he stood, lifting her out of the chair and spinning her around. "You'll come." Then he lowered her feet to the ground, his smile fading. He placed his hand on her belly. "You'll call me and let me know, right?"

She didn't need to ask him what about. She nodded. But she already knew she wasn't pregnant. She hadn't gotten her period or anything, but she just knew.

THREE

November 1996

LATE one night, right before Thanksgiving, Taige rolled out of bed, hit the floor on her hands and knees, and puked. She puked until she had emptied her stomach right there on Rose's worn, polished floors. She puked until she had nothing left inside her, and then she just dry heaved until she almost choked with it.

Rose came running in, woken from a sound sleep. "Damn, girl, what the hell . . ."

She took one look at Taige's face and spun around. Taige continued to hover there on her hands and knees, unable to move, frozen inside. When Rose returned with a wet rag, Taige couldn't even take it. The older, smaller woman had to strong-arm Taige into a sitting position, and she ended up wiping Taige's face like a child's.

"Cullen . . ." She forced the words out.

Rose shook her head, her eyes going wide. "No, baby, please don't tell me . . ."

Taige shook her head. "Call him. It's . . . it's his mother."

There was no answer though, not through that long night. Not the following morning. By ten, she was itching to be with Cullen, and Taige couldn't wait anymore. She convinced Rose to let her borrow the Jeep. The drive to Atlanta was long and agonizing. She pulled over three times to try calling him again on pay phones, but there was no answer. She hadn't ever wanted a cell phone, but on that long, dreary drive, she wished she'd gotten one.

She ended up lost and had to pull over and ask for directions to Georgia State University. Then she had to ask for directions to his dorm. But he wasn't there. His roommate, some vacant-eyed weird guy with a grunge thing going on, answered the door and mumbled, "He left for home. Dunno when he'll be back."

So she had to leave again, get on the expressway and head north, going to the little town where she'd been invited to spend Christmas. She hadn't ever been to Cullen's home where he lived with his parents, but she recognized it from some pictures. It was huge, a sprawling three-story building made from what looked like creek stone, with huge windows and a driveway full of cars. She had to park at the very end, and she made her way up the driveway on legs that shook.

Too late. Too late. Too late.

She knocked, and when Cullen answered, she didn't know what to say.

"You knew." His voice was stark and harsh, and it hit her like a slap on the face.

"No." She licked her lips and shook her head. "Not until yesterday."

"She was killed two days ago." He reached out, grabbed her arm, and pulled her inside, pulling her along behind him, ignoring the people who called his name as he led her up one flight of stairs and then another. When he finally stopped, it was inside a huge room that was nearly as big as Rose's entire house. "Two fucking days ago, Taige. Some sick fuck grabbed her outside the mall, forced her into his car, raped her, and choked her to death. Why didn't you help her?"

Taige shook her head. Tears spilled down her cheeks, and she felt sick inside. *Useless . . .* "I didn't know in time, Cullen. I swear, if I had . . ."

She reached out for him, and he pulled back. He shook his head and said, "Don't. Okay? Just . . ." He turned away from her, and his broad shoulders slumped as he covered his face. A harsh sob escaped him, followed by another and another.

With timid steps, she moved toward him. She touched his back, waited for him to pull away. When he didn't, she slid her arms around his waist and rested her cheek against his back. "I'm so sorry, Cullen."

He reached down and grabbed her wrist. She waited for him to push her away, but instead, he pulled her to him and wrapped his arms around her waist, burying his face against her neck as he cried. "Shhhh . . ." she murmured against his hair, rocking him and stroking his back, his neck, wherever she could reach.

His hands roamed restlessly up and down her back as he cried. He clutched her to him, almost desperately. But as the storm of grief eased, he pulled back. Pulled away completely. "What are you doing here, Taige?" he murmured, easing back from her. He walked away, disappearing through a door on the far end of the room. She trailed behind him, uncertain how to answer that.

"I . . . I wanted to be with you." She peered around the door-jamb into a bathroom that was easily three times the size it needed to be. It had a huge sunken tub on one end underneath a huge window. There was a separate shower that had two showerheads. The toilet was behind a little wall. Cullen stood at the sink, his hands braced on its smooth, glossy black surface.

He laughed, and it was a hollow, jagged sound that hurt her just to hear it. "Be with me. Why?" he asked, lifting his head so that he could meet her gaze in the reflection. "You want to comfort me? Make me feel better?"

Taige didn't have any answer for him. She stood there, staring at him and feeling so damn useless. *Useless.* It was worse than evil sometimes. At least evil accomplished its goal. Useless didn't accomplish anything.

"You knew she was already gone, didn't you? When you headed up here?" He looked away from her, as though he couldn't even manage to look at her reflection.

"Yeah." She had to force the word out, and it was like squeezing it out through a pipe lined with rusty nails.

"When it was too late. Why couldn't it come sooner, Taige? You've saved little kids right in front of my eyes. People that were total strangers to you. Why couldn't you save my mom?" he asked quietly.

He turned to stare at her, and his eyes seemed to burn clear through her.

"Cullen . . ."

He crossed toward her. When he reached for her, Taige held still, hardly able to move. That intensity on his face—it almost scared her. His hands came up, cupping her face and forcing her to look at him when all she really wanted was to look away. Hide. Hide from the shame that he had dragged out from inside her. *Useless. Failure . . .* "You have this amazing gift. But you hide from it, don't you? You hide yourself and screw the people you could help."

Taige flinched as though he had slapped her, jerking away from him. She wished he would have hit her. She could handle being hit a hell of a lot easier than she could handle this . . . this contempt. It cut through with laser-sharp acuity, tearing something deep inside, and she knew it was going to leave a scar. Some wounds didn't ever heal, and this was going to be one of them.

Nervous, Taige backed her way out of the room with some barely formed idea of escape circling through her head. But Cullen followed her, advancing each time she retreated, and when she backed herself up against a fat, wide couch situated under yet another window, he lifted his arms, bracketing her into place. "Nothing to say, Taige?" he asked softly.

Digging her fingers into the plush padding of the couch, Taige stared at him. Her throat felt tight. There was a knot in it that felt the size of a golf ball. It took two tries before she managed to force any words out. "I don't know what you want me to say, Cullen. I'm . . ." *Sorry.* It sounded so lame, so empty. His mother was dead, and she had nothing for him but some trite, meaningless phrase that anybody could say. Frustrated, she brought her hands up and smoothed them down over her hair. The wild curls sprang right back into place, but she was doing it more out of nerves than anything. "I've already told you how sorry I am. I know how this hurts—"

The completely wrong thing to say, she realized about two seconds too late. Cullen's eyes narrowed. His hand flew up, this time fisting in her hair so that if she did move away, she was going to have to leave some hair behind. "You know how this hurts," he repeated softly, his voice incredulous, as though he simply couldn't believe she had just said that.

Her voice shook as she said, "I lost my mama, too, Cullen. I lost my mama and my dad, and I was just a little kid when it happened. I didn't have anybody. So yeah, I do know how it hurts."

Cullen shook his head. "You can't know, Taige. Your parents died in an accident. Yes, a drunk driver killed them, but he didn't do it on purpose. And they didn't suffer. My mom? He raped her. He beat her. He choked her to death. The entire time, she probably knew she wasn't going to get out of it alive. And I couldn't help her; I didn't know anything about it until she was already dead." He dipped his head low, putting his face right into hers. His eyes were turbulent and angry, and they filled her vision so that she couldn't see anything but that furious, tormented gaze. "And the bitch of it all, Taige? It's that I could have done something. Could have done something to help her, to save her. You could have."

"No," she argued, her voice low, furious with denial. She shook her head. There was a scream inside her close to breaking free, but Taige wasn't going to let herself scream. She wasn't going to give in to her tears; she didn't deserve that luxury. "No, I couldn't, Cullen. I can't control how it works; you know that."

"What I know is that you've never tried," he replied. "You don't try to control it. You pretend it isn't even there until one of those dreams comes on you. You don't act—you react."

Anger finally worked its way through the sense of futility. She placed her hands against his chest and shoved against him, but he barely budged. "You don't know what in the hell you're talking about," she snarled. "You don't."

"I know I'm right." He reached up and closed his fingers around her wrists and jerked her flat against him. "And so do you."

"Let go of me." Taige arched back, trying to work her hands between them and shove him away, but he held her so close, she couldn't do much more than squirm against him.

"Why?" He dipped his head. She braced herself. She saw the

fury in his gaze, and the pain. Emotions like that blinded people to everything but the hurt and the pain and the anger. None of them were gentle emotions, and Cullen was caught in the grip of them.

But he didn't crush his mouth against hers. Though he held her tight, his hands were gentle. His grip was unbreakable, but he didn't hurt her. He brushed his lips over the top of her shoulder then up her neck to her ear. "You want to make me feel better, Taige? Is that why you're here?"

She swallowed. "I just wanted to be here for you," she said. Oh, damn. Was that shaky, breathy voice really hers?

A broad, rough palm stroked down her side then slid under the plain black T-shirt she wore. "Then be here," he muttered. "Right here." He straightened and grabbed the hem of her shirt, shoving it up until it was trapped under her arms. He stooped and wrapped his arms around her waist, lifting her up and planting her butt on the back of the couch. He licked her nipple through the black cotton of her bra and then gently bit her. Taige arched, pressing against him. She reached for him, but he caught her hands, pushing them down and holding them at her sides as though he didn't want her touching him.

"Cullen . . ."

He shook his head. "Don't talk," he ordered brusquely. "Don't talk." He pulled her off the couch and turned her around, crowding against her body until she was bent over the upholstered back. His hands went to her waist, freeing the button of her jeans, lowering the zipper. In one motion, he shoved her jeans and panties to her knees, and then she heard the rasp of his zipper. Taige twisted around to push her clothes the rest of the way off, but he fisted a hand in her hair and said, "Be still."

Then he was pushing against her. With her jeans and panties

tangled around her knees, she couldn't spread her legs, and it made his entry rougher. She gasped and arched back, squirming against him as he pushed in, deep, slow, burrowing his way through her tight muscles until he had buried his length inside her. He slid an arm around her waist, pulling her back against him. He muttered in her ear, "Tell me that you love me, Taige." His voice was low, hoarse, and so tormented it made her heart clench painfully.

"I love you."

He rolled his hips against her, and Taige groaned, pressing against him, trying to ride the thick length invading her, but the awkward position made it impossible to do much more than squirm and rock against him. Cullen shifted her again, urging her upper body forward, once more bending her over the couch. Then he braced his hands on her hips, held her steady. He withdrew and then slammed into her, deeper, harder, stealing her breath away. She didn't even have time to gasp for air before he did it again, and again, taking her hard and fast.

There were no gentle kisses, no lingering touches, just his barely reined-in fury and the desperation that bled over into her as well. He held himself back until she came, and when Taige started to scream with it, he dropped even the pretense of control, battering her with bruising force, his fingers digging into her hips. The sound of his ragged breathing, her strangled moans, and the slap of flesh on flesh were the only noises, and then he came, his cock jerking viciously inside her snug heat.

And just like that, it was over. He stepped away. Taige rolled her head on the back of the couch, staring at him through her lashes as he readjusted his pants. Slowly, she straightened. Her muscles felt like wax, and her legs wobbled under her as she pulled her panties and jeans back up. Between her thighs, she ached, and she could feel his semen on her.

"Did I hurt you?" he asked hoarsely. He was standing by the window, staring outside.

Taige shook her head. She was a little uncomfortable, and she'd probably be sore later, but she wasn't hurt. "No."

He nodded. But still, he wouldn't look at her.

She wanted him to. She almost said it out loud, *Look at me, Cullen*. But she didn't.

"You need to leave, Taige."

His flat, unemotional words did a lot more damage than the roughness of the past few minutes, but she tried to understand. He hadn't been expecting her, probably had a house full of family, and other than his dad, none of them knew her. She wanted to be there, though. Wanted to be there for him, and it hurt that he didn't want that from her. "I'll call you tomorrow," she said softly.

Finally, he looked at her. He turned his head and met her eyes and said, "Please don't. I don't want to talk to you, Taige. I don't want to see you again. Ever."

* * *

FROM the window, he could see her, striding out to the Jeep parked at the far end of the drive, her head low, her arms wrapped around her middle. It was chilly out. She hadn't been wearing a jacket when she came in. Did she have one in the car? he wondered.

"Fuck her like that, kick her out of your house, and now you worry she might get cold," he muttered. "Dumb ass." He kept watching her, hoping she'd look back at him just one more time.

But she never did. She climbed into the Jeep and didn't even get the door all the way closed before she threw it into reverse. He heard the faint squeal of the tires even from here. He kept watching, even after she disappeared around the bend in the road, and for a long time after. He had no idea how much time had passed when his father knocked on the door. It could have been minutes, or it could have been hours.

Probably somewhere in between, because most of the cars in the drive were gone, and night had completely settled.

"Did I see Taige?" Robert asked softly.

Cullen nodded.

"She didn't stay long." Robert didn't ask any questions, and Cullen was glad of that.

How could he answer, anyway? *Mom's dead, and Taige should have been able to stop it.* No, that wasn't going to work. He hadn't told either of his parents about the weird things that Taige had been able to do, hadn't ever figured out how to explain it.

When Cullen stayed quiet, Robert said, "Pretty long drive for her to make just to come by and say hi."

"Leave it alone, Dad."

Robert opened his mouth to speak, but then, as though he'd thought better of it, he closed it and sighed. "Taige lost both her parents young, didn't she? I bet she knows all about hurting and grief. Knows how it can make you do or say things that you don't really mean."

"What about things you do mean?" Cullen blurted out. He turned away from his dad and rubbed his hands over his face, wished he hadn't said anything. "Can it make you say things that you do mean, even if you shouldn't?"

"Go after her, Cullen. You've lost enough right now. You don't need to lose her, too," Robert said gently.

But Cullen couldn't do it. Or rather, he wouldn't. He'd seen the hurt in her eyes. Yes, he blamed her, she knew it, and he hated himself for it, but there it was. He couldn't change how he felt. He imagined Taige would even put up with it. Put up with him and deal with the guilt he made her feel and the pain he could cause her.

But, even though he was irrationally furious with her, he wasn't going to do that.

She didn't deserve his misplaced anger, and he loved her. Even more than he wanted to hurt her for failing him, he loved her. Chasing her away was the only way he could keep himself from hurting her, over and over.

His dad finally gave up trying to talk to him and went downstairs, leaving Cullen alone in silence. Feeling lost, he wandered around in endless circles until finally he stopped by the couch, touching the spot where he had been with Taige. He rested his hand against the padded back and murmured, "I'm sorry."

PART TWO

FOUR

May 2008

TAIGE stalked into the kitchen, releasing the holster on her shoulder with one hand and holding the cordless phone in the other. "Damn it, Jones, I said no. I am tired. I just spent four months in hell because of you, and I'm not going back there just yet." On her way past the table, she laid her weapon down.

"Taige—"

She took a deep breath as she opened the refrigerator, staring inside for something to drink. Her belly was an empty, aching pit, but she had no desire to eat. Just a drink. Preferably something strong enough to send her crashing into oblivion for the next eight hours. She wouldn't even mind the hangover too much, provided she had a little bit of peace before it hit.

"You aren't hearing me, Jones. I'm not your lackey. I am not one of your agents you can send running out for coffee or to spy on the neighbors. You want my help; you have to ask me for it. You asked. I just said no. Now leave me the hell alone." She lowered the phone and disconnected it in the middle of Taylor Jones's rant.

Son of a bitch. She couldn't stand him. He had tried to recruit her before she even got out of college, and when he didn't succeed, he sent others to try their hand. Taige had refused all of them, unable to stand the thought of letting them stick her in some specialized unit where they'd use her like some psychic bloodhound and keep on doing it until she either dropped dead from the strain or burned herself out.

Death wasn't the issue for her. Most of the time, she felt more dead inside than alive. Even the burnout part wouldn't be so bad— no voices in her head, no more nagging dreams—but the pace those bastards would work her at would have been something akin to the lowest level of hell. Instead, she agreed to take part in special task forces where the workload was only on the first or second level of hell.

This last, though, it had been the worst. Four months undercover in Chicago. And Chicago in February was cold. She thought she just might freeze her ass before she managed to infiltrate that child-porn ring. Three families, all of them upper-middle-class, all of them foster parents to troubled kids. Troubled kids they drugged and then sold to the highest bidder. Whoever shelled out the most cash got to do whatever they wanted with the kid, and for a little extra, they could even keep the DVD made of the event. Without that extra cash, that DVD might make its way onto the Internet, and God only knew who'd see it out there.

It had taken four months and the overdose of one of the victims before Taige had been able to ferret them out, but finally, they were all behind bars. Whether they would stay or not was up to the judicial system, but at least Taige could close her eyes knowing she had done her part.

It might even help her sleep for a little while. A few weeks, maybe a month or two. Then the guilt would start chasing her again.

She didn't realize she was standing in front of the refrigerator with the door open until she started to shiver. With a scowl, she grabbed a bottle of white zinfandel from the shelf and let the door close. She popped the cork and poured a glass, emptying it in under a minute. Then she filled it to the top again and made her way into her office, bringing the rest of the wine with her.

She didn't boot up the computer or turn on the radio. Instead, she turned her chair around so she could stare out over Mobile Bay and wait for the numbness to set in.

But it didn't come as quickly as it used to.

I worry about you, baby girl.

Often, in moments like these, when Taige was alone, she could hear the ghostly whisper of Rose's voice. It wasn't the woman's ghost, Taige knew that, just memories. There had been long, endless nights of studying when Taige wouldn't have slept at all if Rose hadn't forced her into bed. Days when she would have gone without eating if Rose hadn't sought her out around dinnertime and forced her to eat.

You work yourself too hard. Why are you doing this?

Rose had been dead for three years now, a victim of Katrina. She'd gone to New Orleans to visit a friend who had just lost her mother, one of those friends who hadn't tried to leave until it was too late, and by the time it was clear they needed to leave, they couldn't. Rose had stayed by her side. They had both drowned when the water got too high.

Another one of Taige's failures.

You can't help everybody, baby girl. Come on now, put the wine down and go get something to eat. Take a bath . . . go for a swim . . . you got to do something besides sit inside and brood.

Taige lifted her wineglass in a salute. "If it's all the same to you, Rose, I'm just going to sit inside and brood." She drained the glass and filled it a third time. She hoped by the time she had emptied a fourth, her brain would be getting fuzzy. Otherwise, she was going to have to drink that nasty merlot Dante had brought over when he came down at Christmas last year.

You didn't fail me, Taige.

She closed her eyes and wished she could block out those annoying little whispers. Sometimes, it seemed like Rose had settled inside of Taige's soul, instead of going on to be with the husband she'd lost when Dante was only two. But it wasn't really Rose, just memories of her, just Taige missing her.

But the real bitch was that Taige would have preferred a real ghost and all the nagging and mothering in the world over what happened if she managed to fall asleep before she was so tired she ached with it. When she was that tired, bone tired, she could fall fast and hard into a sleep to rival that of the dead. Dark, dreamless sleep.

Over the years, training and regular use had given her a greater control over her skills, and as her control increased, those abilities had evolved so that she rarely needed to sleep for the visions to come. They came easier now, and she could recall them in fine, vivid detail. Now that she actively sought them, instead of waiting for them to find her, she had more control over them, and they rarely plagued her when she slept.

Unfortunately, though, that left room for something that much more disturbing. The only thing that kept those dreams at bay was sheer exhaustion—or lots of liquor. She didn't have the stomach for whiskey, hated the taste of it, and the smell of beer was enough to nauseate her. So that left wine and cocktails. Cocktails usually required a little more work than Taige liked, unless it was something simple like rum and Coke. It all added up to her drinking a hell of a lot more than she should.

The rhythmic ebb and flow of the waves was having a hypnotic effect on her. She could feel her eyelids dragging down while her body sank into that heavy, drowsy state that came right before sleep. Tired . . .

Her lids drooped low once more, and then she tensed, her body going ramrod straight in the chair. "Damn it," she muttered. She set the wineglass down and scrubbed her hands over her face. Didn't do too much to help. The fog of sleep was already clouding her brain, and nothing short of a caffeine injection or a cold shower was going to do the trick.

Caffeine required too much work. Shoving her tense body out of the chair, she stumbled into the bathroom, stripping off her clothes and dropping them behind her as she went. She left the clothes wherever they fell, shirt, bra, boots, socks, and jeans forming a haphazard trail. Wearing just a pair of plain cotton panties, she flipped on the light in the bathroom and opened the door to the shower stall. She turned the water on full, not bothering to adjust it to a warmer temperature. After stripping off her panties, she climbed inside and let the cool water rain down on her.

It soaked her hair, and Taige realized she'd forgotten to undo the thick braid. Too tired to care, she left it alone. She'd deal with it later. Even with the cool water spraying down on her, she felt like she was in some sort of fog. She gritted her teeth and adjusted the spray, letting the water go from cool to icy. Then she grabbed the mesh sponge from the hook on the wall and soaped it up. The familiar scent of the Molton Brown bath gel filled her senses. She breathed it in as she scrubbed the sponge over her body, hoping she could force herself into wakefulness for a while longer.

By the time Taige finally turned off the water, her teeth were chattering. She decided that maybe coffee wasn't too much work now. Especially now that she was freezing her ass off. She tucked the towel around her body and headed into the kitchen, kicking her boots out of the way. She'd pick them up later. Once she had rested, the whole house needed to be cleaned. It was dusty from her long absence and had that musty smell houses got after sitting empty for weeks or months on end.

She got the coffee brewing and stood shivering in the kitchen as she waited for her first shot of caffeine. Hot coffee splattered on the warming plate and counter as she pulled the carafe out and filled her cup. Folding her hands around it, she let the heat seep into her palms while she took a sip. It scalded her tongue, but she didn't care. She finished off the first cup and poured herself a second before she bothered to get dressed.

As Taige shimmied into a pair of shorts and a tank top, she heard the annoying ring of her cell phone out in the kitchen. She knew that particular ring, and she blocked it out of her mind. There was no damn way she was talking to Taylor Jones anytime soon.

Never would suit her just fine.

By her third cup of coffee, Taige figured she was awake enough to sit down, maybe watch some TV or try a book. She picked up a trade paperback she'd grabbed on impulse at the airport in Birmingham, but instead of curling up on the couch, she headed out to the hammock in the backyard. She could read for a while, then maybe get some housework done.

If she worked hard enough at that, did it long enough, she

could exhaust herself to the point that the dreams wouldn't come. It was either that or dig out the merlot.

Taige was getting damn tired of drinking herself into oblivion.

With caffeine buzzing through her system, she settled down on the hammock. But she hadn't even made it past the first chapter before fatigue came crashing down on her. Her mind started to wander away from the story, daydreams intruding on reality, and she never realized she was drifting off.

The caffeine in her system, the cold shower, none of her attempts to stay awake made a bit of difference under the weight of her exhaustion. She fell asleep with the midmorning sun shining hot on her face, and when the book slid from her slack hands and hit the ground, she didn't notice.

"You push yourself too hard," he murmured as he leaned down and pushed a few wayward strands of hair back from her face.

His voice had changed over the years, deepening just a little. His face had changed some, too, but he was still just as beautiful to her now as he had been when she was sixteen and he had come running to her side the night Joey and Lee had tried to rape her.

She didn't know where Cullen came from, only that one second she was alone, and then she wasn't. They were outside, and Taige was lying on the hammock, with Cullen standing over her and staring at her with dark, unhappy eyes.

In some part of her mind, she panicked. She knew that she'd fallen asleep, and now he was here. Now she'd have to face him, face the memories she tried so hard to bury and the longings that had never faded. But the rest of her? The rest of her was so happy to see him, she figured that if he crooked his finger at her, she would willingly strip herself naked and plant her butt in his lap.

The idea had a lot of merit, but Cullen seemed more inter-ested in scowling at her than making love to her.

"Figures," she muttered. "Even in my dreams, you're going to be a pain in the ass."

"You're one to talk." He glared at her, and Taige had a feel-ing he wasn't impressed with what he saw, somebody far too skinny, far too tired, and now scarred to boot. The midriff tank and low-rise shorts she had pulled on earlier didn't cover the ugly scar low on her belly. It had faded some, no longer the an-gry red it had been a few years ago. The scar tissue was darker than rest of her skin, calling attention to it, and belatedly, she tried to cover it.

But Cullen wouldn't let her. He crouched down by her side and wrapped his fingers around her wrist, pulling her hand away so he could press his lips to it. A shiver raced through her. "You worry me," he whispered, his breath dancing across her skin like a faint, teasing caress. "You don't eat. You hardly sleep. You drink too much."

Tensing, she tried to move away from him. Cullen wouldn't let her, though. He ended up crawling into the hammock with her, cradling her up against him. He made it seem easy, and Taige lay there wishing the damn thing would flip them out onto their butts. "I eat enough. And I drink because I don't want to dream. I hardly sleep because I don't want to dream. You don't like it, then stop showing up in my dreams."

He sighed, and when she looked up at him, she saw that fa-miliar look of frustration, worry, and want. It hurt to see that look on his face. He was just like the ghost of Rose that Taige had conjured up out of her loneliness. Nothing more than a fig-ment of her imagination, and the love she thought she saw on his face was nonexistent.

These dreams weren't any more real than his love for her had been. She knew that, so seeing him looking at her like she was the center of his world was like plunging tiny, needle-sharp shards of glass into her skin.

His hand came up, cradling her face for a long moment, and then he smoothed her hair back. "What happened this time?"

Taige flinched as though he'd jabbed her with a hot poker. She shook her head and tried again to pull away. "I don't want to talk about it."

"You never do."

She sneered at him. "You're nothing more than my imagination, you know. Since I imagined you, wouldn't it make sense that you'd already know what happened?"

Slowly, Cullen's thumb passed over her lower lip. "I'm not your imagination, darlin'. Tell me."

But she didn't want to talk about it. Her gut tied itself into ugly, slippery little knots every time she thought about the videos she'd found and all those girls and boys she had talked to, kids with chunks missing out of their lives, pieces of themselves taken away in the night. That the bastards had recorded it so that every last detail was floating around for the enjoyment of sickos everywhere made it so much worse.

Taige hated the perverts that had paid for the kids for what they had done to them, everything from the drugging to the assaults and the rapes. She hated that the oh so lily-white and pure soccer moms and their fine upstanding husbands had made videos of it, recording the way those kids had been victimized.

Taige wasn't active law enforcement, but she had made sure she was there when the arrests happened, and she had threatened Jones within an inch of his life if he didn't let her observe the questioning. She had left after the first two hours. There had been three couples involved, and most of them wouldn't say a word. Their lawyers had shut them up but good.

One woman though, Deidre Sanger, hadn't seemed to realize how much trouble she was in. Or why. "It's not like they remember it," she'd said. "It's not like they know what happened."

Taige had wanted to go through the mirrored glass and choke the bitch. Deidre had the nerve to act as though they had done the kids a favor by drugging them. Few people could understand how, sometimes, those drug-induced states made it so much worse for the victims. A piece of their life stolen . . .

"Taige." A warm hand curved over her neck, and then a hard mouth pressed a gentle kiss against hers. She shivered and then opened her eyes, stared at Cullen. His lids were low over his eyes but that couldn't hide the frustration she saw there. His hand tightened on her neck, but he didn't say anything else. He just eased her body back up against his, holding her tight. She buried her face in the front of his shirt and wished this was real.

If it was real, she could tell him. She could cuddle up against him and cry herself dry, and maybe the ache in her heart would ease a little. Maybe if she cried hard enough, maybe if she told him all the vile crap she had been forced to wade through for the past decade, she could breathe without feeling like there was a band around her chest. She could sleep deep and easy without nightmares, without guilt.

But it wasn't real. Cullen's presence in her dreams came from years of loving the bastard, even after he'd kicked her out of his life. These dreams were a sham, something brought on by her weak, needy heart, and she hated them.

Suddenly desperate to wake up, to get away from him, she shoved against him, hard and fast. She ended up flipping the hammock over, but she landed on her hands and knees, away from him. He swore under his breath and reached for her, but Taige scrambled away. "I don't want you here, Cullen," she said, squeezing the words through her tight throat and wishing she could scream it at him. Wished she could hit him and do something to ease the pain inside her.

"Yes, you do," he whispered, striding toward her. She brought her hands up, ready to punch him if he came any closer. Cullen was ready to risk it, apparently, because he just kept coming. She swung toward him, and he blocked the first punch. The second one caught him on the chin, but he still reached for her, pulling her up against him.

Taige struggled, kicking at his shins. But her bare feet weren't going to do much damage. She ended up with a sore foot, and that only made her madder. "Let go of me, damn it," she snarled.

"No. I did that once, and I've hated myself ever since," he said, his voice calm and soft, gentle even. Taige leaned forward to bite him, and Cullen jerked back at the last second. Then he flipped her around in his arms, pressing her back up against his front and wrapping his arms around her in a bear hug that effectively pinned her in place.

Seething, she reared back with her head, but he moved his out of reach and kept her from smashing his nose the way she planned. "You son of a bitch, you didn't let go of me. You kicked me out of your life. There's a big-ass difference, and you got no right doing this to me."

"Doing what?" he murmured. He nuzzled her neck. When she flinched and hunched her shoulder to keep him away, he just shifted his focus to her shoulder, kissing the skin bared by the thin straps of her shirt.

Making me still love you. Making me still need you. The words leaped unbidden to her mind, and she almost blurted them out. She had a little bit of pride, though, and she managed to keep them behind her teeth. Barely. "Touching me like this. Talking to me like you give a damn. Any of it."

"You like me touching you," he whispered. Slowly, his arms loosened, and the hands that had been restraining her left her arms to cup her hips. He pulled her back against him, and the feel of him through his jeans had her wanting to strip naked and beg him to touch her.

But she didn't have to beg. Even though she hated herself for being weak, when he slid one callused hand up her side to cup her breast, she groaned and arched into his touch. He squeezed her nipple, rolling the stiff peak between his thumb and forefinger, tugging it lightly. Cullen rested his chin on her shoulder, and together, they stared at the sight of his hand moving under the thin cotton of her shirt. "You like it when I touch you," he repeated, and his voice was hoarse and rough. The sound of it sent shivers dancing down her spine. "And I do give a damn. If I didn't care about you, I wouldn't keep coming to you."

If you cared about me, you never would have left me, she thought. But she didn't say it. She was tired of fighting him. This was inevitable. He would touch her, and she would let him. He would strip her clothes away and she his. He'd make love to her and for a little while, she would pretend it was real and that he did love her, that he hadn't ever left her.

And when it was over, and she woke, she'd feel that much emptier inside, that much lonelier.

His hands grabbed the bottom of her shirt, and she lifted her arms so he could pull it off. The shirt went flying. Gathering the thick mass of her hair in his hand, Cullen bared her neck. She shivered when he bent down and kissed her skin. Then he bit her gently, his teeth grazing her skin and leaving a burning, sizzling path. He spoke, and when he did, it was an eerie echo of one of the last things he'd ever said to her. He'd said it time and again in their dreams, almost as though he had to hear it.

"Tell me that you love me, Taige," he ordered gruffly as he slid his hands around and cupped both of her breasts. He teased the nipples, and each slow tug of his fingers sent need streaking through her, arrowing down and echoing low inside her belly. She squirmed and pressed her butt back against him.

"I love you," she murmured, parroting back the words he needed to hear, words that she had to say. If she didn't need to keep saying them, would she keep having these pointless, painful dreams? She reached behind her and pressed her palms to his muscled thighs, her fingers clenching and digging into the worn material of his jeans so she could tug him closer.

She felt him working the zipper of her shorts, and she bit her lip, holding her breath as he opened the faded denim and slid his hand inside her shorts and panties. He cupped her in his hand and pushed two fingers inside her. She keened out his name and rocked against his hand. Cullen wrapped an arm around her, lifting her against him, and she felt them moving. Opening her eyes, she saw that he'd moved them closer to the deck, and then he slid his hand out of her panties. When he wrapped his fingers around her wrist, she felt the heated moisture there. He guided her hands up, bracing them against the deck floor. Where they stood, the deck's floor came up to her chest, and she leaned against it willingly, letting it support her a little as Cullen stepped back and stripped her panties and shorts away. They fell in a tangle around her ankles, and she went to kick them off. Cullen cupped her hips and leaned against her, muttering roughly, "Be still."

It was déjà vu; she felt like she was reliving that last time with him, and as desperate as she was for him, she almost pulled away.

She had to deal with that pain in real life. Was she going to have to deal with it here, too? Was he going to walk away from her again?

Her body was weak, though. Her sense of self-preservation might be telling her to run, but the rest of her was screaming, *Stay!* Taige remained motionless, leaning against the deck with her palms braced on the smooth, faded wood. She heard the harsh rasp of his zipper and caught her lower lip between her teeth, need and anticipation twining through her. She was so hot and shaky, so hungry and so desperate for him. When he pressed against her, she jolted as though she had been shocked. Her legs were pinned together by the shorts at her ankles, and he had to work his way inside, pushing through the tight tissues and forging his way in, deeper and deeper.

She groaned at the sensations dancing through her. The line between pleasure and pain blurred. She arched back, trying to take more of him. He gripped her hips and pulled back. When he shoved in, hard and fast, the line between pleasure and pain disappeared altogether. She screamed, a startled cry. He did it again, and she whimpered. Again and she twisted against him, unsure if she wanted him to do it again or if she wanted to pull away. Again, and she erupted, crying out his name and coming with an intensity that stole her breath away.

But he wasn't done. He kept slamming into her. With her hands braced on the deck and his hands cupping her hips and holding her tight, she stood there, a willing vessel for him but too satisfied, too drained to feel anything beyond the pounding of her heart and the friction as he shafted her.

The roaring in her ears subsided, and she heard him muttering under his breath. "You're mine, damn it. I want you back. Never lose you again—mine . . ."

Strange words, considering. But then he slid his hand around her hip, spearing through the curls between her thighs, seeking out the hard bud of her clit. She went from letting him ride her and thinking about the weirdness of her dreams and how her heart hurt just being with him like this to hot, hungry, and desperate, as desperate as he was. As though he had just been waiting for that response, he stopped touching her clit, left her hovering on the brink of orgasm. He trailed his fingers, wet from her, up over her hip, the small of her back, and up her spine. Then he bent over her, crowding her closer to the deck and bracing his hand by hers. "I love you," he rasped in her ear. "You're mine . . . aren't you, Taige? Say you're still mine."

"Yours," she agreed, even though deep inside she wanted to scream in denial.

Satisfied, he rode her hard, driving her to another climax before he came, and then he pulled back long enough to pull his jeans up. Taige leaned against the deck, panting for air and her knees wobbling. Then he pulled her into his arms and lifted, carrying her out of the warm summer sun and into the cool, quiet darkness of her house.

*　*　*

IT wasn't a weird way for him to wake up, but it sure as hell was unsettling. Not to mention a little bit embarrassing, Cullen mused as he climbed out of bed and stripped the sheets away. Wet dreams were supposed to stop after puberty . . . right? Whoever came up with that obviously hadn't had dreams about Taige Branch.

Bizarre dreams, dreams that seemed too real for them not to be true.

Bizarre and powerful enough, unsettling enough, that one

dream was enough to hurl him into a black mood that could last for weeks. It was a good thing they didn't happen too often. He'd spent most of his life trapped inside a guilt-induced rage.

Guilt and need colored too much of his life as it was. If these dreams came more often than they did, he'd probably end up on a shrink's couch. And he didn't have time for that.

From somewhere in the house, he heard music, and he glanced at the clock. Seven thirty. Shit. He'd wanted to be up an hour ago. They had too much stuff to do today, and now he was going to be running late.

"Daddy . . ." There was a knock on his door. Years of experience kept him from reacting when the door swung open, and he saw his daughter standing there with an expectant look on her face. He shifted his armload of sheets and blankets a little lower, just in case.

"Gimme a few minutes, Jilly," he said. "Overslept."

She grinned at him and said, "Hurry up, sleepyhead."

She slammed the door behind her, and automatically, he called out, "Don't slam the doors." Then he looked down at his armful of sheets. He didn't have time to mess with them right now, so he carried them into the bathroom and opened the closet in there, dumping them into the hamper. Marci, the cleaning lady, would be in while they were gone, and she'd make the bed with clean sheets, and he could wash the dirty ones when he got back.

Too bad he couldn't deal with the lingering echoes of the dream just as easily.

The haunted look in Taige's eyes bothered him. A lot. She wouldn't tell him what was going on, and Cullen knew from experience that if she wasn't going to share what had caused those shadows, he may never know.

Thinking of her, the weird, too-real dreams, Cullen found

himself walking out of his bathroom and into the office that was on the other side of his bedroom. He opened the connecting door and went to the bookshelf that spanned the entire northern wall. On the top shelf, out of Jillian's reach, was a fat leather album. Inside it were pictures, newspaper articles, some clipped from the paper and some printed off the Web, all of Taige Branch.

He'd seen the first one nine years ago, the day after Jilly was born. He'd been looking through the fat Sunday paper. The nurse came in, bringing Jilly with her, and Cullen had tossed the paper onto the narrow, uncomfortable couch. A section slid to the floor, and when he picked it up a few minutes later, time froze.

Down in the bottom right corner on the last page of the section was Taige. It wasn't a great picture. She had sunglasses on and was looking away from the camera. The bold caption above the picture read, "Local Psychic Saves Kidnapped Child."

It had happened in Mobile. Some thug pulled a woman out of her car at a stoplight and either didn't see the baby sleeping in the back or didn't care. Two days of nonstop searching had turned up nothing. Then a college sophomore showed up at the police department. She'd said she could find the baby. Cullen knew that must have been hard for her, going there and knowing she'd be ridiculed, and after she helped, she'd become the focus of rampant speculation.

As promised, and without any help from the police, she'd found the baby. All it had taken was getting to the mom's side. The paper didn't detail what all had happened beyond her finding the child, but Cullen had done some digging. After the police found the baby exactly where Taige had told them to find her, they had arrested her on suspicion of kidnapping.

The charges were dropped only after they failed to find any evidence at all linking her to the carjacker turned kidnapper, but not until she'd spent a week in jail. Nobody had come to post bail, and by the time Cullen knew a damn thing, she'd been released.

There were other stories, some of them no more than a paragraph or two and others that were nearly full-page stories featuring color pictures and interviews with people who claimed to know her. Dante and Rose had been mentioned in a few, always with something along the lines of "No comment" when asked about Taige Branch. A couple of enterprising reporters had even unearthed some of the kids she had helped when she was younger.

The most recent article was nearly two years old. She'd either gotten better at keeping her name out of things, or she had people helping her on that end. He had a feeling it was a combination of both. Over the past few years it was getting harder to find any information about her, but he had a friend who worked for the FBI. A paper pusher more than anything, but Grant Wilson had confirmed that the FBI did have special task forces, and Taige Branch was often called in to work on kidnappings or other crimes related to children.

He touched his fingers to the grainy image of her face. It didn't seem as if she had aged a day physically, but there was a hardness to her that made him hurt inside. He didn't imagine she'd had much choice but to develop some armor, given the life she lived.

She'd helped so many kids. Cullen knew there were probably far more than those found between these album pages. Ones that she helped and then disappeared before anybody even had a chance to thank her, much less ask her name. She'd done that sort of thing a lot when they'd been together, and he knew how uncomfortable the attention made her.

Taige would avoid it as often as was possible, and when it

wasn't, she'd tolerate it with clenched teeth and a grim look, as though she couldn't understand why people were so amazed by what she did. As though she couldn't comprehend how amazing she was.

Cullen turned to the last page in the album and stared at the picture of her there. It was the best image by far, taken by a reporter for the *Birmingham News*, but it wasn't one he'd cut out of the newspaper. No, this one was an eight-by-ten glossy that he had paid for. "You've got it bad," he murmured. If anybody saw the album, they'd probably peg him for some crazy stalker, and chances are, they wouldn't be far off.

He had subscriptions to every major paper in Alabama because he didn't want to risk missing any information on her, and he regularly Googled her on the Web. Even when he'd been married to Jilly's mom, his obsession with Taige never faded. Fortunately, he'd kept it from Kim, and he only hoped she'd never known that he didn't love her the way she'd deserved to be loved.

He couldn't love her, because he hadn't ever stopped loving Taige—and he never would.

FIVE

JILLY stood with her face pressed up against the acrylic, practically nose to nose with a gleaming white beluga whale. Cullen thought the thing looked more like a toy than a whale, but Jilly was entranced. The whale seemed to be in the same boat. He'd swim upward, spin around, and then come back to stare at Cullen's little girl with besotted eyes.

Cullen was used to it. Animals had that kind of reaction to Jilly, and they had ever since she'd been born. He could remember bringing her home from the hospital when she was three days old, and the old mutt across the street that usually howled and chased anybody and everybody had come running across the street to check out the new baby. But the dog had stopped dead in his tracks about three feet from the baby's car seat, whining low in his throat, staring at Jilly the same way he would have looked at his owner after being left alone for a week.

The whale swam upward again, his long, bulky body amazingly

graceful. He circled around and then headed back down to gaze at Jilly through the acrylic. Jilly smiled at him and reached up, laying her hand against the smooth barrier that separated them. The whale nosed the acrylic, and Cullen heard a few of the parents behind him murmuring.

"*Look at that . . .* "

"*Isn't that sweet?*"

The kids around her weren't thrilled, though. They wanted to see the whale, too, but the big marine creature was totally focused on Jilly. Cullen made his way through the crowd so he could crouch down by his daughter. "Come on, baby. Let's go see the sharks again."

Jilly glanced up at him. "He likes me, Daddy."

"I know, baby. But the other kids want to see him, too." As they left the exhibit, the whale lingered near the glass, staring after Jilly with infatuated eyes.

The whale sharks weren't as entranced with Jilly, but she still enjoyed watching them. She ended up perched on the floor by the great wall, her sketchbook and pencil in hand. By the time they left Atlanta, the sketchbook would be full, and she'd need another one.

According the brochure, the trip through the aquarium usually took a couple of hours. By the time they left the cool darkness for the heat of the Atlanta afternoon, more than four hours had passed. They had one last night left before they headed back home, and if Cullen knew his daughter, he knew where they'd spend the rest of the day: at the zoo.

A hot breeze kicked up as they headed for the parking lot. They stopped at the crosswalk to wait for the green light, and the feel of that hot breeze blowing in his face teased a memory, and for a moment, time fell away. It hit him like that sometimes, memories sneaking up on him and hitting him with the intensity of a sucker punch.

It was like yesterday, standing on an Alabama beach with his arms wrapped around Taige, her mouth sweet and warm under his lips, and her body, so soft and strong, pressed against his own.

A little hand tugged on his, and the memory fell apart around him. Cullen looked down to find Jilly staring up at him with big green eyes. "The light changed, Daddy. We can cross now."

"Yeah. Yeah, it has."

* * *

EVEN as much as Taige despised Jones, she didn't shut the door in his face when he woke her up early the next morning—way early. The sun was already shining, but it wasn't even seven. Too damn early, considering how little she'd slept the night before. Her reflexes were off, so that might explain why she didn't feel too inclined to knock that smug, smarmy smile off his face.

Taylor Jones was just a little too perfect-looking. He had perfectly tanned skin, a perfectly blinding white smile, his hair perfectly cut and styled. She imagined he had a standing appointment at some pricey designer salon for men to keep his hair from growing even one eighth of an inch longer than he liked. His suits were a little more expensive than the typical FBI agent wore, as were his shoes. The man came from money, and she'd heard rumors that he had political aspirations. He'd probably do well in the political arena, too; he had a knack for knowing exactly what to say.

If Taige hadn't seen the bastard in action, she wouldn't believe how utterly ruthless he could be. If he focused that ruthless intent solely on helping victims, she could even admire it. But although he was damn good at his job, he placed his own ambitions just a little higher than the job. He'd ruined the careers of people who got in his way—part of the reason she had decided not to join the FBI. She didn't want to end up some innocent bystander in one of his crusades.

But as focused and ambitious as the bastard was, he knew better than to show up at her door after she'd told him she needed time off. So whatever case had brought him here had to be damn important. Otherwise, he wouldn't risk it. She glared at him, eyes still bleary with exhaustion, but instead of shutting the door on him, she pushed it open wider and let him step inside.

Without saying a word, she left him in the foyer and went to her room. Her wardrobe was fairly monochromatic: a lot of black, interspersed with the occasional pair of blue jeans, and a few things in red and white. She hated shopping, and as a result, her wardrobe was minimal, containing little more than the basics. Pissed Jones off to no end when she showed up on a job wearing her standards, black jeans and T-shirt. Feeling just a little petty, she grabbed a particularly ratty pair of blue jeans, so faded they were nearly white, snug through her hips and butt with a big hole in the left knee.

If Jones's case was something she needed to do, they wouldn't have any time to waste, which meant she'd show up at the job wearing the jeans she usually saved for yard work or cleaning. The black T-shirt wasn't much better, faded to a dark, washed-out gray and hanging on her slender body. On the way out the door, she paused long enough to grab her boots and a pair of socks, just in case.

But it was all for nothing, she knew less than three minutes later.

She sat on the couch, staring at the confidential file, her heart breaking as a pair of innocent, sky-blue eyes stared up at her.

The girl had been kidnapped by her father, who'd been released from jail on parole after serving three years for molesting the girl's older sister. The mom had been pregnant when he went to trial, and it had been her impassioned testimony that had sent the bastard to jail.

Too bad they hadn't kept him.

Taige swallowed around the knot in her throat and then closed the file and pushed it back at Jones. He didn't even need to ask. The look on her face told him everything he needed to know, just like the look on his face told Taige that he was seriously pissed. "You're sure?" he demanded.

"If I wasn't sure, you know I'd say so."

He turned his head, reaching up to pinch the bridge of his nose. As much a bastard as he was, Taige knew he believed in his job, and she had a feeling the little girl's big blue eyes were bothering him as much as they bothered her. Touching that girl's file, she had felt nothing. Staring at the girl's picture, she'd felt nothing but a familiar sense of grief and guilt.

Another child she wouldn't be able to save. She knew, somewhere inside, that she wasn't meant to save this one—this girl wasn't hers—but even that knowledge didn't help her guilt.

Jones looked back down at the file in his hand and then back at her. "You're tired," he said after studying her face. "The last case was a bad one. Maybe if you get some rest today and try again tomorrow . . ."

Taige shook her head. "It won't do any good." But she gestured toward the file. "Leave it if you want. I'll try again, but it isn't going to do any good. If you all find her, it won't be because of me. I'm not going to get a thing."

That was how it worked for her. She'd long since come to accept it, and for the most part, she was even grateful for it. She knew people in the Bureau talked about her, had heard it said, "Branch doesn't find dead ends. Just dead bodies."

Not always, thank God. But enough so that those lost lives had left a mark on her, each one adding to the mess of scars she carried in her heart. Sometimes she was amazed her heart still beat. If emotional scars left the same damage as physical scars, she would have died years ago.

Jones threw the file on the coffee table, and Taige averted her eyes as one photo fell out. Staring at the girl's face wouldn't help anybody. As he headed for the door, she followed him. He opened the door and paused to look back at her, his practiced, semipolite mask back in place. "When can I count on you being ready to work?"

She smirked at him. "You can't. After all this time, you still seem to forget that I don't really work for you, do I?" Then she shrugged and answered his question. "I need a few days at least. Maybe even longer. Four months is a long haul for me."

The skin around his eyes tightened, but he didn't say anything, just nodded and left. He wasn't her boss, but she did have a responsibility to the Bureau. Taige didn't technically work for him; her official title was civilian consultant. Those responsibilities were something she never let herself forget, no matter how tired she got, no matter how bleak things became.

She looked back at the table, and although she didn't want to, she found herself staring at the picture of the girl's smiling face. Things were looking especially bleak right now.

* * *

ALTHOUGH Taige had told Jones it wouldn't do any good, after lunch she made herself sit down and go through the girl's file. Her name was Hannah Brewster. She was three years old, and she'd been at her sitter's when her father showed up, assaulted the sitter, and then kidnapped the young girl. The sitter was still in ICU. One look at the extent of damage done to the twenty-year-old single mom, and Taige knew it was actually a miracle the young woman was still alive. Her own daughter had been at her dad's for the weekend, and Taige couldn't help but feel a little grateful for that. If the sitter's daughter had been home, there might have been two kidnapping victims instead of one.

She pored over the report, spent nearly thirty minutes staring at the file, willing herself to feel something. But there was nothing. When she connected with a case, it was instantaneous; sometimes she knew it was coming even before Jones contacted her. She'd feel a rush of adrenaline, and everything inside of her would seem to focus on the job.

Sometimes all it took was a look at a picture or hearing the victim's name, and it was like an invisible bridge formed between them, a road only Taige could see and follow. Other times, it was more complicated. Like Chicago. Chicago had been bad, but she had known it would be even before she accepted the job.

"I'm sorry, Hannah," she murmured. She touched her fingers to the girl's face and hoped that Jones would have better luck with one of his other psychic bloodhounds. She wasn't the only one, and she wasn't even their best, she knew. But Taige had a talent with kids, so that was probably why he'd come to her first. But she wouldn't be the only one he approached.

Frustrated, she shoved all the reports and pictures back into the file, and then she took the file into her office, stowing it inside the file cabinet. It didn't help much. Putting it away only put it out of her sight, not out of her mind.

She paused by her desk and stared at the empty wine bottle and the glass from last night. The alcohol seemed to call to her, and for a minute, she almost went and unearthed the merlot. But instead, she grabbed the bottle and the glass and carried them into the kitchen. She wasn't going to drink herself into oblivion before one o'clock. Even she wasn't that pathetic.

But she had to do something. Cleaning like a demon seemed to be the ticket. She opened all the windows, letting the hot summer breeze blow through the house and sweep away the musty, closed-in feel, and then she headed for the garage and all the cleaning supplies.

It was a sad, sad state when the only thing a woman could do to occupy her mind was clean.

Three hours later, the house was so clean, Mr. Monk himself would have been satisfied with it. The quirky, obsessive-compulsive fictional detective could have gone through her house with a white glove, and he wouldn't have found so much as a speck of dust or a hair on the floor.

Taige, on the other hand, was filthy. But instead of heading for the shower, she changed into her swimming suit and headed out the back door to the stretch of sand and the gentle waters of Mobile Bay. She dove into the water, swimming under the surface until her lungs threatened to burst, and then she surfaced, shoving her wet hair back from her face and treading water.

A little farther down, she could see a family playing in the sand. Beyond that, a couple of people in the shallows were crabbing. A little girl shrieked, and she turned her head to watch the family. A grin tugged up the corners of her mouth as the father threw the little girl up into the air and then caught her, laughing as the girl screamed, "Again! Again!"

He tossed her, and she went up with a delighted shriek—

Please don't hurt me.

Taige froze as a girl's voice whispered through her mind, insubstantial as mist.

Silence, child.

The man's voice didn't seem real, monstrous and inhuman. How much of that was because of the girl's fear, Taige didn't know.

Taige didn't even have to see the girl to know who it was. The delicate little black-haired darling had been invading her thoughts and dreams for more than a decade, and Taige knew her voice nearly as well as she knew her own. *Come on, honey, tell me who you are,* Taige thought helplessly. *How can I help you if you won't talk to me?*

But it didn't work like that. She didn't even know if the girl was still alive. For all Taige knew, the girl had been kidnapped and killed before Taige was even born. She could be seeing something that happened years ago—or something that hadn't even happened yet. She had no idea, and she knew that she wouldn't get any more than she'd already gotten until the time was right.

You don't act—you react. A ghost from her past, Cullen's voice seemed to echo in her ear as she treaded water and tried not to cry. More than a decade had passed since he'd flung those ugly words at her, words that had cut into her like poisonous claws, and through the pain, she'd known she had to do something. She'd forced herself to go to college, she'd forced herself to learn control, to experiment with her gift and see what she could do. Things that had put her through sheer hell and sometimes, she wondered why she'd even bothered.

Because even after all of that, there were people, children, that she couldn't save. People just like Cullen's mother. People just like her own parents. People like Hannah Brewster.

She couldn't save them.

Useless.

*   *   *

NICE thing about airports that early—it was quiet. The Hartsfield-Jackson Airport in Atlanta was hopping with travelers, business and leisure alike. The hour hand hadn't even edged up on five o'clock in the morning, and all the travelers were tired.

They sipped on coffee, tried to stay awake while reading the paper, and a few diligently worked on laptops. Cullen was one of them, or at least he was trying. The white screen seemed glaringly bright. Of course, that might have something to do with the fact that he hadn't gotten to sleep until midnight. With a three a.m. wake-up call, it was no wonder he was so damned tired.

When he realized he had been staring at the same line for the past five minutes, Cullen finally gave up and shut the laptop down. The faint scratch of pencil on paper had him glancing over. The early hour wasn't affecting all of them. Nice to see.

"What are you working on, beautiful?"

Big green eyes looked up at him. Jillian was as beautiful as an angel, Cullen thought. He'd thought so from the first time he'd seen her, nine years ago, when the doctor wrapped her tiny, red little body in a blanket and placed her in his arms. Jilly's mom had died due to complications from childbirth. She'd held Jillian for half an hour, a miserly thirty minutes, before the nurses took the baby to do a more thorough exam on the newborn. Five minutes after the nurses had taken Jilly, Kim had looked at him and smiled. "Isn't she beautiful?"

It was the last thing Kim ever said. She drifted off to sleep, and while she was sleeping, she'd started to bleed again. The doctors couldn't get it to stop, and Cullen had stood there, stunned into silence, as his wife died.

It had come as a complete and total shock to everybody, including Cullen. How could he lose his wife in childbirth? Women died in childbirth a hundred years ago. Even fifty years ago. But in 1999? He just couldn't wrap his brain around it, even now.

Jilly had inherited her mother's big green eyes, rosebud mouth, and artistic talent. The girl might as well have been born with a pencil and sketch pad in hand. It had been that artistic talent that had landed her in an advanced school when she was only three years old. She had a grasp of light and shadow that many adults lacked, Cullen had been told when he'd met with Arlene Willington.

Fancy way of saying the girl could draw, Cullen had always figured, but Arlene was right. No matter how she said it, Jilly was gifted. Even aside from her skill with a pencil, the girl was special in ways that Cullen couldn't even begin to understand, although he wasn't exactly a stranger to it.

He studied the faces on the sketch pad she showed him and asked, "Are they friends of yours?" Jilly had drawn three kids who didn't look familiar to him: a younger girl who was probably only five or six, and then two older ones, about the same age as Jilly. The boy was black, and he had a wide, mischievous smile. Both of the girls were white, one was probably in her early teens. It was the younger one, though, that really caught Cullen's attention. She looked like a little angel, all big eyes, long hair, and dimples. Although the pencil sketch was in black and white, he imagined the girl's hair was pale blonde. Jillian's talent amazed him. How a nine-year-old could draw something like that, so true to life, was just astounding.

Jilly shook her head. Fat, inky black curls bounced around her heart-shaped face, and she took the sketch pad back. "No. I don't know who they are." She reached out, stroked the tip of one finger down one penciled face. The little cherub. "She was the first one."

A voice came over the speaker, and a bored airline attendant announced a slight delay. Delay. Hell, wasn't that great? Bad weather had grounded their flight yesterday, and Cullen had accepted the red-eye for today. He had a signing and some Q and A deal at a library tomorrow, and he'd really wanted the downtime. It was starting to look as though he just wasn't supposed to have any downtime.

Distracted, Cullen glanced at Jilly and asked, "The first to what?"

"The first to disappear."

A chill ran down Cullen's back, and he stopped, looked at the sketch pad, then back up at Jilly's face. "Disappear from where?"

Jilly just shrugged. "Around." She sighed and bent back over the sketchbook, shutting her worried father out. He was used to it. When she was working on something, she worked with a single-minded focus. Normally, it didn't bother him. Today? Different story. "Where did she disappear from, baby?"

Jilly muttered something under her breath. She caught the tip of her tongue between her teeth, and her eyes scrunched down to slits. Recognizing the signs, Cullen reached out and caught a black curl. He tugged sharply and waited for her to look up at him. At first, her eyes were foggy and unfocused. They cleared, and when he knew she was paying attention to him, he said flatly, "Tell me about this girl."

The firm, I-am-the-parent-and-you-will-answer-me tone still worked on Jilly, for the most part. She glanced down at the sketch pad, but Cullen knew she wasn't seeing the sketch. She squeezed the charcoal pencil so hard her knuckles went white, and Cullen felt a dark, ugly fear move through him. *Not again . . .* Cullen thought as he stared down at his daughter.

Special in ways he couldn't understand, that was his little girl. It wasn't until he'd had Jillian and realized just how special she was that he began to understand how terribly wrong it had been for him to blame Taige for not being able to save his mom. She'd been completely blameless, and while he guessed his misplaced fury might have been understandable, it had still been totally wrong.

This kind of gift was sheer hell, and it still made him sick inside to think about what he'd done to Taige and how much he must have hurt her. He'd undo it all in a second. Often, he wondered if this wasn't the penance he had to bear for doing it, having a child who shared Taige's abilities and knowing he was powerless to protect her from the agony it would cause her.

It had been a year since he'd seen that look in Jillian's eyes, a hot, muggy summer when the little brother of Jilly's best friend disappeared. Braden Fleming had disappeared from his backyard, and he'd been missing for three days.

Cullen hadn't known anything about Braden's abduction until late, late that first night. He'd been called to Jillian's school when his daughter collapsed out on the playground for no obvious reason. Jilly had spent two days in a catatonic stupor that had Cullen so scared he took her to the emergency room. She was admitted to the hospital, and on the second day, she had come out of it, only to look at her father and start crying. The doctors had wanted to admit her for psychiatric tests. Cullen might have agreed, but Jilly looked up at him and whispered, "I know where Braden is."

There had been no logical explanation. Jilly hadn't been home when Braden disappeared. There was no way for her to know that the four-year-old had been grabbed out of his own backyard while he was playing.

No way she had of knowing Braden's abductor was the grandson of the sweet little old lady who lived just behind Cullen and Jilly. But she had known. She'd described a man who sounded vaguely familiar to Cullen. Two hours later, as he continued to rock her and hold her, he had finally figured out who Jilly had been describing.

They'd found the boy, but to this day, Cullen knew Jilly felt guilty. Braden would spend years—possibly his entire life—in therapy, and there were nights when Cullen could hear the boy screaming in his sleep even from two houses down. Although she never made a sound, Cullen knew Jilly also suffered nightmares, but she wouldn't tell him about them. He'd tried putting his daughter into therapy as well, but the counselors had made the problem worse. Jilly retreated more and more inside herself, and finally, Cullen had stopped the therapy.

Gradually, she emerged from the shell she had built around herself. Over the past couple of months, she had slowly started acting a little more like the child she was instead of a miniature grown-up. Jilly had always been a bit—well, different. An old soul, her grandfather called her. But it had been a bit of heaven to see her laughing and playing with other kids, to see her giggle at a magic show or get so excited when he'd told her about their trip. He had a couple of business-related things, the Q and A in Indianapolis, and then a few days in New York City, but before that, they'd spend a few days in Atlanta.

Seeing Jilly excited over anything was an unexpected blessing. She stopped being scared of her own shadow, and sometimes weeks passed between nightmares instead of days.

And now this—whatever this was.

It's nothing, he told himself. *Absolutely nothing.* But his gut wouldn't let him believe that. He scrubbed a hand over his face and looked back at Jillian's sketch pad. She stared at it solemnly and protectively. Cullen laid a hand on her shoulder and drew her close. Jilly cuddled into him and whispered, "He's a bad man, Daddy."

Gaze narrowed, Cullen studied the people around him. "Who? Is he here?" He didn't see anybody unusual, just the typical early morning airport crowd: vacationers, business travelers, and a couple either just recently married or involved in one very hot affair. They couldn't keep their hands, or their tongues, to themselves. "Who's the man, Jillian?"

Her voice shook softly. "He's a monster," she whispered. She clutched the notebook to her chest, and Cullen realized she was trembling like a leaf.

Futile anger rushed through him, and he bent down to catch her small body in his arms. He murmured to her gently and stroked her back. She felt too fragile to deal with this burden she'd been handed. *This isn't fair,* Cullen thought bitterly and wished he was alone someplace where he could give in to the anger building inside. But, despite his rage, he knew how sensitive Jilly was. If he let even a little of his anger show, it would add to whatever else she carried inside. So instead, he just hugged her close. "It's going to be okay, Jillian. Promise."

And deep inside, he only hoped he wasn't lying to her.

* * *

Six weeks later, Cullen had mostly forgotten about the weird episode in the airport. For a day or two, Jillian had been like a little rabbit, jumping at every sound and unable to sleep without Cullen right beside her. But after a few more days passed, she slowly started acting more like herself. And Cullen had forgotten.

It was hotter than hell and so humid that it felt like a weight was pressing down on his chest every time he went outside. The deadline from hell was looming closer and closer, and he still wasn't anywhere near to being done with the last book in his contract. If he didn't hurry the hell up, he wasn't entirely convinced his editor was going to want to see the proposal he had put together for her.

Shoving back from the desk, he rubbed his hands over his face and tried to clear the cobwebs from his brain. He'd dreamed about Taige again last night. She'd been hurt. The dreams made little or no sense, unless he looked at them as yet another form of torture. There was no way imaginable he would have chosen to dream seeing her like that, her left eye puffy, swollen and bruised, and her right hand in a soft cast that went halfway up her forearm.

The dream had disturbed him more than usual, and as a result, when he got up at four that morning, he hadn't felt like he'd slept at all. Instead of going back to bed, he'd settled down to work, and with the exception of refilling his coffee cup every hour or so and fixing some breakfast for Jilly, he'd been there ever since.

Movement caught his eye, and he looked up to see Jilly peeking around the corner into his office. There was a smile on her usually somber little face, and as she edged into the room, he saw the phone in her hand. "Mandy called. They want to know if I can go swimming with them."

Later, it would haunt him as he recalled how relieved he'd been when the Paxton family had shown up to take Jillian to a local water park. Loaded down with sunscreen, money, dry clothes, and a towel, she'd wrapped her arms around his neck, squeezing tight. "Love you, Daddy . . ."

Now, as Kelly Paxton sat across from him on a hard bench, sobbing helplessly, Jillian's words echoed inside his head: *Love you, Daddy . . .*

"Mr. Morgan, I realize how terrible a time this is for you, but I need some more information about where you were today . . ."

Numb, Cullen looked into the agent's face. His voice was rusty as he repeated, "I've already gone over this. A hundred times."

"Let's go over it once more," Special Agent Holcomb said, his voice polite, professional.

Frustrated, Cullen turned away, scrubbing his hands over his face. "I've been at home. Working. Around two, I talked to my agent. Around three, I stopped to take a piss and get a sandwich. Around three forty-five, my dad called." His voice cracked, and he had to stop for a minute. "Dad wanted Jilly to come spend the weekend with him," Cullen said softly. "He hasn't seen her much this summer. I've been so busy . . ."

Although the agent had heard all of this before, he nodded and continued to jot notes down on his notepad. "And your father lives . . . where?"

"Shit." Cullen blew out a harsh breath and then turned to face the agent. "Look, I get what you're doing. I know you need to check me out, and you'll even have to check up on my dad and make sure one of us hasn't been hurting her." Even thinking it filled him with an irrational fury, but he knew they had to ask. Cullen had had it, though. His temper was frayed, he was scared to death, and his overactive imagination, such a blessing when it came to his job, was adding to the grief and terror.

"But I've had it with this. Jillian has been missing for five hours. Have you done a damn thing to find my baby, or are you going to grill me for another five hours?"

"Mr. Morgan—"

The agent's patient expression cracked as somebody new intruded on the scene. Cullen sized him up as another fed in about three seconds, although the man's suit was a little more pricey than what his associates wore. Armani, Cullen knew, and he figured it cost what some agents made in a month. The shoes were Italian leather, and somehow the agent had managed to keep them relatively clean as he made his way through the sand. He had perfectly groomed hair and a smooth, even tan. Considering the blond hair and blue eyes, Cullen was willing to bet the man's tan came from a bed rather than being outside. The new guy didn't much look like the outdoor type.

There was also something vaguely familiar about him, but Cullen was so sick of agents, he couldn't think straight. "Great," he muttered as he stomped away from the agents, not stopping until he reached where the sand gave way to pavement. He stared at his car, wondering if, by some miracle, he could climb in and drive, just letting his gut lead him to his daughter.

But while he had decent instincts, they were just that. It wasn't a gift. He had no way in hell of finding Jilly on his own. There was a flash, a flicker of knowledge dancing just at the edge of his mind, like the first sparks before they gave way to wildfire. Even as he tried to reach out and wrap his mind around it, somebody came up from behind. He turned to meet the steady, congenial gaze of the new agent.

He had friendly eyes and the kind of face that most people would trust. Cullen wanted to hit him until that understanding left his expression. The bastard couldn't understand. Voice harsh with fury, Cullen said, "I can't do this again. I have to do something."

"The only thing you can do is work with us, Mr. Morgan. Look, why don't we go sit down inside? Management has given us use of their offices. We can cool down a little, get something nice and cool to drink—"

Cullen slashed a hand through the air. "This isn't a barbecue. I don't give a damn about cooling off or getting a damn soda. I want to do something to find my baby." His voice cracked again, and Cullen knew he had to get out of there, had to do something. "Oh, God." He covered his face with his hands and sent up another desperate prayer. He hadn't prayed since before his mother had died and he hadn't set a foot in church. But he'd do whatever God wanted if He would just bring Jilly back safe.

"I know this is hard. I can't imagine the hell you have to be going through right now."

Something in the man's voice had Cullen looking back at him. He dropped his hands and said flatly, "No. You can't imagine it. So do something to help me, damn it. What are we going to do to find my daughter?"

* * *

THE bastard, Special Agent Jones, made Cullen go through it another three times. When he finished detailing his afternoon and explaining, "No, I don't have any enemies that I know of, and I can't imagine who could have done this," he looked at the agent and said, "Now do you want to know what I ate for dinner last night and what kind of pajamas Jilly wears?"

With a pleasant smile, the agent murmured, "No. That isn't necessary." He flipped through a rather official-looking file, pausing here and there. "You're a writer. Perhaps you have a rather devoted fan . . . ?"

Cullen shook his head. "I don't have much of a relationship with readers. I don't even have an address where they can write me."

"You never do signings or anything?"

Cullen curled his lip. "I'm sure you have all of that information in your file there." A rather impressive file, considering the short amount of time that had passed since the FBI had shown up on the scene. It felt like years had already passed, but it had only been a few hours since that panicked, terrified call from Kelly had come in. He ran a hand through his hair and tugged on it absently, thinking back to the Q and A he'd done in Lexington a month or so back. It had been right after their trip to Atlanta. "I do a few signings a year. Yeah, I have some persistent readers, but nothing stalkerlike that I can think of."

"What about your dad? He's a successful businessman. Went from working for a CPA firm to being some big-time stock wizard. Surely he's stepped on a few toes."

Cullen shook his head. "Everybody likes my dad. He's just one of those people who doesn't really make enemies. Even his competition likes him. Besides, if this was some kind of vendetta thing or ransom deal, wouldn't we have heard something by now?"

A faint smile curled up the agent's mouth. What in the hell was his name again? Cullen wondered. He'd already forgotten it. "You're a quick one, Mr. Morgan, aren't you?"

Shrugging restlessly, Cullen replied, "Research." He folded his arms across his chest and pinned the agent with a flat stare. "This was a stranger abduction, wasn't it?"

Finally, the agent's polite, professional demeanor cracked just a little. He jerked at his tie to loosen it and then reached for his cooling cup of coffee. "It's too early to say for certain, but it is starting to look that way." He leaned forward, lacing his fingers together. "Mr. Morgan, I'm going to be blunt here. I don't think you had anything to do with this. At all. I think some stranger took your daughter. Nobody other than the Paxtons knew she was going to be here, and although we're looking at them, I don't think they had anything to do with this, either. But, regardless, I need you to be honest with me. You can't hide anything."

"Like what?" Cullen demanded, his aggravation coming through loud and clear.

"Like your daughter's . . . unusual abilities."

Cullen froze. When he spoke, his voice was rusty and hoarse. "What are you talking about?"

Holding Cullen's gaze, the agent lifted up the file, revealing a thinner one, one that Cullen hadn't even seen. Without saying anything, the agent opened the file and revealed the contents. There was precious little. A few pieces of paper and a picture. Braden Fleming's picture. Cullen hadn't wanted anybody to know about Jillian, so when he'd made that phone call to the police's anonymous tip line, he'd done it from a pay phone on the other side of town.

He took the file and was gratified to see that his hands weren't shaking. Damn miracle because on the inside, he was shaking so hard, he thought he might fall apart from it. He didn't want people knowing this about Jilly. He managed to flip through the papers and then give the agent a quizzical glance. "I'm not sure what this is about."

"It's about some statements taken from some nurses at the county hospital where Jillian was treated after she collapsed at school. She spent two days catatonic, and then suddenly, she woke up and told you that she knew where Braden was, according to these nurses who were outside your daughter's room while she was crying about it. Tell me, Mr. Morgan. How did Jillian know about Braden?"

Cullen closed the file and tossed it back on the table. The pages and pictures inside spilled out, but Cullen kept his gaze on the agent's face. "I don't know what you're talking about, Agent . . . Sorry, I forgot your name."

In response, he flipped his name badge around. He said something else, but Cullen couldn't hear it for the roaring in his ears. Taylor Jones.

Like he was watching a slide show that only he could see, Cullen suddenly saw all the pictures and articles over that past year that he had collected about Taige. Most of them made little mention of the feds she worked with, but here and there were a few times somebody within the Bureau had been mentioned. Taylor Jones's name had come up more than once, and there had even been a couple of pictures where both Taige and Jones's face had shown up in the paper together.

A hundred memories rose up to haunt him, to taunt him, and he was suddenly having a hard time breathing. Must have had something to do with the fact that his heart was pounding a mile a minute.

Taige. All that restless, useless energy pulsating through him suddenly sharpened, focused. Finally—son of a bitch, this was something he could control.

* * *

IT was eleven o'clock before the agents decided that he should go home, try to get some sleep, and wait for them to call—and they'd call with an update just as soon as they could. If he hadn't been waiting for just this opportunity, Cullen was pretty damn sure he would have been arrested for attempted murder when he tried to strangle one of the bastards for handing him that line.

"Go home."

"Get some rest."

"We will call you. There's nothing else you can do here."

The dumb shits that came up with that BS ought to have the daylights knocked out of them. His daughter was missing—and they were suggesting he take a fucking nap.

The exit to his house was coming up, and he started to slow down, hitting the turn signal. But at the last second, he shot back onto the freeway, watching as his escort ended up blocked in by an eighteen-wheeler with a rebel flag emblazoned across the grill.

He watched from his rearview mirror to make sure he wasn't being followed, and then he shot off the next exit so he could get back on the interstate, heading north. He wasn't sure if he could make it to the airport and get on a flight to Alabama without the feds catching up with him, but there was no way he was going to drive the six hours to Gulf Shores.

Jillian might not have that kind of time.

SIX

"I'M telling you, the dad hired somebody."

Jones glanced up from his file with a frown. He had to admit, it was suspicious, Cullen Morgan disappearing the way he had.

But he didn't get that vibe off the man. Morgan wasn't just upset about his daughter's disappearance; he was nearly sick with it. Jones had spent more than enough time with guilty people recognize them a mile away. Morgan didn't have that guilt inside him.

All he was carrying around was grief.

But they had yet to discover why Morgan had disappeared. It hadn't taken long to find him, but by the time they found out he went to the airport, he was already en route to Birmingham.

"Doesn't fit, Murphy," he said to the young agent he'd brought with him. Grace Murphy was the eager type, very ready to pin this on the most likely suspect. Jones could argue with her all day long, but Murphy was going to have to learn the hard way, the way most of them did. It was good for her, the way he looked at it. She'd learn that the easiest answer wasn't always the right answer; in fact, it rarely was. After she made enough mistakes, she'd start developing some instincts.

She would need them.

He tapped his pen on the file in front of him, and when the phone rang, he continued to study the lists of names and descriptions of people seen in the water park. Hot summer day, dead of summer, it had been so crowded, it didn't seem possible that a girl could just disappear like this. Didn't seem possible at all.

And that was why he'd been called in. While Jones had none of the unique skills himself, he had a knack for knowing when to call in one of the special task forces. This was going to be one of them, he knew. He was already debating over who to call in. He skimmed the lists and, seeing nothing, started to flip through the grandfather's information.

Whatever had happened in the Morgan family, if it had ever been committed to paper or put out into cyberspace, Jones now had the information. There were holdings all over the world. The grandfather was going to leave Cullen and Jillian a couple of very rich people. Not that Cullen didn't do well on his own. The man was a very popular fantasy author with a huge online following. Internet searches had revealed message boards, MySpace pages, and entire fan Web sites dedicated to the guy's books.

Money. It was always a possibility that somebody had grabbed the girl to use her in some money scheme, but that didn't feel right to Jones. He turned the page, continuing to skim over the Morgan family assets, and a familiar zip code caught his eye: 36547.

He knew that zip code. Taige Branch, a huge asset to the

Bureau and a huge pain in Jones's ass, lived in Gulf Shores. "Hmmmm . . ." Without looking away from the file, he punched the address listed into his computer, pulling up a map. Less than four miles from where Taige had grown up.

Jones knew very little about Taige's childhood. She was remarkably closemouthed about her life, and there had been precious little information he could gather on her that wasn't public knowledge.

That information was pretty much all he had about her formative years. After she'd started college, there had been a decent amount of information, but before, very little. Only that she'd been orphaned at a young age, that she did well in school, and that she had gone to work part-time at a small, locally owned seafood restaurant. She'd lived with her only known relative, an uncle who preached at a nearby church, and she had very much kept to herself.

Coincidence?

Jones didn't believe in coincidences.

"Sir?"

He looked up to find Murphy watching him with a wary gaze. "It's Special Agent Hensley out of Birmingham."

"Do they have Morgan?"

She shook her head. "No, sir. Nobody matching his description got off the plane, although surveillance clearly shows him getting on in Atlanta." Her eyes were wide and glowing with self-satisfaction. Clearly, she thought this was more evidence to her theory that the dad had something to do with Jillian Morgan's disappearance.

Jones was far from convinced, though. He was no psychic. He employed more than a dozen specially trained, highly skilled psychics. While he might not have their abilities, he had damn good instincts. And right now, as he studied the financial data before him, his instincts were singing. He reached for his own phone to call the grandfather, a Robert Morgan. Robert had told his son he'd be waiting at Cullen's house, and Jones had given his men orders to make sure the grandfather remained there for the time being.

In case an attempt at ransom was made, they needed a family member at the house. Since Morgan had pulled his disappearing act, the grandfather was the only option. At the moment, Jones was damn glad he had the grandfather so readily accessible. It answered several of Jones's more pressing questions.

"No coincidences," he murmured as he disconnected from his conversation with Robert Morgan. Sitting back, he studied the board before him while his fingers beat out a tattoo on the table. It had an eight-by-ten picture of Jillian Morgan and below it, pictures of her father, grandfather, and the Paxtons, the people who'd been watching Jillian before she disappeared.

Murphy ended her conversation with Birmingham, and Jones looked her way as she put away her phone. "They found him—well, at least they found out how he ditched them. Guy's clever, we got to give him that. Disguised himself. They're faxing the pictures now. We'll have to . . . What?"

"Morgan had nothing to do with his daughter's disappearance." He glanced down at his notes and then flipped them around for Murphy to read. "The Morgans purchased a condo in Gulf Shores, Alabama, sixteen years ago. They went down there fairly regularly until Cullen's mother was killed twelve years ago, and then the condo was used as rental property for a time. Past few years, the grandfather has taken to going down there more often. They've got great fishing," Taylor mused.

Murphy continued to stare at him, not following. Jones pushed his notepad closer to her and said softly, "Would you like to guess who Cullen dated on his summers in Gulf Shores, Murphy?"

She looked down at the pad, and her eyes widened. "Branch."

Jones nodded. "Taige Branch. He has a history with her, and I'll bet you anything that he's gone looking for her."

* * *

So damn restless, Taige slept fitfully, tossing and turning. She couldn't sleep for the life of her and hadn't been able to for nearly two months now. Ever since Chicago, but Chicago didn't seem to have anything to do with her insomnia.

It was something else. Something new. She was waiting, but she didn't know what for. Mumbling in her sleep, she rolled onto her belly. A jarring pain shot up her arm, and she groaned, automatically cradling her injured right wrist against her chest.

The soft cast that went from her hand halfway up her forearm immobilized her wrist and hand, but it didn't keep it from hurting when she moved wrong. The pain was enough to bring her completely out of sleep, and she lay on her back in the dark room, staring up at the ceiling. She could finally open her left eye again, but it still hurt like the devil. Taige lay there debating between getting up and finding one of the bottles of pain meds the doctors had prescribed or just finding a book and reading until morning.

Wasn't like she was going to be working for the next few days.

Before that thought even made a complete circle through her mind, a chill streaked down Taige's spine. Her breathing hitched. In a smooth, unconscious movement, she rolled out of bed and grabbed the jeans lying on the floor with her left hand. She shimmied into them without hurting her hand much, but she had to lie back to zip and button them, and that hurt.

She shrugged the pain off and grabbed a tank top from the basket of clean clothes she hadn't ever gotten around to putting up. *Hurry hurry hurry.* The words seemed to echo all around her, whispering to her in the dark. She didn't turn on any lights as she moved through her house. Instead, she took up position staring out the huge picture window that faced the front yard.

When the headlights cut a swath through the darkness, Taige held herself still. She didn't recognize the truck, but that was little surprise. Very few people had ever come looking for her. Jones with the Bureau, Dante, Rose before she died; once upon a time, her uncle had sought her out, but that was out of a desire to hurt and torment her just a little more.

But it wasn't any of them.

Taige couldn't have explained how she knew any more than she could explain quantum physics. But she knew. Her breathing went shallow, her heartbeat started to pound, and although she didn't possess much vanity, she ran a hand over her hair. She generally didn't spend too much time messing with her hair, just securing it in a French braid or a ponytail, but with her hand messed up, she wasn't going to be doing too much on her own, and braiding her hair was definitely a two-handed task. So yesterday, tired already of trying to keep it halfway neat, she had spent hours getting the curly mess woven into a series of tight braids. That would keep her from having to mess with it for a while.

Still, she couldn't help but wonder how her hair looked as she stood there, fiddling with her shapeless tank top and fighting the urge to go and change. She pressed gentle fingertips to the nasty bruise ringing her left eye and grimaced. After all these years . . . she'd known she'd see him again. Even when she drove away from Cullen Morgan's home in tears, she'd known it wasn't over between them.

Why he was coming to her now, she didn't know and honestly, just then, she didn't care.

She was so desperate to see him again, it was almost pathetic.

No, it was pathetic. It had been twelve years, and she was all but panting at the thought of seeing him, of staring into those amazing eyes and standing close enough to smell him. How much had he changed? Taige wondered. Instinctively, she knew that Cullen would be as devastating at thirty-three as he'd been at twenty-one. The truck came to a stop close to the house. She couldn't see anything beyond the back bumper, and when the taillights went off, she jerked as though somebody had used a Taser on her.

She took a deep breath and then groaned as her shirt dragged against her nipples. They were stiff and erect, throbbing under the thin layer of cotton. Embarrassed, she folded her arms over them and wished she could manage to get a damn bra on. Her hand hurt too much to manage it, though.

Facing Cullen braless and in her bare feet: how much more disconcerting could it get? She held herself stiff as the knock came, pounding on the door as though he wanted to tear the door from its hinges. It came a second time, and third. Finally, she made herself move, shuffling through the dark living room with her arms crossed over her breasts, the wrap on her cast abrading the bare skin of her left arm and rubbing against her nipples.

Nerves jangled in her belly. No butterflies; this felt more like she had giant gryphons taking flight inside her, gryphons with knife-edged wings. She reached out and closed her left hand around the doorknob and slowly opened it, half hiding behind the door. She kept her gaze focused straight ahead so that all she saw was the way his white T-shirt stretched across his wide, muscled chest.

Through her peripheral vision, she saw that he held something in his hand. Something clutched so tight, his knuckles had
gone white. She hissed out a breath and forced herself to look upward, up, up, up until she was staring into his eyes. It took a little
longer than it should have; he was taller than he had been. At
least by an inch. She was five foot ten—she didn't have to look up
to many people, and she decided then that she didn't care for it
at all.

"Taige."

She didn't say anything. She couldn't. Her throat felt frozen,
and forcing words past her frozen vocal chords seemed impossible.
She just stepped aside to let him come in, and when he did, his
arm brushed against hers. She flinched and pulled away, backing
away until a good two feet separated them. Once he was inside,
she closed the door and leaned against it, resting her left hand on
the doorknob and holding her right hand against her belly and
studying the floor.

He turned to stare at her. From under her lashes, she watched
as his shoulders rose and fell, his chest moving as he blew out a
harsh breath, almost like he'd been holding his breath the same
way she had.

"God, Taige . . ."

His voice sounded almost exactly like it had in her dreams—no,
exactly. In the dim light, she couldn't see his face very well, but
she had a bad, bad feeling that her dreams had been pretty damn
accurate in that aspect, too. Shoving away from the door, she kept
her head down as she moved around him and headed into the living room. He followed behind her slowly. She heard a click, and
light flooded the room. She shot him a look over her shoulder,
just a quick glance, enough to tell her just how dead-on her
dreams had been.

It was almost too spooky; even his hair looked right. It was shorter than it had been when he was younger, almost brutally short. His shoulders strained the seams of his shirt, and she had a flashback to her last dream, when he had crowded her up against the couch, demanding she tell him how she'd gotten hurt. She'd shoved him, pushing one hand against one wide, rock-hard shoulder, and she imagined if she reached out and touched him, he'd feel exactly like he had in her dreams.

"So, are you going to look at me or just let me stare at the back of your head all night?" he asked softly.

She shot him another quick, almost nervous glance over her shoulder, and Cullen blew out a breath.

When he spoke again, his voice was closer. "Aren't you going to ask me why I'm here?"

Aren't you going to speak to me at all? Cullen wanted to ask.

Instead, he waited until she finally turned around and faced him. In the brightly lit room, he noticed two things. The first was that she had her arm, her right arm, in a cast that went halfway up to her elbow. A chill raced down his spine. The second was that her left eye was puffy and nearly swollen shut, a dark, ugly bruise that Cullen suspected was every bit as painful as it looked.

Those dreams—shit.

She spoke, and her voice sounded just as it had in all those dreams. "I already know why you're here. You need my help." A bitter smile curved her lips as she stared at him. "Why would else would you be here?" She glanced at the file in his hand and held out her hand.

Cullen swallowed and lifted it, staring at it with the metallic taste of fear thick in his mouth. "You don't owe me a damn thing, Taige. I know that. I've got no right being here, and I know that, too."

She sighed and dropped her head, covering her eyes with her uninjured hand. "Cullen, stop. You want something. Out with it. I've got better things to do than stand here and have you brooding all over me. So just spill it."

"I . . . look, if I didn't have to have your help, I wouldn't be here. But it's not me that needs you—just . . . just don't—"

Taige cocked a brow. "You don't have much of an opinion of me, do you, Cullen? Whatever brought you here in the middle of the night twelve years after kicking me out of your life has to be pretty damn important, and considering the kind of help you probably need, I'm going to assume there's somebody else involved." She stared at him, her gaze shuttered. "You think so little of me that I'd refuse to help whoever this is just to make you suffer because you and me got some history?"

History . . . Is that what we had? That seemed such a simplified statement. Still, said like that, Cullen felt very much the fool. He looked back down at the file and then at her, watching as she once more held out her hand. Careful not to touch her, he held it out. She took it and moved to sit behind the big iron and glass coffee table before she opened it. She settled down on the overstuffed black couch. If he hadn't been watching her so closely, he never would have seen it as she took a deep breath and set her shoulders, almost like she was bracing herself.

Her eyes, her expression, they were carefully blank as she opened the file. But as she stared down at Jilly's picture, something changed. Her smooth, caramel-colored skin went pale. She looked up at him, and he watched as her eyes darkened to the color of thunderheads. The tension in the room mounted until it seemed too thick to even breathe.

Taige tore her eyes away from the picture and stared up at him. "Who is she?" Taige demanded, her voice harsh and shaking.

"My daughter."

My daughter. My daughter.

The words seemed to echo through her, but instead of getting fainter, they got louder and louder, until the words seemed to shriek inside her skull. Blood pounded in her head, and her vision narrowed down until all she could see was that little face with the pretty smile and solemn eyes. Taige had lost count of how many times she'd seen that face. It had haunted her dreams for years.

"Her name is Jillian. She was kidnapped earlier today, well, technically yesterday . . ."

"I know." Taige looked back down at the picture and traced it with the tip of her finger. "I know her face, Cullen."

Cullen went still. "How is that possible?"

Carefully, she closed the file. She pushed it away. Cullen looked back down at it and then back at her, agony screaming in his eyes. Denial. He thought she was going to refuse him, refuse that little girl. Softly, she told him, "I don't need to see the file, Cullen. And don't look at me like that. I'll find her."

That much, she knew. She shoved up from the couch, automatically holding her hand against her belly as she started to pace in absent circles around the couch. It wasn't going to be long now before it came on her, that dark, eerie knowledge that guided her to the missing. She could feel it hovering just outside of conscious thought, like a thunderstorm brewing out on the Gulf.

Cullen was another storm. She could feel the turmoil inside of him, along with other emotions that she really didn't want to think about. She shot him a quick look and saw that he was still watching her with confused eyes. "You probably don't remember it, but there were several times back when we were together that I kept having weird dreams about a little girl."

His eyes narrowed. The turquoise blue of his eyes darkened, and his brows dropped low over his eyes. "I remember." He grabbed the file from the coffee table and opened it to stare at his daughter's face. "Please tell me that you weren't dreaming about my baby."

She didn't answer, and he grabbed the glossy eight-by-ten photo from the file. He shoved it into her face and said it again: "Tell me that you weren't dreaming about my baby."

Taige reached out and took the photo. She had a sweet face, Taige thought. Soft, delicately pretty. She'd be a heartbreaker when she got a little older. "I can't tell you that, Cullen."

This wasn't happening, Cullen thought. He shoved a hand through his hair, jerking on it hard in hopes that it would clear some of the fog in his head. *You probably don't remember . . .* What would Taige think if she knew that he remembered practically every moment with her in detail so vivid, it hurt? Didn't remember . . . hell, he only wished that were true. He'd lost track of how often he'd wished that his memories of her would fade, even a little, but they never did.

Shit. Yeah, Cullen remembered those dreams. He remembered all too well, and he wanted to scream.

It didn't seem possible that she could have dreamed about Jilly. It had been twelve years, longer really. Nearly fourteen years since the time she had first woken shivering from a dream about a little girl. A dream that would come back and haunt her month after month, year after year. But Jillian was only nine years old.

His voice was rusty. "What can you tell me, Taige? Can you tell me that you can find her?" He stared at her, just now realizing how close she was, close enough that he could see the darker striations of gray in her eyes, close enough that he could smell the warm, soft scent of her. Close enough that he could see the gentle rise and fall of her breasts with each breath she took. Close enough that he could see the compassion in her eyes when his voice broke as he asked again, "Can you tell me that you'll find her and bring her home safe? Tell me that without lying to me?"

She reached up and touched him, laying a hand on his cheek. "Yeah. I can tell you that, Cullen." Then she turned away from him, leaving him standing in the middle of the room as hope hit his system with a force that left him weak-kneed and almost shaking from it.

Taige barely made it to the bedroom before it hit her. She stumbled, falling to her knees as she knocked the door shut with the back of her hand, and then she sagged against it. She swallowed the bile that rose in her throat and tried not to shake as the adrenaline crashed into her.

Her teeth started to chatter as she looked down and realized she still held the little girl's picture. Jillian. After nearly fourteen years, the girl had a name. Taige pressed the picture to her heart and whispered, "Come on, honey. Talk to me now. It's time you and me really talk. Help me out here."

For the longest time, there was nothing.

Absolutely nothing. Just the roaring of the blood as it pulsed inside her head and the pounding of her heart, beating somewhere in the vicinity of her throat. Slowly, the adrenaline surge subsided, and her vital signs dropped down somewhere a little closer to normal. When the gray came rushing up to meet her, she went to it willingly. The gray, it was like a cloud that took her, guiding her until she made a connection with the victims she tried to help.

Sometimes it showed her things that made her so ill, it was a good thing she had no physical body in that space, because she would become so violently sick, she'd be of no use to anybody.

Other times, it showed her things that made her want to cry and things that made her so angry it was a wonder the gray didn't go bloodred with the strength of her fury.

She rarely sank so willingly into it, but this time, she knew it wasn't going to show her something that would destroy another part of her heart. This time, she could help. The gray wrapped around her, guiding her, and she could feel the distance grow as she drifted farther and farther from her physical body. Sometimes distance made no difference, other times, she needed to be closer to the victim before she helped.

There were times when she had to get closer, following the gray's trail, and in the part of her still capable of conscious thought, she worried that just might happen this time, and she hated it. Hated to think she might have to go down and tell Cullen it was going to take some time.

But just when the threads that bound her to her physical body felt stretched tight enough to snap, she stopped drifting. She found herself staring down at a wooden cabin somewhere below her feet, as though the gray was holding her in midair. She drifted down, down, down, through the ceiling, into the dark and there—

There—she found Jillian.

The little girl was tied up but relatively unharmed, lying on a hard, narrow bed that had some very disturbing stains on it. Though the vision she had in the gray wasn't as focused and clear as she'd like, she recognized those stains for what they were: bloodstains.

The air reeked of violence, and she knew bad, bad things had happened here. Awful things, and it was her responsibility to protect that girl. The girl lay on the bed, shivering and huddled in on herself as though she could warm herself. Her face was smudged and dirty, with pale streaks where tears had washed it clean. She looked absolutely terrified.

It's okay, sweetie. I'm going to bring you home. I promise you that.

Shock arced through her when Jilly opened her eyes, staring upward. Taige had the most disconcerting feeling that Jilly knew she was there. Somebody had gagged the child, tying a pristine white cloth around her mouth so tightly, it seemed to dig into her skin. The little girl sighed, her shoulders rising and falling. Taige started to pull back, but as the gray started to guide her back to her physical body, she heard something that shocked the hell out of her: the little girl's voice. Echoing inside of Taige.

I know.

* * *

IT was full daylight by the time she came hurtling back to herself, and judging by the way the light came slanting in through her windows, she figured it was midmorning. Cullen sat on the bed, elbows braced on his knees, staring at the floor.

He looked utterly dejected and completely hopeless. Taige lay there for a minute, taking stock before she went to sit up. At some point, Cullen must have tried to wake her or something. She lay on the bed instead of the floor, and she knew she hadn't made it all the way across the room before she collapsed.

The second she moved, Cullen rolled off the bed and came around the foot of it so he could crouch by her side. He stared at her, his gaze stark. "What in the hell happened? I came in here and found you on the floor. It's been four hours."

Four hours—damn. That was a long time to go under. She licked her lips and shook her head. Couldn't talk yet. Her mouth was like the desert. "Get me some water?" she croaked.

He shoved to his feet but didn't look too happy. His entire body vibrated with impatience, and she could understand that. He left the room, and Taige closed her eyes and rocked forward, folding her arms across her middle. She felt vaguely sick. Something about this whole mess was leaving her with a bad taste in her mouth—very bad. Cullen showing up on her doorstep, seeing the picture of a girl she'd been dreaming about since before the girl was even born. Her head pounded, and everything in her was braced for some oncoming storm.

There was heartbreak looming when she thought about that daughter—and her unknown mother wasn't even part of the equation. Taige deliberately wouldn't let herself think about that yet.

She heard the familiar little jingle of the phone coming closer, and when Cullen came into the room, he had her cell in his hand. He tossed it on the bed beside her and handed her a tall glass of ice water. She guzzled down half of it without pausing to take a breath. "Your phone's been ringing like that for the past three and half hours," Cullen said. "Says it's a Washington, D.C., call, same number. Over and over."

Taige glanced at the phone, disinterested. "It's my boss."

"Your boss."

The phone stopped ringing, and she picked it up, pushing a button and scowling as the list of missed calls came up. Jones must have been calling every fifteen minutes. "Yeah. He's the impatient type."

"Calling three or four times an hour is a little more than impatient." His features were tense, and he glanced at the phone, then at her face, troubled. "I need your help right now, Taige. Jilly needs you."

She drained the rest of the water, and feeling steadier, pushed herself to her feet. "Don't look at me like that, Cullen. I said I'd help, and I will."

"And if that's your boss calling about some other kid?"

Taige narrowed her eyes, staring at Cullen. *Some other kid.* Then she scowled. He knew about her work with the feds. For some unknown reason, that made her damn uncomfortable. "I pick and choose the jobs I take, Cullen—or, rather, the job picks me. It's not up to him who I'm going to be able to help." She went to move past him, shifting her body so she could edge by without making contact, and when he reached out to touch her, Taige jerked away.

He closed his hand into a fist, and it fell to his side. "Taige . . ."

She shook her head. "Don't, Cullen." She didn't know what he had been about to say, and she didn't care. She didn't need to hear it, didn't want to hear it. It was hard enough seeing him like this after twelve years. The sight of him hit her on a deep, visceral level, and she hated that he could still affect her like this. Even after all this time.

Taige knew she hadn't ever gotten over him, and truth be told, she had little interest in trying. It wasn't that she was pining after him. She was just protecting herself, keeping her heart closed off because she didn't want any man to ever have the power to hurt her again.

He was here because he needed her help, and that was more than enough for Taige to deal with. She didn't need any more complications piled on top of it.

She held his eyes for a long moment and then turned away from him, heading to her closet and digging out some clean clothes and her boots. She studied the boots with their intricate lacing and scowled. The boots reminded her that she still couldn't fasten her bra, either. A sports bra wasn't much better, just because the damn things were so tight, she couldn't work it into place one-handed.

And there was no way she was going to spend the next day or two in Cullen's company without a bra. She grimaced, realizing what she was going to have to do. She tossed her boots on the floor and shot him a look over her shoulder and said, "Wait here." On the way into the bathroom, she gave her casted wrist a dirty look. She'd fractured one of the bones in her hand when she hit a guy last week after she'd caught him trying to slip out of town with his girlfriend's daughter stowed in his trunk.

It hadn't been a federal case. Taige had been watching TV when the AMBER Alert was activated. The girlfriend was in the hospital recovering from the beating he'd given her after she tried to leave him. As though Taige had been in the car with the man, she'd seen him sitting behind the steering wheel, unfazed about the woman he'd tried to kill and the girl crying in the trunk.

He was a cold piece of work, that was for damn sure, and Taige didn't regret hitting him, not one bit. But she was completely disgusted about her busted hand and the fact that she was going to have to ask Cullen, of all the people in the world, for help. When she came out of the bathroom a few minutes later, Cullen was standing exactly where she'd left him, his hands shoved deep in his pockets and his legs spread wide. His hair, that same, dark shade of near black, was tousled and standing up on end. As she watched, he pulled a hand from his pocket and shoved it through his hair for what was probably the hundredth time.

He caught sight of her and went still. Taige had her bra on, hanging unfastened over her back, and her T-shirt tucked against her breasts. A dull flush rushed up her cheeks, but she kept her voice empty as she presented him with her back. "I can't fasten this."

Blood drained out of his head as Cullen stared down at Taige, her long, slender, back bare from her neck to the base of her spine where a pair of stark black cargo pants molded her round ass. His mouth went dry as he recalled a thousand dreams where he'd cupped that plump, perfect butt in his hands as he pulled her close against him. Dreams . . . they weren't dreams at all. How it was possible, he didn't know, because Cullen wasn't any more gifted than he was blind. That weird connection between him and Taige was something she must have brought on, consciously or not. Otherwise, there was no way he'd know about her broken hand or her battered face—or the round, puckered scar low on her back.

A bullet wound. Somebody had shot her. He wished something besides Jilly had brought him here, wished he had the right to sink to his knees and kiss the mark some senseless act of violence had left on her. But he was here because of Jilly, and once Taige found his daughter, he was going to disappear from her life, and no doubt, that was exactly what she wanted.

Whenever she looked at him, it was with empty eyes as though she didn't give a damn about him. He lifted his hands and watched, unable to stop himself, as he stroked one hand across her smooth, rounded shoulders. She stiffened, and Cullen cursed himself, reaching for the straps of her bra. She dropped her shirt on the floor, and Cullen quickly averted his eyes, but it was too late. He'd already seen the satiny slopes of her breasts as she adjusted the lace cups around them. Jaw clenched, he fastened the back strap, and the second his hands fell away, they both pulled away from the other as though they'd been burned.

Taige bent and grabbed her shirt from the floor, and Cullen groaned softly as the fabric of her pants stretched taut across her ass. Turning away from her, he stared out the window. "I'm going to need your help with my boots," Taige said.

He looked back to see her sitting on the edge of the bed, sliding her feet into a pair of boots that looked like something that belonged on a soldier, not the woman whose face haunted his dreams. He hunkered down in front of her and started drawing the laces tight, concentrating on that task as though it required all of his attention. Better to focus on it than Taige—or worse, Jillian.

"You going to tell me why I found you on the floor?"

She shrugged. "Works like that sometimes."

"I don't remember it ever working like that before."

He stole a glance at her, but she wasn't looking at him. She was staring somewhere over his head. "That's because back then every time this . . . thing . . . occurred, it was passive. Seeking it out hits me harder." She shrugged.

Harder how? He wanted to ask, but in all honesty, he was afraid to. He really didn't want to know, because even if it was some kind of agonizing hell that she went through, he'd ask it of her a thousand times over if it saved Jillian.

As he went to work on the other boot, the phone started to ring again. She grabbed it and turned it on, held it to her ear. "Yeah?"

Faintly, Cullen heard a voice, and he knew who it was. Taylor Jones.

Taige averted her head, and the voice faded to an indistinct buzz. He started to look back down, and then Taige glanced at him, frowning. "Yeah, actually, I have heard from him. He's here right now."

Shit.

Listening to Jones on the other end of the line, Taige shook her head. "He showed up this morning. We're getting ready to head out now."

"What do you mean, *we*, Taige? That's a civilian you have with you, and the victim's father. This goes against Bureau policy."

She smirked. "Well, I didn't take the case from the Bureau. I took it from him."

"You can't mean to take the girl's father with you, Taige. It isn't safe."

Taige glanced back at Cullen. He wouldn't let her leave him behind, but truthfully, it hadn't occurred to her. It was his daughter, and if it were somebody Taige loved who had gone missing, nobody could keep her away. He had a right to be there. She didn't tell Jones that, though. Instead, she pointed out, "I'm still a little limited here as to what I can do on my own. Only got one good hand."

"Then you'll damn well wait for the team to get there."

With a laugh, Taige said, "No. I don't think so." Then she disconnected the call. She was tempted to leave the phone behind, but she wasn't sure what was waiting for them. If she knew Jones, he'd have a team tailing them using the GPS on the phone, and the backup might come in handy.

But there was no way she was waiting. This wasn't going to turn into an agency case. She wasn't going to let them slow her down with policy and procedure, not when it was Cullen's daughter out there who needed her. She stood up and headed for the door. On the way out, she remembered that soft, strong little voice from her vision.

The little girl. How Taige had realized, with complete and utter certainty, that Jillian had been aware of Taige's presence. *It's okay, sweetie. I'm going to bring you home. I promise you that.* Taige had been making the promise to herself. But the girl had heard her.

Pausing by the door, she glanced back at Cullen. "We're leaving.

And on the way, you're going to tell me more about your daughter."

"More what?" he asked warily.

She cocked a brow. "I think you know what I want to hear."

She saw the knowledge glinting in his eyes. "That could get complicated."

Taking the steps two at a time, she glanced back over her shoulder at him with a humorless smile. "Not a problem. We got a good three-hour drive ahead of us."

SEVEN

"**W**HAT happened to her mother?" Taige rested her head against the headrest as she spoke, closing her eyes to block out the blur of the countryside. They'd left behind the flatter areas of southern Alabama, climbing into the heavily forested area north of Birmingham. They weren't too far from William B. Bankhead National Forest.

The itching in her gut was getting worse, and she knew it was going to go from an itch to downright nausea before the adrenaline finally cleared everything from her system so she could focus on nothing but finding the girl.

The girl. No, not the girl; she had a name now. Jillian. Sweet Lord, Cullen's daughter. It still didn't seem real. None of this felt real, and she kept expecting to wake up and find herself alone in her empty bed once more, alone and aching for the man who didn't want her.

"She died having Jillian. She started hemorrhaging; she never even made it down to surgery." Cullen's voice was oddly flat and, unable to help herself, Taige looked at him.

His face was as expressionless as his voice, and she wondered how much grief he was keeping hidden under that calm mask. For the past three hours, ever since they'd left the house, he'd been remote, almost distant. It was a few minutes after two now, and she would bet that he hadn't looked at her once since they'd stopped half an hour ago for gas.

At her house, he'd shown fear and desperation, but now it was as if those moments hadn't existed. She couldn't really even pick up on any emotion from him at all. She'd never been able to read him the way she could other people. Over the years, her mental blocks had gotten strong enough that she no longer picked up so much random emotion, but there had only been a few people in her life like Cullen, people she didn't have to shield so strongly against. Under any other circumstance, it was a welcome respite, but right now, she wished he wasn't such a closed book.

Then again, this was a blessing. She didn't know if she could have dealt with the pain it would cause her if she knew how much Cullen had loved this wife of his. "I'm sorry," she finally said, looking away from him and closing her eyes again. "That must have been awful for the two of you."

"Harder on Jillian than me," he murmured. "I hate her growing up without her mother."

Deep inside, she felt something wrench, almost like some rope was tied around her gut, and it had been jerked, pulling on her until she had no choice but to follow. "We need to head west now," she said, opening her eyes. They were on a long, empty stretch of the I-65, heading north. There were no major interstates for a good while, but it didn't matter. They needed to go west, and they needed to do it now. Up ahead, she caught sight of an exit ramp.

Highway 940 wasn't much more than a two-lane highway that would lead them to a town not really big enough to be called such. But that was where they needed to go. She pointed ahead. "Get off there."

"What are we looking for?"

She shrugged. "I don't know yet."

A little bit of impatience edged into his voice as he asked, "Then how do you know we need to get off here?"

Taige bit back the pithy response that came instinctively and kept her voice calm as she said, "I know what I'm doing, Cullen. I've been doing it a long time, and I'm good at it. That's why you came looking for me, right?"

Cullen blew out a sigh. He cut across the interstate, hitting the exit ramp and not slowing down until the very last second. It was midafternoon, but there wasn't a car in sight on the highway as he turned left, punching the gas until the speedometer was edging up over seventy. He took the turns at a speed that would have made Taige nervous if she hadn't been feeling the same uneasiness.

"Can you—" His voice broke off, and he shoved a hand through his hair. Taige glanced at him and saw that his hair was standing completely up on end.

Cocking a brow, she asked, "Can I what?"

"Has he hurt her?"

Sympathy and understanding flooded her. If Jillian had been hurt, Taige didn't know what she'd say to him just then—he was already so tense. That calm mask he wore was just that, a mask. She'd dealt with distraught parents before, but Cullen—he was different. No matter how this ended, it was going to affect Taige in ways that no other case, no matter how heartbreaking, had done.

Part of her wanted to run and hide from that fact. This man had caused her enough heartbreak. It might seem infantile to some, still mooning over a man who had dumped her twelve years ago, but Cullen was the only man who had ever been able to get close to her. She hadn't been interested in having that again, but the few times she decided maybe it was time to get back to life, even time to start having a life, the man she thought she might want turned out to be like glass to her, so transparent she either had to keep her mental shields in place or her thoughts were swamped with memories and emotions that weren't her own.

None of those guys had been shallow. There had only been a few, and they'd all been pretty hot. All of them smart and decent guys. But one touch was all it had taken to shatter any hope of having a relationship. It just didn't work trying to get with a man when she touched him and realized he was thinking about what kind of panties she wore.

It made it that much harder to look at Cullen now because it drove home the reminder of just how fricking perfect he'd been for her—and how little he'd loved her.

Even though she couldn't read him, she could read his tension, and it was so thick and heavy in the car, it was choking her. Feeling his gaze on her, she closed her eyes and reached out.

Taige found her quicker this time, and adrenaline started to pound as she realized how close they were. Through the gray, she saw Jillian, and the girl was as Taige had seen her last time, three hours earlier. Dirty, pale, and still. Taige tried briefly to make a connection, but Jillian was sleeping, lost in a deep, deep sleep. Still, the brief surface connection she made was enough to let Taige know that Jillian hadn't been hurt.

They would be in time—this time. Cautious, she expanded her search, looking for the man who had grabbed Jillian. The cabin was small, a couch that opened up into a bed, a kitchen with a minuscule, meticulously cleaned sink. Jillian lay behind the only door in the cabin, besides the main door at the front. That room disturbed Taige, way down deep.

It was a bathroom, but it wasn't the kind of bathroom Taige would have expected to see. The room itself was large, nearly the same size as the other room that served as both kitchen and bedroom. The cot where Jillian lay was tucked up against a wall. The tiles were a bright, blinding white—almost everything was white. Everything but the cot itself, the sink and shower fixtures, and the shiny drain cover in the middle of the floor.

The floor sloped down in the middle.

The showerhead was the removable kind, the sort that came with a head that detached, but this thing looked industrial-grade, more like something used for power washing than personal hygiene. The hose itself was long, so long it could have spanned the entire width of the room.

Her belly churned as she examined the room as closely as she could through the gray's connection. *Take me closer,* she commanded, but it wasn't the room itself she wanted to observe.

She had to reach out, make a deeper connection.

A warning voice screamed at her from inside her skull, but she pushed forward, reaching out, out, out . . . The warning voice was suddenly drowned out by screams of the damned. Young voices, older voices, all of them screaming and begging for help as pain rained down on them like water. She heard the harsh crack of something striking flesh, a voice garbled, an ugly voice that turned her blood to ice.

Sliding farther and farther into that morass of pain, Taige

panicked and jerked away, but it was too late. The screams forced themselves inside her head, echoing through her heart and soul.

Who are you . . . ? Who did this . . . ?

There was no voice, however, to answer. They were all long dead, and the man who had killed them had left nothing of himself behind for Taige to find.

She heard a strange rattling sound and then Cullen, shouting her name. Hands squeezed her arms brutally, and she realized Cullen was shaking her hard. So hard it felt like her teeth were rattling around inside her skull.

"Damn, Cullen," she wheezed out. "Are you trying to shake my head off of my shoulders?"

His arms came around her, and now, as hard as he had been shaking her, he was holding her, a big hand cradling the back of her head and holding her tight against him. "Damn it, what was that? You looked terrified."

Weak, she shoved against his chest, trying to get some air between them. He let go only to cup his hands around her face and stare at her. "What in the hell was that? Damn it, you started screaming, and you wouldn't stop. I didn't think you'd ever stop."

Taige swallowed, and her raw throat rebelled. She looked at the digital clock on the dash: 2:59.

Her jaw dropped. "How long . . . ?"

"You closed your eyes about thirty minutes ago. You started crying," he said softly, reaching up to wipe away tears she hadn't even been aware of. "And about ten minutes ago, you started screaming. You started screaming, and you didn't stop." He pushed her hair back from her face. "What happened to Jillian?"

Taige shook her head, and he growled, "Don't lie to me."

She reached up and covered his hand with hers. "I'm not. Jillian's not hurt. He's not even there."

* * *

HE would have driven right past the gravel road if Taige hadn't tensed up, her back arching up off the leather seat. Her hand flew out and grabbed him. Short, neatly trimmed nails bit into his forearm. "Here."

He didn't see anything. He slammed on the brakes in the middle of the road and looked around him. "Here where? There's nothing here."

She pointed off the roadside, and through the high weeds, he saw the gravel road. He turned off the road and muttered, "Glad I didn't go with that sedan." The big Tundra ate up gas, but it took the rough, poor excuse for a road like a dream. As the road started to climb, he glanced over at Taige and saw she had worked forward, even with the seat belt on, so that she sat on the edge of the seat. She had her hands curled around the edge, knuckles gone white.

"Turn," she said, her eyes closed. She didn't open her eyes as she pointed to the right. It was another sorry road, more of a trail than anything, and it climbed up, up, and up.

There were no more turns, the road going up at such a high angle, it climbed up the side of the mountain. It kept going up until the ground leveled out. They were damned high. Cullen climbed out of the car and looked around, staring at the cabin in front of him. He noticed the generator, saw a huge water tank, an empty spot in front of the cabin where it looked like somebody parked regularly. But the cabin itself looked damned empty. As secluded as this place was, if somebody had been in that cabin, they would be at the door.

Or maybe not, Cullen thought. If the sick fuck who had taken his baby was inside that house, the last thing he would want to do was announce his presence to anybody. "Don't suppose I can convince you to wait in the car, huh?" Taige asked as she came up to stand beside him. She'd put a holster on, and Cullen could see the butt of a gun peering out from under her right arm. With her weight resting lightly on the balls of her feet and a grim, intent look on her face, she looked as much a warrior now as she had that first summer when he'd watched her break through the waves like a mermaid, a drowning child in her arms.

"No. You can't convince me to wait in the car."

As one, they turned their attention back to the house. "Can you use that gun left-handed?"

"Almost as good as I can with my right hand," Taige replied. She closed her eyes, and her shoulders lifted and fell as she took a deep, slow breath, followed by another. "But I don't think I'm going to need it. She's in there alone."

"How can you be sure?"

Her misty gray eyes slid toward him, and Cullen blew out a breath. "Okay, dumb question."

She rolled her shoulders, looking like she was getting ready to step into the ring with a professional boxer, but she didn't look scared or even worried. She pulled the gun from the leather shoulder holster, palming it in her left hand.

"I thought you said he wasn't here." Instinctively, Cullen shifted and placed his body in front of hers. Pointless, considering she was the one with the weapon. A very mean-looking weapon at that, matte black, and she held it like it was part of her.

"I did. And I'm certain he isn't." Then she slid around him and planted herself squarely in front of him and gave him a hard look over her shoulder. "But I've been wrong before. Now, please, stay behind me. We're both worried about your girl. Don't make me worry about you, too."

So I'm supposed to worry about you? he wondered. But he kept the question behind his lips, and when she started to walk toward the house, he stayed exactly two steps behind her, close enough that he could grab her and throw her behind him if he had to.

The door was locked. He watched as Taige tried to open it by shoving against it. It didn't even budge. The door boasted three shiny, rather new-looking locks. She glanced at him and asked, "Don't suppose you can pick locks, can you?"

Cullen scowled. "Hell, no. Can you?"

She lifted her casted hand and said, "One-handed? Hell, no." She stepped back and studied the house. Cullen took her place and shoved against the door. It was like pushing against a brick wall. He took a step back and threw his weight into it, striking it with his shoulder, and it still didn't give.

"Don't bother. If he's been using this as a place to keep his victims, he's going to do his damnedest to keep people out. That door is probably reinforced, and those locks are heavy-duty."

Cullen ignored her. If his little girl was on the other side of that door, the door could be made of titanium, and he'd find a way through it.

"Cullen."

He heard the thud of footsteps on the porch, heard gravel crunch and the truck door open and shut. He glanced back as Taige came striding back toward the porch. His shoulder throbbed, and the door still felt as solid as a redwood.

The sound of glass shattering finally had him looking around. Taige stood in front of a small, narrow window. She had her left hand wrapped in what looked like a T-shirt, and she was using it to knock shards of glass from the window. She glanced toward him and shrugged. "I'm already bruised and battered enough," she said.

As she unwound the T-shirt wrapped around her forearm and hand, he saw that she held her gun and had used it to break the window. Little shards of glass rained down as she dropped it onto the porch.

Still holding her Glock, Taige peered through the window. It was exactly as she'd seen in those few brief moments from earlier, one room that served as kitchen and bedroom, and a wall that bisected the house nearly in half. The door was in the middle of it, and Taige's heartbeat kicked up a few notches when she saw it.

Jillian—

She pulled back and slid Cullen a glance before ducking inside, first one leg, then the other. She wobbled a little and ended up smacking her busted hand on the wall when she went to catch her balance. Pain streaked up her arm, and she just barely managed to keep from crying out. Biting down on her lip, she did her best to push the pain aside and focus on the situation at hand.

It was hot in there. Dangerously so. The windows were closed, and although there was an AC unit in the back window, it wasn't on. The air was close and tight, and there was a faint scent of something that set her teeth on edge.

Taige felt a mad vibration on her hip, and she looked down at her cell phone. Moving to the door, she undid the series of locks before pulling her phone off the clip and reading the message. Jones. Impatient bastard. He was a good hour away still, according to the message, although there was a helicopter en route that would be there within thirty minutes.

I plan on getting them out of here in less than ten, Taige thought grimly. Despite the heat in the room, she felt chilled, and the skin on the back of her neck was crawling. She opened the door to let Cullen in, and she stepped to the side as he came through the doorway, taking in the room with one quick glance.

His mouth compressed down to a thin, tight line as he started for the door. Taige shoved the phone into her pocket and rushed to cut Cullen off. She hadn't seen any kind of trap on the door earlier, but looking through the gray didn't always allow for the clearest view, and she wasn't going to take the chance that something nasty was waiting to happen if somebody opened the door unwittingly.

She slammed a hand against Cullen's chest and said, "Slow down."

He went to move her aside, and Taige shoved him. "Wait a damn minute, Cullen. Let me make sure it's safe."

He looked down at her, and there were a few seconds when she wondered if he was really even aware of her as a person. He eyed her as though she was nothing more than an obstacle in his way. Even though she understood, it hurt. Softening her voice, she said, "Just let me check the door, okay?"

There had been a case three years ago when a dad, a certified lunatic who was convinced the government was trying to brainwash his wife, had killed her and then kidnapped his three kids. For three months, the guy had gone off the map. It wasn't until after the mother's body was found that Taige was brought in. She led Taylor's unit to where the man was hiding his kids, but there had been a trap rigged to the door. When one of the agents opened it, bullets started flying. If it had been anybody other than a very cautious law enforcement agent, they would have needed some body bags.

Taige still had some bad moments over that one, but it had taught her a very important lesson: people were fucking crazy.

By the time she was satisfied the door was safe, several minutes had passed, and she could all but feel Cullen's impatience as she wrapped her hand around the knob and turned it.

Slowly. Easing it open an inch at a time and standing off to the side, just in case. It opened completely, and she felt her legs go watery as she saw Jillian lying on the cot, her face slack, her chest rising and falling. It was every bit as hot in the bathroom as it was in the main room, and a nasty, cold ball of fear settled in Taige's belly as she saw the girl's flushed red face.

She started toward Jillian. Two steps, though, and she froze in place as screams started to echo through her head. Screaming voices, begging for help, begging for death; children begging for their mothers before their voices were forever silenced. A moan rattled up through her tight throat, but she wasn't aware she'd made a sound. Bile churned in her gut, and she fell to her knees, vomiting on the floor.

Her eyes were wide open, but it wasn't the gleaming white tile she saw—or rather, it was, but the tile was covered in blood. Not streaked, but covered so that the white wasn't even visible. Face after face flashed through her mind, and she could hear their voices.

Help me . . .

Don't hurt me . . .

I want my mommy.

There was a laugh, ugly and monstrous. The man's voice was distorted, and try as she might, Taige couldn't see his face. She saw his hands, big and cruel-looking, rising and coming down. Taige flinched away as she felt their pain. So many—there were so many.

"Son of a bitch," she gasped. "You son of a bitch."

Tears blinded her, and she had to wrench herself out of the

vision. Her skin crawled as she shoved herself to her feet and stared at the room. The stink of vomit permeated the air. Staring at the narrow cot, she saw them. Children, ranging from mere toddlers to teenagers: black, white, Hispanic, male and female.

Slowly, she turned her head and stared at Cullen. He held Jillian in his arms, patting her face and talking to her in a voice thick with tears and terror as the little girl continued to lie there, unresponsive. "She needs a doctor," Taige said, her voice barely above a whisper.

Lying in this close, confined heat, the girl was dehydrated. At least. Taige closed the distance between them, and although part of her didn't want to touch the girl at all, she reached out and laid a hand on Jillian's narrow chest. The girl was breathing far too quickly, and her heartbeat was weak and erratic.

But the girl's soul was powerful. Taige felt it wrap around her like a blanket warm from the sun. Relief rushed through her, and she almost sagged to her knees. Thank God. Then she pulled her hand back and turned to stare at the room. There was a cabinet under the sink, and Taige crossed to it, opening it up and finding white washcloths, as brilliantly white as the tiles. Grabbing a stack, she turned on the tap water and soaked them through, carrying them back to Cullen and the girl.

She laid one the girl's forehead. Jillian whimpered but didn't open her eyes. "You got water in the truck?" she asked, draping the other rags over his shoulder.

He lifted his head and stared her, his eyes practically sightless. "Yeah," he murmured. Then he looked down at Jillian. A sense of hopelessness wrapped around him like a shroud.

She ached for him and wished she could do something, anything, to take this from him. Taige wanted to wrap her arms around him and promise that everything would be okay, but she didn't make promises she couldn't keep. Instead of trying to comfort him, she made her voice hard and flat as she said, "Cullen, she's just dehydrated. Get her to the hospital. There was a county hospital two exits back on the highway." Digging in her pocket, she pulled out one of the cards that Taylor constantly nagged her to carry. She shoved it into Cullen's pocket. "Taylor's number is on it. Call him after you get Jillian some medical care."

His voice was rusty. "Aren't you coming?"

She looked away from him and crossed her arms over her chest, automatically cradling her splinted hand. "No. I'm not done here. Not yet." Then she softened, unable to help it as she reached up and laid a hand on his cheek. His flesh seemed as chilled as she was: shock. "Cullen, she's going to be okay. Just pull it together and get her some medical care."

Finally, his eyes focused, and when he looked at her again, she knew he saw her. Cullen nodded grimly, and he turned away, cradling his daughter against his chest as he left, walking away with long, quick strides.

She held herself still until she heard Cullen's engine turn over, and then she looked back at the bathroom. "Where are you?" she asked softly. She could feel them pushing at her, screaming to her, but if she opened herself up to them again, she wasn't sure she could pull herself out on her own, and it was too dangerous to do it now.

Taylor, damn him, knew how to handle her if she slid too deep inside the visions. Until he was here, she had to keep herself centered. But she couldn't remain still, either. The phone at her hip buzzed again. This time, she answered it.

"Jillian's alive. Her father has her. Taking her to the emergency room."

"Damn it, Taige. You know she needs—"

Interrupting, Taige said, "She needs fluids. She's dehydrated. Seriously dehydrated." Another wave of agony washed over her, and she almost buckled under the weight of it. She had no idea how tortured her voice sounded when she said, "It's bad here, Jones. So bad."

Jones was quiet for a moment, and then he said, "Are you in trouble?"

She shook her head. "Not yet. But I will be if you don't hurry."

"Get out of the house until the team arrives, Taige. That's an order."

But Taige didn't like orders. Especially orders that came from Taylor Jones. "Get your ass here now." Then she disconnected and turned her back on the bathroom. Whatever had happened in there, she wasn't going to let herself see just yet. But the main room, she would look there.

Look for traces of the monster who'd done this.

* * *

"Are you ever going to learn to listen?"

"I don't work for you, remember?" Taige said as she glanced up from her focused study of the floorboards and wished she had some tools: a crowbar, a shovel, something. There was something under the floor of this house, and considering how edgy she was, considering the voices that continued to scream at her, she suspected she knew what it was.

Bodies. How many, she had no clue, but their cries were a dull roar inside her head, and she had long since stopped trying to differentiate between individual voices. She tapped on one of the floorboards with the butt of her gun and said, "There's something under here. I think he buried their bodies."

"Their?" Jones asked from the doorway, his bland, professional face falling away for a minute and letting her see some semblance of humanity. "Whose?"

Shaking her head, she murmured, "I don't know. But there are a lot of them. She wasn't his first, Jones. Not by a long shot."

Shoving to her feet, she glanced around the plain, Spartan cabin. "There's no sign of the owner here. No vehicle when we got here, no personal belongings—no imprints. I can't sense anything from him. It's almost like he doesn't even exist."

"You can't see his face?"

Taige shook her head. "No. A glimpse of his hands, but there was nothing there to identify him beyond the fact that he's male. Even his voice doesn't sound real to me. It's too ugly, too distorted."

Taylor scowled and stood aside, letting his team come in. The team that had arrived on the helicopter had been ordered to wait until he arrived now that they knew the girl was safe. Jones gestured to the floor and said, "Ms. Branch thinks there is something under the floorboards. See if there's a crawl space or something for now. Let's get to work. Ms. Branch, if you don't mind . . ."

He gestured to the open door. He said nothing else, but she got the picture loud and clear. Oooohhh . . . he was pissed. Smirking, she headed for the door. "What, can't I stay and play with the big kids, Daddy?"

"The big kids work for me, remember? You don't." He parroted her own words back at her as he followed her outside. Once they were on the porch, he said, "Fill me in, Taige. And don't bother telling me that this wasn't a Bureau case. The only reason you got here with him instead of with us is because he slipped away from his tail."

In a mockingly respectful tone, she replied, "Then maybe you should train your men better, boss." Taige wrapped her arms around her belly and wished there was someplace she could sit down. She was damn tired, and her legs felt like wax. "Cullen Morgan is a private citizen with no training. If he can evade your agents, then you have a problem."

Jones's eyes narrowed, and if Taige were actually an official part of his team, she just might have gotten a little nervous. He gave agents that look, and demotions came rolling along like a river. But she wasn't part of his team, she wouldn't ever be part of his team, and the most he could do was not send her any more cases.

Which would suit her just fine.

Taige wasn't naive enough to actually think that would happen, though. She'd been trying to get him to fire her for the past five years—longer. Hadn't happened yet, and she was under no illusions to think that might change any time soon.

She waited for him to press the issue, but instead, he went off on another tangent. "I believe the two of you had some history."

Taige shrugged. "Long time ago. Had nothing to do with this beyond the fact that he suspected I could help. I haven't seen him in years."

"Are you familiar with his daughter?"

Rolling her eyes, Taige said, "Now didn't I just say I hadn't seen him in years? I didn't even know he had a daughter. How can I be familiar with her?"

Jones didn't look terribly convinced. "So you don't know anything about her abilities?"

She didn't bat a lash as she lied, "Nope."

Taige knew that nothing on her face had given her away, but

she also knew that he hadn't believed a word she'd said, either. It didn't matter. She didn't care if he believed her or not, and in another few minutes, he was going to be plenty distracted. Sliding a look back at the house, she said, "Bad things happened in there, Jones. I can feel them pushing at me. Can't fight it much longer."

He nodded. "I had expected as much." He glanced around and finally cupped a hand around her arm, gestured to his car with his other hand. "I don't imagine you want to sit down in that place."

No. No, I don't, she thought grimly. Jones opened the back door and she crawled inside, cradling her injured hand to her belly. Curling into a fetal position, she stopped fighting and let the madness take her.

Bad didn't even begin to describe the torment that awaited her. Sheer hell didn't describe it. It was an evil unlike anything she had ever felt in her life, and Taige had dealt with a lot of evil. She felt their presence screaming at her, felt their pain. The shock.

Beatings, harsh and pitiless. Days of starvation and dehydration. The ugly blackness of despair as the mind finally accepted what the body had already known. Death waited, and the only question was when it would come and how painful it would be.

The young children were the worst though. They never stopped believing that somebody would come for them. That they would be saved. But they weren't. They died screaming, broken and alone.

All until Jillian. Jillian broke the cycle.

Taige came out of her stupor screaming and crying. Her entire body twitched and jerked. It was a familiar feeling, and one she didn't really care for. The bastard had used a Taser on her again. Sending Jones a dirty look, she said hoarsely, "I think you like having a reason to zap me."

Jones cocked a brow. "Taige, I may be a bit of a bastard, but I have no desire to cause a woman harm." Then he shrugged. "But you weren't coming out of it. You've been under more than an hour, and you screamed for a good twenty minutes. You weren't stopping."

Yeah. She knew that. But just because she knew a physical blow was sometimes the only way to bring her out, that didn't mean she had to like it. Her limbs shook with exhaustion as she climbed out of the car. Glancing at the brightly lit house, she asked, "Have they started looking under the floorboards yet?"

"No. There was a crawl space, but somebody sealed it with concrete. We won't be able to do anything until we tear up the floorboards." He looked back at her and said, "There's nothing to be found in that house that will lead us to him, is there?"

Taige shrugged. "You'd be better to ask one of your precogs that, Jones. But I really don't think so. This guy, he's too careful."

With a bitter smile, Jones muttered, "We'd noticed. They've been keeping me updated. We haven't found a single hair. Not a fingernail. The one thing we did find was a receipt under the refrigerator, dated three years back. It was from one of those old-fashioned cash registers, didn't have so much as an address on it. Just the date." Shaking his head, Jones said, "What are we supposed to do with a receipt? Nothing but prices, a date, and a total."

"No fingerprints, I assume?"

Jones's flat look was answer enough. Sighing, Taige shoved away from the car. Her head was pounding, her throat felt raw from screaming, and she wanted to sleep so badly, she almost hurt from it. But instead, she locked her legs and said, "Before they tear it up, I want to go over it once more, okay?"

He gestured to the house. "Be my guest." As she walked off, he called out, "You need to give me an official report, Taige."

"I wasn't here on Bureau business," she said over her shoulder.

Sliding in front of her, Jones blocked her path. "You look like hell, Taige. You need some downtime."

Taige shook her head. "No, I don't. What I need is to find something that can lead me to the bastard who did this." Then she walked off, her head down and her gut already churning. "If you're smart," she muttered to herself, "you'll just stay out of this part."

But Taige hadn't ever claimed to be a genius. Once more, she walked back into that hellish house, watching as the team went over everything with a fine-tooth comb. No, it was more detailed than that. They might as well have used X-ray vision, because they peered between the cracks in the floorboards, they checked out the walls, they moved out the few appliances and took them apart.

She joined them, skimming the back of her hand along surfaces so she could have physical contact without adding her prints to the mess. Everything would be dusted for prints, and if they found hers among them, they'd rip her a new tail. It had happened before.

Physical contact could strengthen her gift, and all she really needed was just a faint link. Not much, just a little. She could get a memory flash off something a killer had touched months, years earlier.

But there was nothing. After the first two hours when she went crawling across the floor on her one good hand and her knees, Jones had told her to take a break. She hadn't. She kept going, searching for something that couldn't be found, and she had no intention of quitting.

It was midnight before she finally acknowledged what most of the team had accepted hours ago. Taige would find no trace of the kidnapper here. There might be trace physical evidence—and oh, did she mean trace. So far, they hadn't even found an eyelash.

And there wasn't even a sliver of a psychic trail.

She sat on the porch, numb inside, as she watched the crime scene techs going over the yard. More teams would have to be brought in.

She wouldn't be on hand for those, though. She'd done her part, done what little she could. The visions had showed her precious little this time, but it was a damn good thing she waited, because once the gray sucked her under this time, it hadn't wanted to let go. Jones probably hadn't enjoyed using that Taser on her, but she also doubted that it would give him any bad moments. The man was relentless, pitiless, and driven.

Still aching from the Taser jolt, Taige stood off to the side and watched as they pried up for the first floorboard. Taige had told Jones the harsh, ugly truth: there was a graveyard of bones under the floorboards of the main cabin. And she had no idea how many bodies.

Right now, she didn't want to even see the first one. Turning on her heel, she left the house and went out onto the porch. The air out there was cooler, just a bit, and the stink of death wasn't so strong. But she didn't dare relax. Worn out, she sank down on the front steps and braced her elbows on her knees.

She was so damned tired.

Breathe, girl. Just breathe. One breath in. One breath out. She might not be able to sleep, but if she tried hard enough, maybe she could zone out for just a minute or two. Except every time she drifted just a little closer to a mindless state of rest, the screams would start again.

"You ever going to stop being the Lone Ranger?"

Taige managed to smile as Desiree Lincoln settled down beside her. If Dez wasn't such a sweetheart, Taige could have hated her on the spot. Dez bore a startling resemblance to Halle Berry, and she almost always had a smile on her face. She worked with Jones's unit, and technically, she was considered part of the crime scene investigative team. But Jones didn't work with typical agents, plain and simple. Dez's particular skill wasn't the kind that Taige would have taken for all the wine and chocolate in the world. Dez made a connection with victims who had already died, and that was why she was here now.

Dez glanced at the house and murmured, "I hear they think they're going to find some bones."

Grimacing, Taige said, "Not some. A lot." Inside, she could hear them working. It would be hours yet before they were ready for Dez, hours away from finding all the bodies. But Dez always liked to be there from the first.

If Taige was right, the bones beneath the floorboards of the cabin were going to take a long time to sort out. Jones probably hoped Dez would help shorten that time frame. She probably would. Dez, like all of the people Jones had grabbed for his secretive unit, was damn good with her abilities. More, she had an ethereal way about her; all the death she dealt with rarely seemed to faze her. Taige had once asked her how she could do what she did and still seem so at peace.

Dez had told her it was because by the time the victims came to her, they were all way past suffering. Then she'd smiled and told Taige it was easier that way. At that point, she couldn't do anything to add to their pain; therefore, she couldn't fail them.

In their line of work, failure meant people died.

"Scoot your skinny butt over, Lone Ranger. Tell me what's going on in there."

Obligingly, Taige scooted over enough so Dez could sit down, and when Dez wrapped an arm around her shoulder, she willingly accepted the silent offer of comfort. "Wasn't trying to be the Lone Ranger, Dez. I just couldn't wait."

"These poor babies calling you that hard?"

Taige shook her head. She shot a grim glance over her shoulder, staring inside the open door as Taylor barked out orders left and right. From time to time, he reached up and rubbed at the back of his neck. It was one of those rare times when the bastard actually seemed almost human. All this death was enough to do it, though. Even Dez looked a little grim, and for her, that was unusual. "It wasn't them that pulled me here; it was the girl."

"Hmmm. Yeah, the little cutie that was grabbed from Atlanta. You felt that?"

"Nope." She braced her arms on her knees and leaned forward. "It was her father."

Dez's midnight brows arched up. "Her father. Well, that's a different turn for you."

Taige grimaced. "Not exactly. I knew him. We . . . we sort of had this thing when we were younger." Exhaustion pressed down on her hard like a weight, but there was no way in hell she was going to rest here. Those few minutes when she had tried to just zone out had been rough. Really going to sleep? That would be like walking willingly into hell. All around her was the lingering touch of death. Even if her gifts didn't intrude on her sleep, the negative energy here sure as hell would. She was going to have enough nightmares as it was. Taige had no intention of letting the sad, angry atmosphere of this place color those bad dreams any more than she had to.

"A thing, huh?" Dez smiled. "Saw his picture in the paper. He look as biteable in person as he is on paper?"

Biteable. Despite her exhaustion, she couldn't help but smile. "More so."

Feeling Dez's eyes on her, she looked back over her shoulder. The appraising look on the woman's face made Taige squirm. "So that's the deal."

"What?" Taige demanded defensively.

"I always wondered why you don't talk about guys. You're hung up on some sexy boy from high school."

She didn't bother denying it. "It wasn't high school. His parents were loaded; they had a summer house close to where I grew up."

Dez made a face. "Oh, please tell me he wasn't some rich boy looking to piss his folks off by dating a black girl."

Taige's face softened a little. "No. He wasn't like that. Cullen . . ." Her voice trailed off while she tried to figure out just how much she wanted to tell Dez. She hadn't discussed that last day with Cullen with anybody. Not even Rose before she died, and the good Lord knows, Rose had asked. And asked. And asked . . . Especially after—

Oh, Taige, girl. Don't go there. She had enough shit inside her head without remembering that period in her life.

"He broke your heart."

"Yeah." Taige blew out a soft breath and rubbed her hands over her face. "Yeah, he did."

"So, speaking as your friend, should I totally hate this guy?"

Taige laughed. "Cullen isn't the kind of guy you can hate easily. God knows I certainly tried to hate him."

"So are you going to tell me what happened?"

Taige dropped her hands and stood up. Every muscle in her body screamed at her as she did it. She hurt so much that every movement was a small lesson in agony. Right now, the pain was a blessing. A sweet blessing, because it distracted her from the pain of her own memories. Blowing out a sigh, she said, "There's not all that much to tell, honey. He lost somebody—and I wasn't able to help."

She heard Dez moving up behind her and turned around, lifting her hands to ward Dez away. "Don't, Dez. Okay? I'm not up to this right now." *I don't know if I'll ever be ready for it.*

"You don't get to pick and choose who you are able to help, Taige. You know that."

She blinked away the tears stinging her eyes. "Yeah. I know that. Still doesn't make it any easier when I can't help."

* * *

It was nearly three a.m. before she got away from the crime scene. It probably would have been later if Dez hadn't pushed the issue. She'd taken a break from her gruesome job and was outside for some fresh air. While she was walking through the maze of yellow tape and portable outdoor lights, Dez saw Taige leaning against a plain black van. Taige had been weaving on her feet, fighting to stay awake as the exhaustion weighed down heavier and heavier with each passing second.

Dez had turned on her heel and stalked back into the house, grabbing Jones by the collar of his suit and jerking him away from the tech he was berating. "You want her to collapse out there?"

If Taige were an optimist, she could have said that him leav-

ing the scene to drive her into town was a sign that he was human. But she knew better. He saw it as an opportunity to go find
Jillian's dad—and Jillian. Which was how Taige had ended up in
the waiting room of the county hospital. Jones had told her that
she could get a hotel room and put it on her expense account, but
since she didn't have a car, she was stuck waiting for him.

"Asshole," she muttered, watching his suited back disappear
through the doors. The triage nurse at the desk hadn't wanted to
let him back, but he'd flashed his identification from the FBI, and
Taige had seen the woman's eyes round in surprise. A second
later, the door was buzzed open.

If Taige hadn't been so bone tired, she would have followed
him back. She wanted to check on Jillian, and she wanted to see
Cullen, but it felt like she had cement blocks strapped to her feet.
She'd fallen asleep in Jones's rented car on the way in, but that
thirty minutes had done more damage than good.

Now, though, in the quiet of the predawn morning, sitting in
an armchair that was covered with that easy-to-clean fake leather,
she was almost comfortable. The chair was a little harder than
she preferred, but at least it was better than the straight-backed
chairs or benches that were in most emergency rooms. The only
sounds were the low voices coming from the staff at the triage
desk and a sniffling child. The little boy's face was flushed from
a fever, and he had a nasty, deep cough that made Taige's chest
hurt in sympathy.

The tired mom glanced at Taige, and Taige tried to smile
back, but she was just so tired. The little boy started to whimper
again, and the mom automatically rocked him, singing softly:
"You are my sunshine . . . my only sunshine . . ."

A sad smile curved Taige's lips. Her mother had used to sing
that song to her.

"You make me happy . . . when skies are gray . . ."

Taige felt her lids drooping, and she tried to move around. Body was too heavy, though, and as her head fell forward, the woman's song echoed in Taige's mind.

"You'll never know, dear, how much I love you . . ."

Sleep didn't ease up on her as it had in the car. It sucked her under like a leviathan emerging from the depths of the ocean, grabbing her, and pulling her down deep and hard. Although the mom kept on singing, Taige heard nothing, saw nothing, just the black oblivion of deep sleep. How much time passed as she slept, she didn't know. It could have been hours. It could have been minutes. Then the darkness eased, and she knew she wasn't alone anymore.

Still caught in the grip of sleep, Taige sensed Cullen's presence as he joined her in her dreams. He looked as exhausted there as she felt, standing at the door of the emergency room. He paused there, looked back over his shoulder like he didn't want to leave, and then he came forward, his steps slow, almost clumsy.

Straightening in the chair, she forced herself to smile at him. "How's Jillian?"

He shrugged. "Sleeping right now. They've got her on IVs. You were right. She was seriously dehydrated." A scowl darkened his face, and he murmured, "That boss of yours is an ass. He wants to talk to her, but neither the doctor nor I are willing to let him wake her."

"Jones is definitely an ass," she agreed, her forced smile fading away. "He will have to talk to her, Cullen. They need to know who hurt her." But even as she tried to explain that to him, she wondered why she bothered. In real life, she needed to deal with reality. These were her dreams; she didn't have to be logical here.

A grimace twisted his mouth. "Yeah, I know. And if she can help, I want her to try. I don't want another parent to have to go through this kind of hell if I can stop it. Just . . . not yet."

"Have you talked to her?"

Cullen nodded. "She opened her eyes—"

Hands closed around Taige's shoulders and shook her. Still trapped in the dream, she stared at Cullen's face, and he said something else, but it wasn't Cullen's voice. It was Jones. "Damn it, Taige, wake up. You know you shouldn't sleep here."

"Wha . . ."

She groaned and smacked at Jones's hands as he shook her again. Awake now, she squinted up at him and then looked at the clock hanging on the wall over his shoulder. Ten a.m. She'd been under probably close to six hours. And she could tell, just by how stiff her body was. Sleeping in an armchair was always a bad idea. Groaning, she straightened up. Her stiffened muscles screamed at her, and she pressed a hand to her low back, scooting to the front edge of the cushion so she could stretch a little.

"What in the hell are you still doing here?" Jones demanded.

Tired and cranky as hell, she snarled at him, "Where am I supposed to be? You dump me here, and it's not like there's a yellow cab outside waiting to take me to the nearest Holiday Inn."

"There's a Motel 6 a few blocks down the road."

Shoving up off the chair, she got in his face and demanded, "What, you really think I was going to walk there or something? Damn, Jones, what bug crawled up your ass this morning?"

His eyes narrowed. Sometimes, she knew, he wondered why in the hell he tolerated her. If she actually worked for him, he could discipline her for the attitude she gave him. She mouthed off enough to know she could have been fired ten times over—if she were an employee. But since she was more of a freelance type, he didn't have that much authority over her, and he also knew that if he never asked for her help on a case again, she could care less. Took away a lot of his fun, she was willing to bet. Which made it all that much more fun for her.

His voice was pleasant as he said, "You know, Taige, one would think you could understand that I'm in a bind here. You broke procedure doing what you did. You could have endangered that girl even more. Maybe one of the bugs up my ass, as you say, is because I'm trying to figure out how to keep you from getting into a world of trouble."

Taige snorted. "Oh, come off of it, Jones. You and I both know that what your superiors care about is results. Just like you and I both know that I'd never have gone to get her if I hadn't thought that was the best thing for her." She eased around him, searching for the coffee carafe she'd glimpsed last night. It was on a small table under the TV mounted to the wall. Taking one of the small foam cups from the table, she filled it half full and took a sniff. Strong. Stronger than she liked, and she had a feeling it would eat away the lining of her stomach if she drank too much.

But right now, she needed the caffeine. She added twice as much sugar as normal, and three times as much cream. Still, it was strong enough to make her blanch, and the caffeine hit her system with the force of a sucker punch. "Damn. These medical types make their coffee strong."

She turned around and met Jones's gaze. He was still scowling at her, and she gave him a sweet smile. "So why did you wake me up?"

He looked around and then jerked his head, a silent summons that she follow him. In the time since she had fallen asleep, the number of people waiting in the emergency room had gone up considerably. She made her way past two elderly patients in wheelchairs, a girl sitting doubled up in a chair, and a very, very pregnant woman as she followed Jones to the double doors by the triage desk.

The nurse buzzed the door, and as Taige walked by, she saw the dirty look the nurse shot at Jones's averted back. Yep, Taylor Jones made friends everywhere he went. He led her into a small office, one he'd obviously appropriated for his personal use. He gestured to a chair and told her to sit.

She didn't. She hated it when the bastard tried to throw his weight around with her. He dropped into his chair and gave her an irritated look. "Sit down, Taige. You need to give me your report, and you look like shit."

"My, you are in a bad mood. Cussing and everything," she said with a cheeky grin. She sipped at her strong, overly sweet coffee and added, "I'll stand."

He gave her his most intimidating stare. She didn't even blink. He broke first, leaning over the desk under the guise of opening a file. "You'll need to fill out your official report, but right now, I need your impressions on the kidnapper."

Taige's mouth thinned out in a flat line, and she shook her head. "Can't. Already told you that. I didn't so much as get one look at him. That place, it's like it's been wiped clean of his touch. I can feel the evil of him, but not him."

Jones looked up, and she saw a muscle ticking in his jaw. "You got nothing?"

* * *

She waited until Jones disappeared into the bathroom before she slipped out of the office and made her way down the crowded hallway. She kept her chin up, shoulders back, and she took a minute to loop the lanyard holding her badge in place around her neck. It displayed her official identification with the FBI and that, coupled with her confident stride, kept anybody from stopping her as she sought out Jillian and Cullen.

It didn't take long. Busy as it was, the county emergency room was small. She sensed Cullen's presence before she actually saw him and turned to find him sitting behind a curtain that partially blocked him from view. Keeping quiet, she moved to the curtain, intending only to glance in and see Jillian for herself. After dreaming of this girl for more than a decade, for longer than Jillian had even been alive, it was hard to believe those dreams might actually be over.

Very hard.

But Jillian lay on the bed, her pretty little face peaceful, once more the soft, fragile ivory that Taige remembered from her dreams and no longer stained with the hot red flush that had come from the heat and dehydration. Cautious, Taige lowered her shields and reached out to Jillian.

The girl slept with the deep, dreamless sleep of the exhausted. Taige didn't sense any torment, any bad dreams, or any fear. All she could pick up was a sense of peace now that Jillian had her dad with her. The bad dreams would come, of that Taige had no doubt. Hopefully, it would be a while. The mind had a way of protecting itself, and maybe Jillian would forget for a while, at least until she was a little older, a little more ready to deal with what had happened.

Taige certainly hoped so.

"Hey."

Startled, she turned her head and saw that Cullen had opened his eyes. He stared at her, his lids hanging low over his eyes. "You look exhausted," she said.

His lips quirked in a smile. "You, too."

Nodding toward Jillian, she asked, "She woken up yet?"

Cullen shrugged. "For a minute. Saw me and told me she knew I'd find her. Then she went back to sleep and hasn't woken up since. The doctor said not to worry." His mouth twisted in a sullen scowl. "How in the hell can I not worry?"

He glanced at Jillian and then stood up slowly, arching his back and groaning a little. He slid out of the small, curtained room and leaned his shoulder up against the wall, staring at Taige with intense eyes. "I don't how to say thank you."

Taige wished she could move away a little, get some distance between them, but she couldn't, even though she tried to make herself. Her body seemed to be reaching out to his, and it was all she could do not to touch him. She'd made it this long without touching him, but that had been because she'd been focused on Jillian and saving her. Now that Jillian was safe, it was harder.

Quietly, she said, "You don't need to say thanks for anything, Cullen." She glanced back at Jillian and sighed. A faint smile, almost amazed, curved her lips. The relief she felt was unreal. "It's kind of hard to believe all of this is over. I've seen her face so many times. I'm just glad she's finally safe."

Cullen's eyes darkened. "You saved her life, Taige. Saved mine—it would have killed me if anything happened to her. I owe you a hell of a lot more than thanks." He looked away for a minute, hooked his thumbs in his pockets. A harsh breath escaped him, and he looked back at her. Under the thick fringe of his lashes, his eyes were stormy. "One thing I do owe you is an apology. What I did to you when you came to see me about Mom, it was wrong. All of it. For blaming you." A faint rush of blood darkened his tanned face. "And for what happened before you left."

She swallowed. The knot in her throat was going to choke

her; she knew it. Taige turned away from him, nervously toying with one of her braids. "It's over with, Cullen. It doesn't matter now."

His voice was rough as he murmured, "The hell it doesn't." His hand curved over her shoulder and he turned her to face him. He cupped her chin in his hand. The feel of his hand, callused and warm, against her flesh brought a rush of sensation. All at once, it eased the ache that had lived inside her for years—and added to it. She tried to pull away, and Cullen's eyes narrowed.

He glanced over her shoulder at Jillian, and then he grabbed Taige's hand, guiding her to the small room across the hall. It was outfitted with a TV, a Coke machine, and four chairs. Her bathroom at home was bigger than this, and as Cullen tugged her inside, she felt panic closing in on her. Jerking her hand away from him, she put as much distance between them as she could. It wasn't much. She figured she could climb onto one of the chairs and get a few more inches between them, but she wasn't willing to go that far—yet.

"Can't you look at me?"

She shot him a look over her shoulder and then focused her attention on the wall in front of her with an intensity that bordered on ridiculous. She heard him coming up behind her, and everything inside her went on red alert. Cullen sighed, and she felt the warm caress of his breath just before he reached up and cupped her shoulders, slowly turning her around. She wouldn't look at him. Instead, she focused on the faded white cotton that stretched over his chest.

"It does matter," he said softly. "Don't look at me and expect me to believe that you aren't still pissed off at me. You've hardly looked at me. You won't speak to me unless you have to, and any time I come within three feet of you, you move away."

Her voice was hoarse as she murmured, "I'm not pissed off at you, Cullen." Taking a deep breath, she steeled herself and looked up at his face. Damn—that face. It had haunted her dreams ever since that gray November day, and she knew it would haunt her for the rest of her life. As she stared at him, Taige realized that she'd been right. She had always suspected she'd never get over Cullen, and she'd been right. "Never have been, really."

His hand came up, and she braced herself, but whether she was trying to keep herself from pulling away or from leaning toward him, she didn't know. Gently, he traced his finger along the line of her mouth. "You really are amazing," he murmured.

Her throat went tight. A bittersweet ache spread through her as she remembered a time when he had said that and held her in his arms and made love to her. Apparently, she wasn't amazing enough. If she was as special as he'd always made her feel, he would have stayed with her . . . right? She would have been able to help his mom, and him.

"I did it again," he said, his voice tense. He cupped her chin and forced her to look at him. "What did I say this time?" he asked, his voice hollow.

Taige lied. "Nothing."

"Then why do you keep looking away from me?"

She glanced over his shoulder, through the glass wall that allowed them a full view of Jillian's bed. The curtain was still half-open, enough that Taige could see the girl sleeping. Damn. Too much to hope for that Jillian might have woken up. She touched her tongue to her lip and tried to find some answer that would satisfy him without making her look like the hopeless idiot she knew she must be. "It's nothing you did or said," she finally told him. The little white lie wasn't going to kill her, right? "This is just really—awkward."

He brushed his thumb over her lips, and his gaze settled on her mouth. For a second, she thought he might kiss her. He didn't, though, and she couldn't decide if she was grateful or disappointed. He let go of her chin, but he didn't move away. Instead, he feathered a gentle caress over the swollen, discolored skin of her left eye. "How did this happen?"

With a faint grin, she said, "A pissed-off jerk who didn't like me interrupting his plans."

His eyes narrowed down to slits, and the force of his anger hit her like a tidal wave. Trying to lessen the impact, she moved away so that he wasn't touching her.

"And your hand?"

She shot him a mischievous glance over her shoulder. "That happened because I didn't like him hitting me. I popped him and managed to fracture a bone in my hand." She wiggled her fingers a little and winced at the resulting pain. "Doesn't seem fair that he pops me one but when I get him, I break a bone. You males have heads like granite."

Her gaze was drawn to the child sleeping on the other side of the glass. "She's a special girl, you know."

Cullen stroked a hand down Taige's hair, a familiar gesture that managed to drive another razor-sharp shard into her already broken heart. His voice was a little deeper, a little rougher than normal. "Believe me, nobody could be more aware of that than me."

With a grimace, Taige murmured, "I don't know." Jones hadn't shown up, but she knew it was just a matter of time. He knew there was something strange about Cullen's daughter, otherwise he probably wouldn't be on this case. Strange was his specialty. Taige wasn't so certain that boded well for the little girl. "Jones is going to want to talk to her."

"He's already tried." A weird sense of déjà vu moved through her as he added, "That boss of yours is an asshole. He wants to talk to her, but neither the doctor nor I are willing to let him wake her. He wasn't too thrilled with it."

Shaking it off, she glanced up at him and said, "He will need to talk to her."

Cullen blew out a harsh breath. "Yeah. I know. And if she can, I want her to help. I don't want another parent going through . . ." His gaze locked with hers.

The weird sense of déjà vu exploded into something else entirely. Something that shook her to the core. His eyes narrowed, and he reached up, caught her chin in his hand, staring at her.

She was pale, and Cullen thought she looked every bit as shaken as he felt. "The dreams," he muttered. He caught her face in his hands and forced her to look at him, staring into her pale gray eyes. The ugly, dark bruise around her left eye made her iris seem that much paler, and as he watched, the pupil flared, enlarging until just a sliver of gray was visible.

Taige tried to jerk away, and he wouldn't let her. "You had the dreams, too, didn't you?" he demanded.

Her voice shook as she reached up with one hand to jerk on his wrist, trying to break his hold. "Let go of me."

Slowly, he shook his head. "You have," he whispered, dismay spreading through him. Dismay—and something else. She'd always held herself apart from him in those dreams. But through those dreams, he'd gotten to know her, gotten to know the woman she had become. She was pulling away from him not because she was angry at him or because she didn't want anything to do with him.

She pulled back because she still loved him.

She hadn't ever stopped. That knowledge hit his system with

the equivalent of an electric charge, setting his blood on fire and making him itch to touch her, to pull her close and cover her trembling mouth with his. He leaned in, desperate to kiss her—for real, this time, not just through some dream connection. As hot, as powerful as those dreams had seemed to him, it wasn't the same as really touching her.

Slowly, he slanted his mouth over hers, using his grip on her hair to angle her head up and back. He didn't close his eyes; after this long, he wanted to see her, wanted to see if he affected her the same way she still affected him. Her lashes fluttered over her eyes, and she moaned into his mouth, a hungry, kittenish sound. Slowly, he pushed his tongue into her mouth and gorged on the taste of her. *Too damn long,* he thought distantly.

God . . . Taige . . .

He wished they were someplace else—wished things were different so he could have the time to hold her the way he wanted, time to strip her naked and make love to her, over and over, until the ache inside him eased. Until he'd erased the pain from her eyes, and, maybe, magically undone the damage he'd done to her all those years ago.

But instead, he pulled away, slowly, his lips lingering on hers until he had to either step back or lose control.

He pushed a hand through his hair and swore, his voice shaking. "Damn it, Taige."

She swallowed. He could see her throat working as she did it, and then she licked her lips, her lids drooping as though his taste affected her, just like her taste was enough to turn him into a raving lunatic. "What are we going to do about this?" he asked, his voice quiet but intense. He stared at her, waiting for her to look at him.

But instead, she turned away. Walked away. She reached the door, and without looking back at him, she said softly, "Nothing, Cullen. There's nothing to do." She started to open it, and then she stopped.

She did look at him this time. One quick glance. "Jones is going to try to get your daughter."

Startled, Cullen repeated blankly, "Get?"

Taige nodded. "He came looking for me in college. He's recruited some kids straight out of high school, and I've heard rumors that the FBI finds some kids even younger than Jillian and watches them, waits for them to grow up, grabs them for their specialized units."

"You mean . . ." Cullen glanced at his daughter, and then he glanced at Taige's battered face. Oh, hell, no.

"You know what I mean," she said softly. Her mouth twisted in a bitter smile as she said, "Jillian has this amazing gift. Jones expects a person with a gift to use it."

In his mind, he heard the words he'd hurled at her that day. *You have this amazing gift. But you hide from it, don't you? You hide yourself, and screw the people you could help.*

Yeah, she'd hidden some. But he'd had no right to expect more than she already gave. He hadn't understood the hell she lived with until he saw his daughter going through it.

Slowly, he shook his head. "I don't want that for her. I don't want her forced into a position where she's used as some kind of tool." *Like what I did to you,* he thought silently. "If she makes the choice, then it's hers, but I won't let him force it on her."

Taige cocked a brow and said, "Then you'd better make sure you keep him away from her. He'll have to talk to her about this, about his case. But after that's done, keep him away from her. Right now, you can. She's just a child, and you're there to protect her." Her eyes darkened, and her voice fell to a soft whisper as she added, "She deserves to be a child, Cullen. Don't let anybody take that away from her."

She jerked the door open and paused once more, looking back at him. "And stay the hell out of my dreams."

EIGHT

"**D**IDN'T I tell you to stay out of my dreams?"

Taige glared at Cullen, her arms crossed over her breasts.

He glanced around and shrugged. "Easier said than done. That's assuming I wanted to stay out of your dreams." He closed the distance between them and touched his fingers to her lips. "This is the only way I can be with you. The only way you'll let me. You won't call me back. You returned the letters I sent you. I tried to send you flowers, and you wouldn't accept them."

He dipped his head, kissing her quick and light before she could move away. "So for now, this is all I can do."

Turning her head, she stomped toward the house. She didn't know why she bothered; she knew she was dreaming and knew that when she opened her eyes, she'd be lying on the beach towel where she'd fallen asleep. Hell, the way her luck was going, she'd wake up as red as a damn lobster.

"What in the hell is that supposed to mean . . . for now?" she asked as he fell into step beside her.

From the corner of her eye, she saw him shrug. "Just that. Sooner or later, Jillian and I are going to get back to our life. Sooner or later, I'm going to stop hiding her away. When that time comes, I'm going to show up on your doorstep." He reached out and caught her hand, forcing her to stop. "And when that happens, you're going to have to let me in. You're going to have to deal with me."

Pushing her hair back from her face, she sneered. "I already have dealt with you, Cullen. There's no damn reason for you to come down here. You said your thanks. Your daughter is safe. Go live your life, and let me live mine."

A grin canted up the corners of his mouth, and he whispered, "Life? That's exactly why I'm counting the days until I come back for you, Taige. You are my life."

He moved closer, close enough that if she leaned forward, their bodies would be touching. She held herself still, completely still, even though everything inside her yearned for him. It should have been so easy to reach out to him, so easy, but it wasn't, even when she had thought he was little more than a figment of her lonely imagination. Now that she knew these were a little more than the average dreams, it made it that much harder to give in.

Staring into his clear blue green eyes, she held his gaze and then took a slow, deliberate step back. "I'm not your life, Cullen. I never was."

A faint grin curled his lips upward, and he reached up, caught a wayward curl, and tucked it behind her ear. "I miss your braids," he said softly. Then he skimmed a finger over the soft, delicate skin under her left eye. "The swelling's gone."

She gave him a sardonic smile. "Been a month. It ought to get better."

Cullen shrugged restlessly. "A month? Yeah. I guess. Seems longer—and not. I see your face almost every time I close my eyes. And I see that bruise some bastard left on your face." He caught her right hand and lifted it, staring at her wrist, finally out of the soft cast. "And I can't help but think how many times I've dreamed about you and seen marks on your body."

Taige saw his gaze slide over her body, linger low on her torso. Stiffening, she pulled away, but she didn't move fast enough. He caught her in his arms and pulled her against him, turning her so he could lay his hand on the scar from the bullet that had ripped through her abdomen a few years ago. "I remember dreaming about you in the hospital. I thought it was just a nightmare. That's all I wanted it to be, but it wasn't a nightmare; you were shot."

Closing her eyes, she tried not to let his nearness affect her. It was like swimming upstream—up a stream that had long since flooded its bank—and although she was strong, the current was pulling her along, and she had no choice but to go with it and hope she didn't go under in the process. He was pulling her under, pulling her in, and she was powerless to resist. Against her back, she felt the heat and strength of his body, the slow, steady cadence of his heart, and his breath drifted over her naked shoulders like a caress. When she'd left the house earlier, she'd pulled on a plain black tank suit, and the thin material did nothing to camouflage the effect he had on her. Although he hadn't done anything more than cover the bullet scar with his hand, her nipples were stiff peaks, stabbing into the thin material of her swimsuit.

"You were shot," he murmured, as though he was unaware of the effect he had on her. "Because of what you are, what you do. What I forced you into."

Taige tugged against the arm he'd wrapped around her belly, but he wouldn't let her go. "You didn't force me into this, Cullen. It was my choice."

"And what I said to you, what I accused you of, had nothing to do with that choice?" He rested his hands on her hips, stroking absently. He didn't even seem to realize he was touching her, and that was just another little torture, because she was so damned aware of him, she could hardly follow the conversation.

"So what if it did?" Taige stiffened her body and tried again to pull away. This time, he let her go, and she got a good five feet between them before she turned to look at him. "You gave me a kick in the ass, a much-needed kick."

"You didn't need to be forced into a life where you're constantly risking your neck, your safety—your sanity. You live in hell, doing what you do."

Bitterly, Taige thought, *I've lived in hell all my life. It's pretty much about all I know.*

But that wasn't entirely true. The few years she'd had with him hadn't been hell. Not until she failed him.

She glanced at him from the corner of her eye as she turned to stare out at the rolling blue green waters of the Gulf. The water was rougher than usual today, and the waves crashed into the sand. Turning her head, Taige stared back over the beach where they had walked. Already, the waves had washed away their footprints. It was like they had never walked there. If only something could come and wipe away her memories that easily. Memories of Cullen, memories of the people she'd failed to save—including his mom.

"I'm not in hell, Cullen," she said quietly. Granted, there were times when she would agree with him, times when she was certain she did indeed live in hell. But then there were times like when she had looked through the curtain in the hospital and seen Jillian's sleeping face. She hadn't dreamed of the girl once in the month since she had left Cullen in the hospital with his daughter.

Looking back at what she'd done with her life, she knew it was worth it. It would have been worth the heartbreak, the rage, and the tears if she saved even one life. Instead, she'd gotten to see dozens of kids safely home to their parents. Kids she had pulled out of their own hell. Whatever hell she had to live in, it was worth it for that.

"If you could give it up, would you?"

Startled, she looked back at Cullen. All the distance she had put between them just moments ago was gone, and he stood so close, she could see blue and green striations in his eyes. She could smell the warm, musky scent of his skin, and she could almost feel his mouth on hers.

His lips moved, and Taige had to bite back a moan as she fought the urge to cover that mouth with hers. "Would you?" he asked persistently.

Dazed, she tried to remember what he'd asked. Would she give it up? "Give up the ability to see things?" She averted her eyes. She couldn't think when she looked at him. "No. No, I wouldn't give it up."

Self-preservation kept her from looking at him, but it also left her unprepared for his touch when he reached out, curved a hand over her neck. He drew her close. The feel of his hand on her flesh weakened her to the point that she couldn't resist—that she didn't want to. "Always so strong, aren't you, Taige?" he murmured, his thumb rubbing back and forth over her neck.

No. She didn't feel strong at all, staring in his blue green eyes and wishing he was actually here with her, not in some dream, even if they were both sharing the dreams, and that was something she still didn't want to think about. "It doesn't have anything to do with being strong, Cullen. It just has to do with being me. I can't change what I am any more than you can change who you are."

"Hmmm." His gaze dropped down, lingering on her mouth. "I don't know that I'd want to change you." His thumb stroked over her lower lip, and she felt an answering throb deep inside. "But I'd do damn near anything to change how much you've been hurt. From me, from this job of yours, from life."

Turning her head aside, Taige said in a flat, unhappy voice, "Life hurts, Cullen. That's just a fact. Nobody can change it."

"But it shouldn't hurt," he whispered. His hand moved to her chin, bringing her face around so that their eyes met. "It's going to, but there ought to be just as much pleasure as pain. How long has it been since you felt the pleasure of life, Taige?" He didn't wait for an answer.

Instead, he kissed her. With his free hand pressed to her back, he pulled her up against him. She groaned into his mouth, and in response, he growled rough in his chest. The tension in the air seemed to heighten. Taige could sense the wild hunger inside him. It echoed her own, and she braced herself instinctively, but Cullen kept his kiss soft, seductively slow. He lifted his head just a fraction. She could feel the warmth of his breath on her mouth, could still smell him, still taste him as she licked her lips. "I want to show you some pleasure, Taige."

The word *no* seemed to freeze inside her throat. She wanted to say it. It was circling inside her head, but when she tried to force it out, she couldn't. Her body was rebelling against her, willing to go along with whatever Cullen might want. As he slid his hands under the straps of her swimsuit, she stood motionless and let him strip it away. When he sank to his knees in front of her, she looped her arms around his neck and cuddled him close as he kissed her belly. "I miss the taste of you," he said on a sigh. "I should have kissed you, really kissed you, before you walked away from me."

He shot her a dark look and added, "But I'm coming back, Taige, and when I do, we're making up for some lost time."

That arrogant, confident tone grated against her pride, and she wanted to sneer at him. Instead, she found herself sinking down so that she straddled his hips. She wanted to laugh at him, wanted to do something to hurt him like he'd hurt her. Knowing that he shared these dreams made her want to do that very badly: inflict some measure of hurt on him. But instead of doing that, she found herself leaning into him and kissing him, watching him from under her lashes.

He cupped her butt in his hands, and the feel of his rough, callused palms on her flesh was a sweet sensation. Almost as sweet as the one of his bare chest pressed against hers when Cullen finally pulled his shirt off and pressed their torsos together. "If you make love on the beach in a dream," he murmured as he rolled forward and urged her to her back in the hot sand. "Will the sand bother you?"

Taige laid a hand against his cheek. "Cullen, just touch me. I need that. I don't need talking or apologies or jokes."

Turning his head into her palm, he kissed her. She felt the rough growth of stubble under her palm as he asked, "And if I need it? I need to see you smile at me again. I need to hear you laugh. You never laugh enough."

Staring into his eyes, she slid her hands down his chest and freed the button of his jeans, dragged down his zipper. Then she slid her hand inside his pants and closed her fingers around his swollen flesh, dragging them up, then down—just once. "I need you inside me. I don't need to laugh."

She stroked him again, and Cullen groaned, reaching down and gently tugging her hand away before pushing to his knees so he could shove his jeans and underwear out of the way. He came into her, hard and full, stretching her. For a minute, Taige almost felt complete. But this, even if he shared the dream with her, wasn't real, and nothing but the love he'd taken from her was going to make her whole again.

Tears burned her eyes while she stared up at him. "Don't cry," Cullen muttered, dipping his head so he could press a kiss to one eye then the other. He shoved back onto his knees and slid his hands down her thighs, over her calves, until he could grasp her ankles. He pushed her legs wide, draping her knees over his shoulders as he leaned against her. "Please don't cry."

He kissed her tears away and rocked slowly against her, raining soft, gentle kisses on her face and murmuring to her. His voice was gentle, the words the romantic, heart-stopping things that a woman loved to hear as a man made love to her.

"You're so beautiful.

"I love you so much.

"Kiss me . . . damn it, I've missed you . . ."

It seemed like each word was a knife in her heart, and there was a part of her that was filled with hate. Directed at herself for being so weak, directed at him for the power he had over her. But the other part, the much larger part, was melting. Melting under the warmth of his hands on her, the sweet, seductive way he kept whispering in her ear. Rough fingers trailed gently up along the

line of her thigh, and he shifted his weight, sliding his hand between them.

When he circled his roughened fingers around her clit, it felt
like he'd somehow changed her blood to liquid lightning. It exploded through her, and she screamed. Instinctively, she tried to
move against him, but the way he held her—her knees hooked
over his shoulders, one big hand palming her ass and holding
her tight against him, and his upper body crushing hers into the
sand—she couldn't move. "Come for me, Taige," he murmured,
his voice a rough whisper in her ear.

She had no choice, not when Cullen continued to stroke her
like that, not when he continued to shaft her with slow, surging
strokes that took his cock deep inside her body. Her hands tightened on his shoulders, nails digging into his flesh, as the climax
slammed into her with the force of a category-five hurricane. Her
vision went dark, and the roar of her blood pounding in her ears
all but drowned out the sound of Cullen shouting her name.

Inside, she felt the rhythmic jerking of his cock and then the
hot wash of his semen as he came. His back arched as he pressed
deep, and for a moment, he remained just like that, unmoving,
the power of the moment holding them both suspended.

Time slowed down, the moment crystallized, and for a few
brief seconds, she felt happy. Almost at peace.

But then thought intruded, memory returned, and she wasn't
making love with him on a beach, she was only dreaming about
it, and when she woke, she'd be alone again.

Alone.

Slowly, he guided her legs down, and then he collapsed against
her with his head resting on her belly.

Taige felt her heart slamming away inside her chest, felt the heaving of Cullen's chest as he struggled to breathe. He pushed up onto his elbow after a few minutes passed, and the sight of that smile on his face ate at her. Cullen was too damn beautiful for words, and that sleepy, sated smile reminded her of a time when she'd actually believed in his love for her. Believed in the promise of it.

"Let me up," she whispered softly, pushing at his shoulders.

"Taige—"

I'm not going to cry over him again, she told herself. Jerking her gaze upward, she stared at the flawless blue sky overhead. "I'm waking up now," she said.

"Damn it, Taige—"

Deliberately, she closed her eyes. Digging deep, she found the iron will that got her through life no matter how hard it got, no matter how much it sucked. She hadn't ever had much control of the dreams with Cullen. But she'd control them now. Knowing that he shared those dreams gave her a strength born of desperation, and she forced herself into wakefulness.

Her eyes opened, and she automatically squinted against the blinding glare of the sun, but the sun no longer shone overhead. It was late. She didn't have a watch on, but she pegged the time at close to eleven, maybe a little later.

Which meant that she had probably been asleep a good four hours. She'd come out to the small private strip of beach around six, and she'd swum for a little while before flopping onto the towel to relax and read.

The vestiges of the dreams were falling away, but she could still feel the warmth of his hands on her body, the silken brush of his lips across her face and shoulders, and deep inside, slow, rhythmic pulses continued to ripple through her, aftershocks from the climax Cullen had given her in her dreams.

She blushed furiously, recalling how many times she'd come into wakefulness just like this, her body sated and the bed beside her empty. Or the sand. If he was actually with her, these dreams wouldn't be the torture they were. But he wasn't with her. Knowing that he'd shared all those dreams had her squirming with embarrassment.

Although Taige never really relaxed, in her dreams, she'd let her guard down with him a little. He always wore her down, and she'd figured since it was just some dream-Cullen and not the man, it wouldn't hurt. But knowing that he actually shared those dreams, that it was him and not her lonely mind working overtime, she almost feared going to sleep.

With a groan, she sat up and went to bury her face in her hands. It hurt, though, and she jerked her hands away and looked down at herself. It was too dark to see, but she suspected when she looked in the mirror, her caramel-colored skin would have a rosy hint to it. Too rosy.

"That's what you get, falling asleep on the beach in July," she muttered. "And ain't this just perfect?" Gingerly, she touched her skin.

It felt damn hot. It had been a while since she'd had a sunburn. Her skin wouldn't burn as easily as some people's did, but she could still burn, and oddly enough, it was a small relief. Her skin pulled uncomfortably as she gathered up her towel and bag. It was going to keep her from resting too well for one night, so that was one night where she wouldn't have to worry about Cullen showing his face in her dreams.

It was a sad thing when a woman couldn't even count on her dreams for escape.

* * *

THE moment Taige had looked into his eyes and said softly, "I'm waking up now," the dream had fallen to pieces around him, and now he lay on the couch, the TV still on and in the middle of a *Law & Order* marathon. It was late, pushing midnight, and the last thing he remembered was flopping onto the couch a little after eight when he'd put Jillian to bed.

It was early for her to go to sleep, but ever since he'd brought her home, she hadn't been able to go to sleep without a light on, and she'd seemed to sleep better when he was still moving around, and the house wasn't terribly quiet.

His blood was still hot. Hell, he was hot, but it had nothing to do with the temperature of the room. It was cool in the house. Both he and Jillian were hot-natured, and he kept the air-conditioning running cool. But his entire body was sweating, and it seemed as though his skin was warm from the sun. And from Taige—damn, it was like he could still feel the warm, wet caress of her sex as he rode her. Still hear those soft, sexy little moans as she climaxed.

Still see the pain in her eyes. He'd smiled up at her, half forgetting the twelve years of distance that he had put between them until he met her gaze and watched as gray ice formed in her eyes. *I'm waking up now.*

And then she was just gone, and less than a heartbeat later, he was waking up.

Cullen rolled to a sitting position and leaned forward, bracing his elbows on his knees. He stared at the polished hardwood floors under his bare feet and brooded. There was no way he was going to sleep for a while. Taige wouldn't be asleep either. He gave the phone a considering glance and wondered what she would do if he called.

"Probably hang up on me," he muttered.

One thing was certain, he had a damn hard road ahead of him. But even that knowledge wasn't enough to deter him. He'd had twelve years without Taige, and those few hours they'd spent together as she led him to Jillian had convinced him of one sure and certain fact: he didn't want to spend the rest of his life without her.

But it was going to be a while before he could even try to start smoothing things over with Taige, before he could start trying to convince her to give him another chance. Both he and Jillian were still trying to deal with the trauma of what had happened. Jilly would scream in her sleep, haunted by nightmares. Those screams would wake him from a dead sleep, and he'd go to her room to find her thrashing on the bed, held captive by the dreams.

She was going to a counselor, but it didn't seem to help much. Cullen wasn't going to quit it this time. It might take years for Jillian to move past that trauma, if she ever did.

No. Not if. She would. Jilly was strong. It was just going to take time. Cullen had his own demons to deal with. His guilt over not protecting her. The helplessness that plagued him. It wasn't him that had saved Jilly, it had been Taige. Cullen had been all but useless, and it ate at him. It was a father's job to protect his child, but he had failed at it.

As much as Cullen wanted to hear Taige's voice, he looked away from the phone and shoved to his feet. He passed a long, sleepless night. Knowing that sleep would elude him for the most part, he didn't bother going to bed. For a few hours, he worked in his office, knocking out another chapter on the book that was due at the end of the summer. Then he made a sandwich and ate it before watching TV and dozing through another *L & O* rerun.

By morning, he was bleary-eyed and damn thankful that it was Saturday. His dad was coming to get Jilly. It was going to be the first time she had left the house without Cullen since the kidnapping. It would be good for her—and him. By the time Robert Morgan showed up at the house at ten, Cullen was dragging. Still, he crouched by Jilly's side and studied her face. "You sure you're going to be okay? I can come with you."

She gave him a smile. "No, Daddy. It's just me and Grandpa this time."

He nodded and then leaned, kissed her cheek. "You call me if you need me, okay?"

"She's going to be fine, son," Robert said as Cullen straightened up. "We're going to get some pizza. See a movie. Maybe I'll let her con me out of a toy or a book."

"Or both," Cullen said with a faint grin. He knew his dad, and he knew his daughter. Jillian had Robert so completely wrapped, if she asked for the Eiffel Tower, Robert would find a way to steal it for the girl.

On his way on the door, Robert paused. "You should get some rest, Cull. You look awful."

Cullen just smiled, but after they left, he paused in the hallway and stared at the mirror hanging over the console table by the front door. Awful. Yeah. That about summed it up. He'd lost probably ten pounds in the past month, and the bags under his eyes were bordering on ridiculous. Last night's sleeplessness hadn't helped, but Cullen had been looking a little worse for wear for a month now.

It wasn't going to get better for a while, he suspected.

He moved through the house, picking up toys, clothes, and shoes. The cleaning lady was due in Monday, but Cullen didn't pay her to pick up after his daughter. Normally, he got after Jillian to do it herself, but he'd been coddling her. Logically, he knew he needed to quit doing it so much, but he couldn't seem to control it.

He dumped clothes down the laundry chute, toys into a basket by the steps for the trip back to her room, and cleaned up toast crumbs, cereal, and spilled milk from the breakfast bar. That done, he headed for the stairs at the front of the house. He was going to get some sleep. Real sleep. Sleep that didn't involve Taige, sleep that wouldn't be interrupted when his daughter's screams woke him.

But he hadn't even cleared the landing when the doorbell rang. Cullen heaved out a sigh and headed downstairs. Whoever it was would just have to come back. But a peek through the Judas hole and the sigh turned into a flat-out, ugly swear.

"What in the hell do you want now?" Cullen demanded as he opened the door to Special Agent Taylor Jones. Using his body to bar the way, he kept the agent out on the porch. Part of him really wished he didn't dislike this guy so much; Jones was busting his ass trying to find the man who had kidnapped Jillian, but he was so damned overbearing, and he didn't seem to care that his questions would put Jilly through that trauma again. He came back to the house once a week, and the first week, he'd been there almost every day.

"Thought you might like to hear the progress we've made," Jones said, showing off what Cullen thought of as the whitest, fakest smile in the South.

With a grunt, Cullen stepped aside. There probably wasn't any progress, but now was as good a time as any to let the agent come inside. The man was not going to stop trying to bully Jillian, and with Jilly not being there, now was an excellent time to make that known.

"I don't suppose you've given any more thought to what we discussed," Jones said as he followed Cullen into the kitchen at the back of the house.

"Hell, no. I already gave you my answer on that."

"You do know; I could take this before a judge. She's the only surviving victim of a serial killer. We need to find out what she knows."

Cullen said, as he'd said a hundred times already, "She doesn't know anything. If she did, I'd be happy to let her help you. I want that bastard caught. But she doesn't know anything." He smirked and added, "And you're welcome to try taking this before a judge. You ought to know by now that my lawyer is the best around, and she isn't any more interested in letting you bully Jillian than I am."

"Well, just keep it in mind," Jones said. But his voice was preoccupied. They sat at the table, one on either side, and met each other's stare levelly. Cullen knew that Jones had a job to do, and he could appreciate the man's desire to find Jillian's kidnapper. Jones probably knew that Cullen's main concern was Jillian's safety and happiness. The father would do whatever was necessary to protect his child.

"Is that all you wanted to say?" Cullen asked, making sure the man had nothing else.

Jones shook his head, a queer little smile on his face.

Cullen, already silently forming his thoughts so he could lay his cards on the table, didn't like that smile. "Then why don't you tell me the rest?"

"While we were here back in June, one of my agents found a sketchbook of Jillian's."

"She loves to draw. She has a lot of them."

"Hmmm. Well, I was particularly interested in this one." Jones reached into his briefcase and pulled one out.

"What in the hell were you doing, taking . . ." His voice trailed off as he stared at the sketch pad. He recognized it. The date on the front of it corresponded with the dates when they had been in Atlanta. For no particular reason, he remembered the sketch Jillian had shown him at the airport.

"The first to disappear." A young girl, younger than Jillian. Then two others.

"Disappear from where?"

"Around."

Voice rusty, Cullen asked, "Why do you have her sketch pad?"

Instead of answering Cullen's question, Jones flipped open the sketch pad and asked one of his own. "Care to explain this?"

He didn't bother clarifying what he wanted explained, and it wasn't necessary. Cullen stared down at the sketch, feeling like he had been sucker punched. It was the one from the airport. But it no longer had three kids.

It had four, and Jillian was the fourth. Still trying to take in that particular shock, he was left floundering as Jones removed something else from the briefcase, three pictures, to be exact. And each picture bore a striking resemblance to one of the faces that Jillian had sketched.

Jones tapped his finger on the one that looked the oldest. It had that yellowish cast to it, and the background was that fake, woodsy looking backdrop that had been used in a lot of school portraits in the seventies. Her hair was long, parted down the middle—again giving him the idea that the picture had been taken a good thirty years earlier.

"Her name was Leslie. She disappeared from Birmingham

when she was ten. Back in 1974. As of this summer, she was still presumed dead."

Something about Jones's voice made Cullen's gut knot. "Presumed?"

Jones acted as though Cullen hadn't said a word. He pushed another picture toward Cullen. This one was the black boy with the impish smile, and Jillian had captured the mischief in the boy's smile almost perfectly. "Kendrick. Disappeared from Atlanta in 1982. Presumed dead."

Cullen asked hoarsely, "What do you want me to say, Jones? You already know about Jilly. Obviously. But she can't help you. She's tried. And I won't let you traumatize her."

"Amy. Disappeared 1992. Perdido Key, Florida. Presumed—"

"I get the picture. Why in the hell do you have this, and what do you want me to say?"

Jones leaned back and stared at Cullen. "Your daughter knew something was going to happen to her, Cullen. Did you know?"

"She didn't know!" Cullen shouted, shoving back from the chair. But then he looked down at the sketch pad and wondered if he knew what he was talking about. It was there, plain as day, sketched out with the talented strokes of Jillian's charcoal pencil. "Oh, God." The strength drained out of him, and he sank back down into his chair, covering his face with his hands and trying not to puke.

She'd known. Somehow, some part of her had known, but Cullen hadn't recognized it for the warning it had been. "You all found this the day she disappeared?" he asked, his voice rusty.

"My agents were here with your father. They found it on her bed. She left it there, almost like she knew they needed to see it."

Cullen shook his head. "I don't understand. I don't get it."

Jones's gaze fell away, and that polished, cool veneer left his face for just a second, letting Cullen see the man under the mask. "We've been working on identifying the bodies that were buried under the cabin where Taige Branch found Jillian," Jones said softly. He pulled yet another piece of paper from his briefcase, but this one he didn't offer to Cullen. "There are more than twenty bodies buried under there, and just about all of them are children or young teens. The first positive match came back yesterday."

Jones looked up and met Cullen's eyes as he laid the page down on the table and pushed it toward Cullen. Almost afraid to look, Cullen shifted his gaze downward.

Leslie King.

Most of the jargon on the report was too medical in nature for Cullen to follow, but he saw one thing clearly enough: bones found at the crime scene in Otisco, Alabama, were positively confirmed as the remains of Leslie King, a child missing now for more than thirty years. It had been confirmed through DNA.

"Shit."

Jones grimaced. "That was my first thought as well."

* * *

TAIGE read the report and looked up at Jones with unreadable eyes. "So why am I hearing this? You never officially put me on the case."

With that neutral, polite smile, Jones said, "Taige, you put yourself on the case all on your own." He laid three other reports out. They were preliminaries as well, and staring at the names revealed nothing to Taige. She might as well have been reading a list of names out of the phone book.

But he wouldn't be here just to update her on the case. He would have done that on the phone or not bothered. Taking a deep breath, Taige reached out and touched one of the pictures that Jones had placed facedown.

She didn't even have to flip it over. It jolted down her back, and she hissed. Her instinct was to jerk her hand back and cradle it against her chest. It was almost like she'd touched a hot stove. Pain streaked through her, but instead of pulling back, she flipped the picture over and found herself staring at a young, dark face. He had a mischievous smile. Even as the pain swarmed her system, she was more aware of that smile than anything else.

At least until she heard his scream.

This time, the gray didn't come and wrap her gently in its embrace. It was a violent possession, and she knew she'd be ill when it was over. But she was powerless to fight it, and she knew why Jones had brought the pictures instead of calling her. He'd been hoping for this.

She fell into the boy's head like a stone falls into water. Taige's physical connection to herself grew weak, replaced by the one forged between herself and the boy. He lay on the floor, screaming and crying, begging for his mama. There was a man, but his face was distorted. Whether through fear or a child's eyes, she didn't know, but there was no way she would learn anything about the man that would help identify him.

Pain streaked through her back as something struck her. The initial blow didn't hurt so much; it was the fiery pain that came after. Even as lost inside the boy as she was, Taige knew what was happening. Somebody was beating him, not with their hands, but with a belt. A leather one, with a metal buckle. She had a few faint scars from the times when she'd been similarly whipped, and in the small part of her that was still cognizant, she didn't know what she wanted more: to weep or to tear into something with her bare hands.

Not something. Someone. Some ominous, faceless man who beat a small boy with a fury. And it was fury. It wasn't some lust for causing pain, although Taige suspected the man did enjoy inflicting the pain. She could hear his harsh, labored breathing, but it sounded more like the gasps of a man in the throes of passion than exertion. Fury drove him. Though she couldn't see him, and though her gift was one of thought, not emotion, she could feel his fury. It beat at her, crawled over her, digging into her flesh like a thousand little knives.

The boy screamed again and again, until his voice gave out, and then he went silent. He retreated into the safety of his own mind—and Taige felt it when his mind finally gave out. Inside, he stopped living. Although his body still bled and his heart still beat, what had made the boy alive was gone. As Taige came clawing back into awareness, she knew that it had been a blessing.

She was on the floor, a quivering, sweaty mess, and she shoved to her knees. Before she could lurch to her feet, her stomach rebelled. Jones was there, shoving a pot under her just before she would have puked all over the floor. It was a sense of fastidiousness that had him holding her hair as she puked, not compassion, but she was thankful, nonetheless. Her eyes burned, and her throat felt raw as she sat back on her heels.

"God." Closing her eyes, Taige said a prayer under her breath. A prayer for strength to do what she had to, a prayer for justice, a prayer to stop the man before he killed again. She'd saved Jillian, but that wasn't enough now. She had to save them all, stop this man before he could hurt another soul.

When she opened her eyes, she saw Jones watching her with faint amusement. "Considering what your uncle did to you in the name of God, it's a wonder you pray at all."

"My uncle did it, not God, Jones," she said tersely. Slowly, every muscle in her body protesting, she pushed herself upright. Taige doubted she had the strength to stand, though. Instead, she rested there on her heels and waited until her breathing slowed. She jerked her chin back to the coffee table where two more pictures still sat. "Those pictures of the boy or other people?"

"Others. Two girls. Did you see anything?"

She shook her head jerkily. "Not much. Not him." Taige didn't need to clarify. She didn't like Taylor Jones, but she knew him well, and she knew what he had been hoping for when he showed her those pictures. "I can't help you find him—not yet. The boy couldn't see him."

"His name was Kendrick."

Kendrick. Taige squeezed her eyes closed and tried to block out the sound of his screams. "He had a sweet smile."

Jones didn't respond to that. Instead, he rose to his feet and went back to his briefcase. "I have the original file from his case. He disappeared in 1982 from a mall in Atlanta. He was there with his mother, picking out clothes for school. He would have started third grade that year."

"Third grade," Taige murmured. "He was so young."

Jones glanced at the pictures and then back at her. "I'll warn you now. One of the girls was even younger."

With a grimace, Taige said, "I need a drink."

"You drink too much as it is."

Her legs still felt way too unstable as she shoved to her feet. Three unsteady steps had her back to the couch, and she collapsed on it thankfully. "Considering the shit you dump on me, it's amazing I still have a functioning liver." She started to ask how young, but then she shook her head. It was best she not know much before she looked at the picture.

"Did you notice anything unusual about the boy?"

Frowning, Taige asked, "Like what?"

"Like the fact that he was like you."

Taige blinked. "Like me how?"

"Gifted." Jones leaned back into the dark blue leather of his chair, watching her closely. "His mother ran away with him when he was two, because his father was using him to help win at the races. The boy knew which horse would win, which would lose. All before he could even tie his shoes."

"Could it be just dumb luck?"

Once more, Jones glanced at the coffee table.

Taige felt something sick spin inside her.

"It could, but you and I don't believe in coincidences, do we? Jillian is gifted. Kendrick was gifted—and at least one other victim that we've identified."

No. It wasn't coincidence. Taige reached up and wiped a hand over her mouth. She felt numb inside, chilled from the fear. Three victims. No way was that a coincidence. Which meant the other children were probably gifted as well; more, it meant that the killer was probably gifted. It usually took one gifted person to recognize another.

"It isn't over," Taige whispered, more to herself than him.

But Jones responded anyway. "No, it isn't. But I think you already knew that."

NINE

THE scream woke Cullen out of a dead sleep. He raced down the hall toward Jillian's room and hit the partially opened door with the palm of his hand, shoving it with a strength that sent it flying. He heard it hit the wall, but the sound barely registered as he crouched by Jillian's side and pulled her into his arms.

"Wake up, Jilly. Come on, baby, wake up," he whispered, his voice harsh, almost thick with tears. The knot in his throat threatened to choke him, but he didn't know what would kill him first: the knot or the poison of the rage that flowed through him. This was killing him.

Every night for the past week Jilly had awakened screaming from the nightmares. Every damn night. And each dream made him feel more and more helpless. He had to do something. Had to.

"Daddy . . ." Jilly moaned, and he pulled back just enough to see her face as her lashes fluttered open.

"I'm here, baby. I'm here."

"He's going to hurt her, Daddy. Don't let him."

Cullen stroked a hand up her back and whispered, "He can't hurt you again, baby. I won't let him."

But she shook her head, shoved against his chest with a strength that was almost unnatural for a child so young. "Not me, Daddy. It's Taige. The lady that helped me. He wants to kill her. He knows she helped me, and he hates her."

It took several hours to get her back to sleep, and as the night stretched out in front of him, Cullen lay on the bed beside Jilly, her head cuddled on his shoulder. Staring at the wall, he replayed those words in his mind. *Not me, Daddy. It's Taige.*

Not once did he doubt Jilly. He'd never doubt that eerie, bizarre knowledge again. No, it certainly wasn't doubts that plagued him now, just conflicting desires. He needed to be with Jilly. She needed him right now, needed him to keep her safe.

Don't let him.

Don't let him hurt Taige. His little girl somehow thought he could protect the woman who had saved her, and in his heart, that was exactly what he wanted to do. Did Taige really need to be protected? He'd watched as she went, steely eyed, into a house, and he knew that she'd do whatever was necessary to get the job done, to save a child she didn't know. He remembered all the bruises and injuries he'd seen on her over the years, through their shared dreams, and he didn't doubt Taige's strength, her courage, or her spirit.

But, despite her gifts, despite her skill with her fists and with a gun, Taige was just a woman. She bled, she breathed just like anybody else, and she was only one person. Cullen didn't know exactly what he could do to help her, didn't even know it was expected of him by anybody other than his daughter. And himself.

But if he didn't do anything, and Taige was hurt, he'd never forgive himself. It would destroy a part of him, and what was left wouldn't be worth much.

As dawn slowly broke over the horizon, he stared at Jilly. The sun slanted on her small face, painting it a soft, sun-kissed gold. Gently, he leaned down and brushed his lips over her temple. Jilly's lashes fluttered open, and she looked at him, gave him that sweet, heart-stopping smile. She'd owned his heart from the first time the doctors had placed her in his arms. From her very first breath, she'd owned him.

But she wasn't alone inside his heart, and that was what was killing him. Much like it had been with Jilly, Taige had forged a place inside of him in a way that even twelve years apart hadn't been able to dim. He loved that woman. He couldn't let anything happen to her.

"Sweetheart, I've been thinking. Grandpa's been wanting to take us to Ireland again. How would you like to go with him, all on your own?"

It's too soon, his head screeched. Jilly still needed him.

Her hand came up and patted his cheek. "I'll be okay, Daddy."

Cullen caught her hand in his, and he squeezed it gently. "Of course you will. You're my girl. You're going to be more than okay."

She grinned, and for a minute she was just a little girl, with a mischievous smile and big, sparkling eyes. "That's not what I meant. I'll be fine with Grandpa while you go help Miss Taige. I don't want to go to Ireland, though. Not yet. Not without you. It's too far away." She curled up against him and whispered, "I like Miss Taige. She's always had the nicest voice."

"How do you know her voice, sweetie? You were asleep when Taige led me to you."

Jilly snuggled closer. "I heard her voice a lot. She talks to me in my dreams."

Apparently today was just going to be another very unsettling day, Cullen decided. Resting his chin on her head, he asked, "How long has she been doing that?"

"Always."

Always. Cullen squeezed his eyes shut.

"Daddy?"

He opened his eyes and met Jilly's level green gaze. "Yeah, baby?" he asked, his voice hoarse.

"It's going to be all right," she said softly. She puckered up her lips and gave him a soft kiss on the cheek. "I see her sometimes in my sleep, but she looks happier. She's so lonely, but she's just been waiting for us."

"Waiting for us to what?"

Jilly smiled once more and said simply, "To be her family." Then her eyes darkened. "But you two have to stop him first."

* * *

THE sound of the doorbell came far too early, as far as Taige was concerned.

She rolled out of bed with a groan and staggered to the door, grabbing a pair of jeans from the floor. Her weapon was still sheathed in its holster, slung over the bedpost at the foot of the bed. For some reason, she stumbled back to the bed and grabbed it. It took three tries to get the damn thing in place, and she almost didn't mess with it. On her way to the door, whoever was at the door rang again. And again. And again.

"What in the hell are you doing?" she grumbled. "Leaning on it?"

She undid the locks without checking the Judas hole. Grumbling, she jerked the door open, something suitably cutting on the tip on her tongue. But when she saw who it was, the words froze in her throat. Son of a bitch. Without saying a word, she grabbed the door and went to slam it shut, but Leon reached out and caught it, then used his foot to wedge the door open.

He gave her a pious look and produced a piece of paper from inside the somber black sport coat he wore. Though he wasn't Methodist or Catholic, Leon Carson dressed more like a priest than anything else, all black, from head to toe, no matter the season, no matter the occasion. "We're having our annual revival," he said, his voice deep and serious. "Seeing as how you aren't out practicing your evil on the innocent and the weak, I thought it would do you well to attend. Or are you still beyond salvation?"

"Your idea of salvation?" she returned. "Absolutely."

He shoved the paper at her once more, and she flicked it a disinterested glance. "You wave that at me once more, Uncle, and I'll make you eat it. I'm not coming to your revival."

"You don't even care that you're damning yourself to hell," Leon stated.

"Well, if you're going to be in heaven, then I want no part of it." With an irreverent smile, she added, "But I really don't think you're going anyplace other than hell yourself."

"Blasphemy," he hissed, lifting a hand to shake a finger in her face.

Taige was tempted to reach out and grab it, twist it just to see how much she could make him squirm before she either let him go or broke the bone. "It's not blasphemy, Uncle. It's a fact. If He welcomes you into the pearly gates, then everything I've been taught about God and Jesus is a lie, and whatever He offers, I don't want it." She glanced down at his foot and then gave him an angelic smile. "If you keep your foot there, you just might lose it."

Leon curled his lip in a patronizing sneer. "Are you so far gone that you'd threaten a man of God?"

Taige's own mouth curled into a sneer, but she suspected hers wasn't so much patronizing as downright mean. Staring into his eyes, she drew her gun and without looking away from his eyes, she leveled it at his foot. "If you were a real man of God, Uncle, you and I wouldn't be as we are. Would I threaten you? Absolutely. But here's another question you should ask. Would I shoot you? Hell, yes."

Slowly, Leon retreated, and she noticed something she hadn't noticed before: he'd aged. A lot. It seemed every single second of hate showed in his face, and hate had aged him far faster than time ever could. He didn't seem as big as she remembered, but he was still larger than life, and she could remember in acute detail how strong his hands were, how he knew exactly where to hit to make it hurt the most without leaving much of a mark.

In a soft, solemn voice, she promised him, "The next time you come near me, I'm going to leave a mark on you. Think of how many you left on me, Uncle, and know that I mean it. Sincerely."

She watched him pull away before she closed the door gently. Then she turned around and leaned against it. Her lids lowered, and she heaved out a harsh sigh. Then, slowly, she headed back down the hall, intent on a shower and at least a half pot of coffee. Maybe even the whole damn pot.

It wasn't until thirty minutes later when she was standing in front of the cabinet that she realized. Damn it. She'd forgotten to buy more coffee. With a groan, she bent over and let her head thunk against the counter. Damn it. She desperately needed her coffee.

* * *

SOME *days* . . . Taige thought miserably as she climbed out of her car to see her uncle coming out of the Winn-Dixie. She almost climbed back into her Jeep, but the thought of retreating from him, even from an unwanted confrontation, ate at her. So instead of climbing back into the car, she locked the doors and pocketed her keys.

"Just walk by him and don't say a word," she mumbled under her breath.

Leon, though, couldn't resist an audience. He'd always saved the beatings for private, but deriding her in front of others had been almost like a hobby to him. He reached out as she walked past. His skeletal white hand landed on her arm, and she doubted the people passing by could tell how he dug his fingers into her flesh.

"It would seem as though it's God's will that you and I spend some time together today, my dear niece," Leon said, lifting his voice so that it carried.

He did have a compelling voice, almost mesmerizing. Taige could see why his church congregation was twice the size it had been ten years ago. When he wasn't dealing with his niece, Leon had a charismatic quality that was undeniable. But Taige didn't consider him the sharpest crayon in the box. After all, he honestly thought she would behave since she was surrounded by people.

Jerking her arm back, she glared down her nose at him. "Maybe the Almighty is putting you in my way just to see if I can withstand temptation."

Leon sighed and shook his head. "Beloved child, you never could withstand temptation. That is why you walk this evil road."

"Spare me." Rolling her eyes, she went to push past him. She glanced around, trying to keep it casual, and she saw easily five people pretending not to watch him. Apparently Leon realized he had a good audience, because he wasn't going to let her push him aside so easily.

His pale hand closed around her arm, and bony white fingers once more dug into tender flesh. "You can't keep walking this evil road, Taige. It will destroy you—and everyone you touch."

Without missing a beat, she tossed back, "Oh, yeah? It hasn't destroyed you yet, and I keep waiting for that."

With a theatrical sigh, he shook his head. "You would even bring down destruction on a man of God, if you could. Are you so far gone that I cannot reach you?"

"Shit. Are we back to that song and dance again?" Dropping her voice, Taige leaned in and said softly, "Are you so damn stupid that you've already forgotten what I said I'd do? Take your hand off of me, Uncle. Now. Or you just might have to say this week's sermon through a straw."

He smiled. It was faint, there and then gone again, and nobody but Taige had seen it. Slowly, he let go of her arm. "Your reckoning is coming, girl. Coming fast."

"No faster than yours, Carson."

The voice from behind her was both welcome and unwanted. As Leon's hand fell away, she turned to see Cullen standing there, his thumbs hooked in his waistband, legs spread wide, and his eyes narrowed on Leon's face. He looked like a boxer ready to brawl, she thought. She stared at him, but he hadn't so much as looked at her yet.

No, he was totally focused on Leon. He closed the distance between them and stared down at the shorter, skinnier man. In his youth, Leon had probably had a strong, wiry build. She knew well enough just how strong he was, but all the years he'd spent practicing his fire and brimstone spiel had softened his body, and now, standing in front of Cullen Morgan, he looked weak, almost frail.

"You know what I'm going to do to you if I see you touching her again?" Cullen asked, his voice pleasant, almost friendly.

Leon sneered. "Even after all these years, that harlot niece of mine has control over you, doesn't she? You succumbed to temptation, and now you're as damned as she is."

Cullen's hand shot out, and he fisted the sturdy black cloth of Leon's shirt. Jerking Leon forward, he said in a soft, deadly voice, "You want to watch how you speak of her, Carson. You might have half the town thinking you're a benevolent, God-fearing man, but I know better, and I'd sooner knock your teeth down your throat than look at you." He gave Carson a hard, fast shake before he turned the older man loose. "You don't want to touch her again, old man. You do, you're going to deal with me."

Anger did a bad thing to Leon's common sense. Dropping the pretense he always used in public, he lifted a bony hand and pointed a finger at Cullen. "I've tried to warn you, tried to keep you from the evil you want to surround yourself with. But you're no innocent lamb led astray. You seek out the evil, embrace it. You'll burn with it when the time is right." Muttering under his breath, Leon stormed away.

"Why didn't you just hit him?" Cullen asked, his voice cold and flat as he turned to face Taige. "He needs it."

"Yeah, but I don't need the headache." She frowned at him. "What are you doing here?"

Lifting a brow, he replied, "I'm looking for you."

"Why?"

"Unfinished business." His voice softened as he looked her over from head and toe, and Taige had to suppress a shiver. Nearly a hundred degrees and so damn muggy breathing was a chore, and he could make her shiver with just a look.

Then she focused on what he had said, and she felt something dig at her heart. "We don't have any unfinished business, Cullen." Damn, he wasn't going to try to pay her or something, was he? A niggling suspicion wormed through her, and she narrowed her eyes at him. "I don't want any money from you."

A reluctant grin tugged at the corners of his lips as he shook his head. "I'm not here to pay you." That hard, sexy mouth of his flattened out into a thin line, and his eyes scanned the parking lot. He held his hand out to her and murmured, "We need to talk."

Taige really, really didn't want to touch him. She'd worked hard to avoid doing just that as much as possible in the few hours she'd spent with him last month, but there had been a good excuse for avoiding physical contact. Now? There was no logical reason for refusing to put her hand in his. Other than the fact that she really didn't want to touch him.

"Scared of me, Taige? Or just pissed at me?"

Yes. No. In that order. But was Taige going to tell him that? Oh, hell, no. She took a deep breath to steady herself and then reached out, placed her hand in his. Instinctively, she braced herself for the onslaught of memory flashes that came with physical contact, and just as quickly, Taige forced herself to relax. She hadn't ever been able to pick up anything concrete from Cullen, and now wasn't any different. When she lowered her mental shields, she caught a few faint flickers, but none of them were solid. None of them of were defined.

"Where to?" she asked and hoped he didn't notice the way her voice shook just a little.

* * *

THEY ended up at an oyster house that Cullen remembered from his summers there. The red and white striped awning hadn't changed, and the restaurant still had the best salad bar and excellent fried oysters. Too bad he had next to no appetite. He sat pushing the food around on his plate and wondering why he'd thought getting a bite to eat would break the tension.

"Where's Jillian?"

He looked up to see that Taige had eaten about as much as he had: next to nothing. Her eyes glimmered against the warm gold of her skin, framed by long, spiky lashes. Cullen's mouth went dry as he stared at her. Seeing her had the same effect on him as it had twelve years ago: hot need and a tenderness that turned his bones to mush. He was torn between wanting to pull her against him so he could cuddle her close and wanting to strip away her clothes so he fuck her brains out.

Only with Taige had he ever experienced anything besides lust. She hadn't been the first girl he'd slept with, but she'd been the first girl to really matter to him. The first one he'd loved. The only one he'd loved.

"Cullen?"

He blinked and realized she'd asked him about Jillian. And was still waiting for an answer. "With my dad."

"How is she doing?"

Shrugging restlessly, he leaned back from the table and crossed his arms over his chest. "She has good days. Some not so good. Nights are hard on her. She doesn't want to be left alone." He grimaced and added, "Hard on me, too, because I have a hard time leaving her alone."

At that, Taige lifted a brow. Her mouth, soft and kissable, bowed upward in a gentle smile. "Then why are you here? You need to be home with her. She needs you right now."

Cullen pushed his plate out of the way and then leaned forward, reached out, and caught her hand. He laced their fingers and said, "I'll be honest; a huge part of me needs just that. But . . . she needs to feel safe more. There's only one thing I can do to give her that."

"Ahhhh." Understanding came into her eyes, and she squeezed his hand, gently, and then pulled back. She didn't like him touching her. It was almost impossible to miss that. She'd hesitated before putting her hand in his earlier. As soon as she could, she'd pulled away, and now she was doing it again, all the while giving him a false, bright smile. The smile faded from her face, and she said, "You need to understand that nothing you can do is going to help her nightmares. Nothing you do can undo what happened. Even if he'd been there that day, and you killed him then, she'd still have a hard time. The only thing that works is time."

"Putting that degree in psychology to good use, aren't you?" he asked grimly.

Now both brows arched. "How did you know about that?"

Lifting one shoulder in a shrug, Cullen said, "There's nothing you've done in the past twelve years that I don't know about. If it's public knowledge, I found out about it. What wasn't public, I learned through all those dreams." He paused and then softly added, "You trust me more in those dreams than you do now."

Taige shook her head. "It doesn't have anything to do with trust. I do trust you."

"As far as you trust anybody?" he said ruefully.

"More than I trust anybody," she corrected. With a scowl, she demanded, "What in the hell do you care what I've been up to the past twelve years?"

The look on his face did bad, bad things to her insides, Taige decided. There was a lambent, lazy look in his eyes, and her skin heated under the warmth of his gaze. She knew that if they were someplace private, he'd probably be trying to do more than look. There were twelve years between them, but those years might as well not have existed, thanks to the dreams that had kept them connected. She knew him better now than she had when they had been together, knew when he was mad, when he worried—when he wanted.

And now he wanted—oh man, did he want. She hadn't ever had a man look at her quite the same way Cullen did. His lids drooped low over his eyes, and he murmured, "You know why I care, Taige. You might not let yourself see it, but you do know."

Averting her eyes, she asked quietly, "Why are you here, Cullen? Exactly what do you want from me now?" *I found your daughter. I gave you my heart, my soul, my body. I don't have too much left to give you.*

She kept that latter part quiet, although she suspected he already knew most of that, just like she knew that if he asked, she'd probably give herself up to him all over again.

"Your help."

"Help with what?"

Bracing his elbows on the table, Cullen leaned forward. His blue green eyes pinned her in place, and she couldn't have looked away from him if she had to.

Softly, he said, "Finding him."

* * *

CULLEN stood on the step just behind Taige as she unlocked the door. She'd left her hair down, and he wanted to lean forward and bury his face in it, feel the soft, wild curls and just breathe her in.

Instead, he tucked his hands in his pockets, and when she finally opened the door, he held back until she gave him an impatient look and demanded, "Are you coming inside or what?"

He took the two stairs at once and ended up standing so close, he could hear the soft, shaky sound of her breathing. "What are the other choices?" he asked before he could stop himself.

"Huh?"

"Coming inside . . . or what? What does the 'or what' entail?"

She dropped her gaze and moved away, shoving the door wide open and stalking inside. Her booted feet made muffled thuds on the wooden floor as she crossed it, not turning back to him until she had put a good five feet in between them. "Don't go getting cute, Cullen. I said I'd try to find him. Nothing else."

"With me."

She gave him a frown.

He clarified and said, "You're going to try finding him with me. I'm not being left behind on this."

Taige shook her head and stomped into the living room. Cullen followed and rested a shoulder against the arched doorway, watching her as she sat down and started unlacing her boots. They were black, thick-soled boots like a soldier might wear, and they should have looked ridiculous on her. Instead, they suited her. Or rather, they suited the woman Taige had made herself into. She'd gone from a girl with no particular goal in life beyond getting through each day to a dedicated warrior. The promise of the woman he'd glimpsed in her before either of them had even been old enough to consider themselves adults had come to life, and she was more than he'd ever thought she could be. And he'd always thought she could become a great deal.

The cost had been damn high for her, though. She'd risked her life, her sanity, her heart, time and again. Whatever the cost to her, she'd done what she had to do, and she'd done it alone. Not this time. This time, he'd be with her. When it was over, he had every intention of keeping her. If she'd let him.

"Cullen, you have no idea what you're asking. Besides, Jillian needs you."

"And I told you that Jillian needs to feel safe. She won't be able to do that while he's out there." He moved over to her, hunkering down in front of her and taking her other foot, loosening the laces and slowly pulling the boot away. Taking both boots, he set them aside and then focused on Taige's face. "I'm going with you on this."

She cocked a brow. If he didn't know her, he wouldn't have seen through her bravado as she said, "Exactly how are you supposed to help me? Got any law enforcement experience? Got a permit for a gun? Do you have eyes in the back of your head, or have you suddenly become psychic?"

"I don't need a gun, or law enforcement training to watch your back, Taige." Unable to resist, he placed his hands on her knees and squeezed gently. "I saw you that morning after I told you about Jillian. You were all but helpless. You need somebody with you."

"I'll get somebody from the task force."

"And if it takes a while?" He cocked his head, studying her. "I'm willing to hire you, pay whatever you want for as long as it takes. You freelance for them, so you can take however much time you need on this. Can anybody else?"

She glared at him. "And you'll take all that time away from your daughter?"

Cullen shook his head. "No. I'm not going to disappear from her life until we find him."

"So you plan on taking breaks from watching my back?"

You went and got catty on me, sugar, he thought. But he couldn't really blame her. "No. I plan on making sure you take breaks and take care of yourself." Slowly, he slid his hands to the outside of her thighs and watched her pupils flare as he started to rub his hands up and down, edging higher and higher. "You could come home with me. Spend some time with Jillian. She could use somebody in her life who knows what she is dealing with. Somebody who understands her."

Her gray eyes narrowed and flashed hot. "That's low. Using that girl to get to me."

"No. It's a fact. What would be low would be if I used her to get close to you so I could seduce you back into my bed." Leaning in, he stopped just a breath away from her mouth before he added, "I plan on seducing you before the night is up, just so you know. I'm going to fuck you blind, until you can't see or hear or feel anything but me. Then I'm going to make love to you, soft and slow. Then I'm going to start all over again. You'll welcome me back into your bed, Taige, and sooner or later, you'll welcome me back into your life."

Taige's breath hitched, and her eyes widened. He felt the reaction in her body, even though he never once looked away from her face. Her body temperature seemed to spike, and the heat coming off of her set his already hot blood to boiling. The scent of her seemed to grow stronger, and blood tinted her cheeks a dusky pink.

"You sound awful damn sure of yourself," she said. Her voice was husky and rough, unsteady. The sound of it reminded him of the way she moaned when he was inside her, soft, broken little moans that spurred him on.

He dipped his head and licked her lower lip. Then he nuzzled her neck and murmured, "Any reason I shouldn't be sure of myself? You going to kick me out?" He leaned back and studied her face. "Might serve me right, and if you tell me to go now, I will. But that doesn't mean I'm giving up."

Taige looked away, her hair falling to shield her face from him. "I'm not going to be your plaything again. If you need somebody to warm your bed, look elsewhere."

Cullen laughed and reached up, fisting a hand in the soft, sexy curls framing her face. Gently, he tugged her head around to face him. "You were never a plaything, Taige. And if all I wanted was a willing woman in my bed, I could find one. But I don't want any woman, Taige. I want you. I always have."

Slowly, he lowered his head and covered her lips with his. He licked the seam of her lips and coaxed her to open them for him. She did, slowly, almost reluctantly, and Cullen groaned as the taste of her hit his system. He hadn't ever had a woman who tasted as sweet as Taige. Never needed another woman like he needed her. She was like a drug: hot, potent, and devastating.

When she kissed him back, he felt it in every pore of his body. His skin felt too tight, too hot, too small, and he burned for more. He skimmed his other hand up her body and rested it just under the curve of her jaw. She felt so hot under his hand, so silken soft.

It didn't seem possible that she was truly as soft as she had seemed in memories, in dreams, but she was.

He needed more.

Slowly, he straightened up and waited until her eyes met his before he ran his hand down the placket of buttons on her shirt. It was simple white cotton, veeing down in the front where six plain buttons held it closed. It ended right where the waistband of her jeans began. The shirt had driven him nuts over the past few hours, because every time she moved, he caught glimpses of smooth golden flesh. It was demure enough, not dipping low enough at the neckline to give him even a glimpse of her breasts, but the body underneath it was curved, sleekly strong, and he remembered all too well the way she had fit against him.

He freed the first button, holding her gaze all the while. He'd stop, for now, if she told him to. It might take a two-hour swim in the Gulf before the fire inside him cooled, but he'd stop. Yet as he moved on to the second, then third button, Taige sat in front of him, frozen. Her hands were on the couch beside her, arms locked as though she had to brace her weight to keep from sinking backward. The shirt parted as he freed the last of the buttons, and he lifted his hands to smooth it down her shoulders.

As the shirt fell away, he stared at her nearly bare torso. Her bra was simple and white, no lace, no frills, nothing but a soft sheen that glowed against her skin and cupped her breasts lovingly. She reached behind her back, but he caught her wrists in his hands, bringing them back around, and eased them to her sides. Then, still staring into her eyes, he reached around and freed the clasp of her bra.

She shivered as he stripped the bra away and tossed it over the back of the couch. He cupped her breasts in his hands, ran his thumbs over the already stiff peaks, and watched as her head tipped back. One of those soft, sexy little moans escaped her throat, and he gritted his teeth and tried to rein his hunger in. Dipping his head, he skimmed his lips over her throat, down the delicate line of her collarbone. He pressed his lips to the plump upper curve of her breast, savoring the warm, sweet taste of her. She tasted of soap, the ocean, and Taige. Her nipples were stiff, swollen, a warm, rosy brown, shades darker than the smooth slope of her breasts. Taking one in his mouth, he bit down gently.

Arching up against him, she cupped a hand around his nape, holding him close. Damn, her taste. She was hot and sweet under his mouth but it wasn't enough. Cullen was dying on the inside and had been for years. This was the most alive he had felt since he'd chased her away from him, but still, he needed more. Damn it, he had to have more. He slid his hands down her sides, his fingers digging into the curve of her hips. Slowly, he tugged her forward as he trailed a line of kisses down her belly. Soft skin and muscle rippled under his touch, and when he slid his fingers inside her waistband, she jerked.

He straightened up and met her gaze. Their eyes were level, him kneeling in front of her while she sat on the edge of the couch. Her pale gray eyes darkened like thunderheads over the ocean as he cupped his hand between her thighs. "I need you naked, Taige. Right now." He leaned forward and kissed her through her jeans. "If you're going to pull back, now is a good time."

He braced himself for just that. But instead, she lifted shaky hands and freed the button on her jeans. "You know I've never been able to resist you," she said in a husky voice. Her lids drooped low over her eyes as she hooked her hands in her jeans, but before she could push them down, he covered her hands with his, easing her jeans down himself.

She was still wearing her underwear, and he cupped her butt

in his hands. Under his palms, her skin was warm—and bare. Cullen swore hotly as he traced the line of the thong that she wore. The soft black cotton clung to her hips, rode between the cheeks of her ass. Lowering his mouth, he kissed her through the cotton and hissed as he found the material already wet.

Sliding a look up at her, he said in a voice gone rough with need, "Lie down." Taige did, but she was too far away. Grasping her ass, he pulled her hips to the edge of the couch, guiding her knees over his shoulders. Cullen tugged the thong aside as he blew a soft puff of air against her. Tight black curls shielded her sex from him. Already starved for her, he pressed his lips against her and used his tongue to open her folds. Slick, hot, and wet, and as he used his mouth on her, she got hotter and wetter, so hot she seemed to singe him and as wet as a spring storm.

Circling the entrance to her body, he held her steady as he pushed his tongue inside her. Taige screamed and bucked, her hands clutching his head and holding him tight against her. She rocked upward as he shafted her with tongue and fingers, as he suckled on her clit, as he pushed her closer and closer. He felt the warning spasm of her body, felt the powerful climax coming on her even before it hit her, and as it broke over her, he continued to lick and kiss.

His hair tumbled into his eyes as he levered his body up over hers. Lifting her lids, Taige stared at him, her body still shuddering from orgasm. He shifted her body around so that she lay full-length on the couch and then, before she had even caught her breath, he knelt between her thighs, covered her body with his, and pressed his cock against her. "Look at me," he demanded. Through her lashes, she did, staring at him, hardly able to believe this was happening.

It wasn't a dream, wasn't a memory. It was real; he was real, his body hot and heavy, one big hand wrapped around the base of his cock as he pressed close, and then their gazes locked, and he pushed inside. Taige screamed. He was thick, so hard it seemed to bruise her, and he was relentless, forging deeper and deeper until he was sheathed inside her to the hilt.

She groaned and thrashed under him, working to accommodate him. Twelve years was a damn long time, and she felt as though everything in the world had ceased to exist, everything but the couch they lay on, the man above her, and the thick length of his cock throbbing inside her. Unable to breathe, she worked her hands between them and shoved against his shoulders. Her hips wriggled and Cullen swore heatedly. "Damn it, be still."

Looping his arms under her shoulders, he caught her head between his hands, holding her still as he kissed her. With his hips, he pressed down to still her frantic movements. Taige whimpered and pressed backward into the couch as much as she could.

"You're tight," he muttered against her mouth. He didn't try to kiss her, just rubbed his lips back and forth over hers, roaming upward to kiss away the salty tears streaming from her eyes. So tight, she wrapped around him in a snug, silky embrace, wet, soft, and the most sinfully sweet pleasure he'd had—since the last time he'd had her.

Silky sweet—and he was hurting her. He could see it in her eyes. Even though she was still as hot as fire beneath him, and even though he could feel the power of her need, he was hurting her. Damn it, how could he not? She was virgin tight, and once he'd pushed the first inch inside her, he hadn't been able to stop until she had taken all of him.

It damn near killed him, but Cullen didn't follow the needs of his body and take, take, take, taking her until they were both too breathless and tired to move. Slanting his mouth over hers, he braced his elbows on the thick leather cushion on either side of her head, taking some of his weight off Taige.

He eased his hips back, withdrawing until only the head of his cock was wrapped in her warmth and then, slowly, surged forward. When he felt her tighten around him, he stopped, withdrew, working his way inside her, and slowly, she relaxed around him. Her arms slid up over his shoulders, and her mouth sought out his. When her nails started to bite into his shoulders, he started to move faster.

Taige's body bowed up to meet his. Their breathing came in short, ragged pants, and neither of them could see anything for the other. Cullen stroked a hand down her thigh and guided her knee up over his hip, then cupped the curve of her ass in his hand, and held her tight against him. He felt her body clench around his.

Deliberately, he changed rhythm. Taige slid her hands down his back and clutched at his hips, squirming against him. "Damn it, Cullen . . ."

He reached behind him, caught her hands, and forced her wrists down beside her head. "After twelve years of dreaming of this, this is going to last longer than a few minutes." Not much longer, he knew, but longer. And later, he'd do it again, take her as many times in the few hours as he could. Bind her to him again. Remind her of how good they'd been together before he'd screwed it up.

Settling into a shallow, teasing pace, he nuzzled her neck and licked away a bead of sweat from her throat. Her skin glowed, and under his hands it had gone damp. Her body arched and strained against his, and the snug, wet clasp of her pussy around his cock seemed to clutch at him as though she could keep him from pulling away.

Cullen circled his hips against hers and stared at her face, watching her. Too damn beautiful. She moaned, a soft, sexy little sound that throbbed through his system like the beat of a drum. Lashes fluttered low, hiding her eyes. Dipping his head, he bit her lower lip and murmured, "Open your eyes, Taige. Look at me."

Slowly, the fan of her lashes lifted, and she stared at him with a blind, foggy gaze. "Tell me that you love me," he rasped.

"Cullen . . ."

He slanted his mouth across hers, kissing her deep and hard. Then he lifted up, tossing sweaty hair back out of his face. "Tell me you love me," he growled against her lips.

She shifted under him, tugging on her wrists and squirming. "Let go of my hands."

Cullen didn't want to. He didn't want to do anything but demand an answer from her, but he'd already done that twice, with no response. Slowly, he loosened his grip on her wrists. If he could have pulled away then, he might have. His heart was like ashes inside his chest, and he wanted to pull back, hard and fast. Instead, he hunkered down low over her, burying his face in her neck and cursing the need that wouldn't let him pull away.

A strong, slender palm stroked up his back. The other hand still lay over her head, and she sought out his, entwining their fingers. Her free hand curled over the back of his neck, and then her head turned, her lips brushing against his cheek. "I love you, Cullen. Did you actually think I could stop?"

Any control he might have had left died in that second. Turning his head, he sought out her mouth. Hooking his arm around the back of her neck, he whispered against her lips, "You're mine, Taige. Mine." Then he pushed his tongue into her mouth and kissed her until all rational thought faded away.

He moved higher on her body so that each deep, hard stroke had him rubbing against her clit. Canting her hips upward, he changed the angle of his thrusts so he could hit the buried nerve bed inside her pussy. She lit up like the sky on the Fourth of July, screaming in his mouth, her nails raking down his shoulders, and her back arching. As she came, Taige bucked under him, hard, convulsive little jerks. Cullen banded his arm around her waist and held tight, riding her through it, chasing his own orgasm with blind fury.

It erupted from him, and he spilled himself into the wet, receptive depths of her body. Her sheath continued to spasm and clench around his cock, milking him dry. It was as though she was pulling fire from inside his body, a pleasure that was damn near painful in its intensity.

When it ended, he collapsed against her, burying his face between her breasts and sucking in badly needed air.

He couldn't think, could hardly focus on anything but the little aftershocks rolling through his system. The one coherent thought he was aware of: *I'm never letting you go now, Taige.*

* * *

MINUTES passed—or maybe hours, and Taige continued to lie on her back, staring at the ceiling. She'd gone from self-disgust to acceptance to anger and all the way back again. Right now, she was right smack in the middle of acceptance. Eventually, she'd be pissed off again. At him. At herself. At everything. But right now, she was content to stroke a hand up and down Cullen's back and listen to him breathe.

Her thighs ached, and deep inside, she felt raw and a little sore. Twelve years was a damn long time, she mused again. And Cullen hadn't been gentle with her. She hadn't wanted him to be. That greedy desperation eased the ache in her heart, even though it left her body stiff.

I'm never letting you go now, Taige. Catching complete thoughts like that outside of a direct connection wasn't normal for her. It was probably just the physical contact, the very close physical contact that had let her subconscious establish a strong enough connection for her to pick up on that one, clear thought. Just the one, nothing before and nothing since. She was aware of his fatigue, and she'd felt a distant echo from him as they made love. *Sex, Taige. Just sex,* she corrected herself. She'd felt the echo of his pleasure and the burn of need, but she wasn't convinced of anything other than that he wanted her.

A lot.

At least that was what she tried to tell herself. But those few words, *I'm never letting you go now, Taige,* had managed to undermine all the instincts that demanded she protect herself. Inside, she was in turmoil, practically at war with herself. Half of her demanded that she stop being so damn cynical and just see what happened with Cullen. The other half came back with, *Tried that route before, and he dumped me on my sorry ass and stomped all over my heart,* and that part wasn't at all interested in turning said broken, trampled heart back over to him.

His breathing changed. It brushed over her flesh and made her shiver. Stirring, he lifted his head and stared at her out of bleary eyes. "Crushing you," he muttered, his voice thick.

Taige smiled and slid her fingers through his tousled hair. "I'm fine."

"Hmmmm." Lowering his face, he trailed his tongue over her belly in an absent, erotic little pattern. "You're not fine. You're perfect. Delicious." Pushing up on his elbow, he rolled his weight to the side, pressing up against the back of the couch. "You're wet with me. I didn't use a rubber." His lashes drooped over his eyes, and he said, "Seems to be a bad habit with us."

Taige shrugged and tried to dismiss what was clamoring for attention in her heart. Wouldn't matter even if she did acknowledge it. Dreaming and yearning to have a baby of her own, somebody to love and cuddle and protect, was pointless, because it wasn't going to happen.

"You're too quiet," Cullen said. His voice didn't really change, but she heard something there nonetheless.

Looking up, she met his eyes. He watched her with a soft, loving gaze that made her want to scream. Stiffening, she tried to pull away, but he wouldn't let her. "Don't worry about it," she said brusquely.

Heat shimmered through her, and she hissed when he pushed his finger inside her, stroking in and out of her pussy. "I'm not really worried," he whispered, dipping his head to flick his tongue against her clit. "No matter what happened, I wouldn't be worried."

Squeezing her thighs together, she tried to pull back from his caressing hand. "Nothing will happen." Her throat was closing up on her; she could feel it. Eyes blurry with tears, she reached down and grabbed his wrist, trying to pull him away. "Let me go."

"Don't look so scared, Taige." He nuzzled her belly and spoke in a soft, cajoling voice. "You still love me. I still love you. If something happens, we'll deal with it. God knows, I'd love to see you pregnant with my baby."

Her laugh was bitter, so harsh it hurt her ears just to hear it. "It won't ever happen, sugar. I can't get pregnant." This time, when she jerked away from him, he was surprised enough that she managed to pull free. She ended up on her ass by the couch, and too upset to even be embarrassed, all Taige did was shove to her feet and walk blindly in the direction of her room.

She didn't even make it to the doorway when he stopped her, grabbing hold of her arm and trying to turn her around to look at him. When that didn't work, he planted his body in front of her and caught her face between his hands. "What?" he asked hoarsely.

Blinking back the tears, Taige said, "Just let go of me, Cullen."

"Not until you explain that."

This was going to choke her. She knew it. She'd force the words out, and they'd lodge in her throat and choke her. "I got pregnant that day I came to see you when your mom died. I didn't know about it." Forcing the words out was about as easy as it would have been to regurgitate broken glass, and she figured it was every bit as painful. "I lost weight, was sick a lot, but figured I was just depressed. Then I collapsed at school. I was taken to the ER, and they found a tubal pregnancy, but it was too late. The tube had ruptured." Mechanically, she recited the details, unaware that the tears had finally won the battle, and they fell unchecked down her cheeks.

Cullen lifted a hand to touch her, and she flinched away. "Don't," she said harshly.

"Have to," he said, pulling her against him.

His hand rubbed in soothing circles over her bare back, but she held herself stiff in his arms, unable to relax, hardly able to breathe. He was quiet for a long while, and then, finally, he blew out a sigh. His arms tightened around her, and he murmured, "I'm sorry, Taige."

She didn't know what to say. Hell, what was there to say?

"Can you tell me about it?"

Woodenly, she said, "There's not much to tell. The tube rup-tured. The baby never had a chance."

"And you? How were you?"

Alone. But she kept that to herself. "I'm still around, aren't I?" There was really no point in explaining that she'd nearly died. What good would that do either of them?

He cupped her chin and forced her to look at him. "You're not going to talk about it yet, are you?"

Taige averted her eyes. "There really isn't that much to talk about, Cullen."

"Yeah, there is." He shifted, moving around so that he stood behind her, keeping one arm wrapped around her waist. The other hand he pressed to her belly. "I'm no doctor, but I remember anatomy well enough. There are two tubes; only one is gone."

Reaching down, she caught his hand. "Yes. One is gone." She guided his hand lower and laid it down flat against the scar low on her belly. That bullet had ripped through her abdomen, dam-aging the other ovary beyond repair. "On the other side, there's no ovary, Cullen. A bullet saw to that. So it looks like you lucked out all around. You don't need to worry about me getting knocked up, even if we spend the next ten years fucking like rabbits."

Then she jerked away from him and stormed down the hall-way.

* * *

Looks like you lucked out all around.

Cullen sat on the beach, feeling like he'd been wrung dry.

Going from an emotional high to an all-time low in the matter of minutes was hell. He thought that maybe he could have done the Iron Man triathlon and still not feel this worked over.

Taige had been pregnant. Nineteen years old, alone, and pregnant. He didn't know jack shit about tubal pregnancies, but something about the way her face had looked when she talked about it made his gut knot inside. Then there were the tears that had rolled down her cheeks and the way she pressed a hand protectively to her belly as she murmured, *The baby never had a chance*. She'd wanted the baby. He knew that as well as he knew his own name.

Fury gnawed nasty, ugly holes inside him. That faded, puckered scar low on her belly: he'd thought of the pain she must have gone through, and he thought of how easily she could have died, but he hadn't known that whoever had shot her had robbed her. Robbed her of the chance to get pregnant.

And how much of this was his fault?

If he hadn't thrown her out of his life that last day, he could have been there with her when she lost the baby. He wasn't so impressed with himself to think that maybe if he'd been with her as he should have been, it never would have happened. But she'd been alone, and pregnant, because he was a selfish bastard.

It had been his words that pushed her into the career she chose. He didn't give a damn what she said to the contrary, and he knew she had saved lives, done a lot of good for others. Because of what he'd said and done, because of how he'd acted, Taige had gone into a career that broke her heart regularly, that was dangerous, and that had taken away her chance at having a child.

He thought of Jillian, how she regularly broke his heart and how she regularly made him so damn proud, how he loved her so much it felt like his heart would explode from it. Then he thought of Taige, how protective she was, how fierce and how she loved with everything she had inside her. She would have been the kind of mother every child should have, and that had been stolen from her.

The sand muffled her footsteps, and Cullen didn't realize she was standing behind him until she said, "Are you going to sit out here all afternoon and all night?"

Slanting a look at her over his shoulder, he shrugged. "Occurred to me."

"Going to be hard to help me if you plan on spending the time counting the waves."

"I'm sorry, Taige."

Her eyes met his for a split second, and then she looked away. "For what? Counting waves?"

"You know what."

Blowing out a ragged breath, Taige moved closer and sank gracefully to the ground. She kept a good two feet between them. "Don't, Cullen. Okay? Just don't. All of it is over and done with, and for the most part, I'm okay with it. I've got a lot of bad shit inside of me, and maybe this is God's way of making sure I don't pass it on."

"That's a load of crap," Cullen said in a flat voice. "You don't have a damn thing bad inside of you."

"We'll just have to disagree on that one." She shrugged. "It's something I've mostly dealt with, so just let it go."

He could tell by the way she held herself that she wanted some distance, might have even needed it. But he needed to touch her. Rolling to his knees, Cullen crawled across the sand until he could kneel in front of her. Her hands felt cold under his. "I don't know that I can let this go, Taige." Cullen still couldn't believe she'd been pregnant and that now she'd never be able to conceive a baby again. It just didn't seem fair.

"Try," she said grimly. Her eyes were stark and cool, the dull, leaden gray of a winter sky. Everything about her had gone cold and distant.

Apprehension gnawed at him, but then she twined her fingers with his. "Things are moving a little too fast for me right now, Cullen," she murmured. Her gaze lowered, and her lashes shielded her eyes from him. "I know I threw a lot at you, but none of it is easy for me to talk about. I just can't do it right now. I don't even know which way is up. I need some time to level out."

A sigh escaped him. Reaching up, he cupped her chin and lifted it so he could see her eyes. "This isn't done, Taige." Cullen stroked her lower lip with his thumb. He bent his head and pressed a kiss to the corner of her mouth. "We got enough going on right now, that's for certain. But this isn't done. And while you're leveling out, there's something you need to keep in mind. I meant every word I said before, when I told you that I still love you and that I want you back in my life."

Cullen slanted his mouth over hers, cupping his hand over the back of her skull and holding her still. Under his mouth, she was soft and sweet. She sighed into his mouth, and when he slid a hand up her side and cupped her breast, she arched into him with a moan.

Urging her backward, he covered her body with his. Her hands slid under his shirt, her fingers cool and agile, stroking over the sensitive skin of his lower back and then dipping under the waistband of his jeans. "You certain you want to do this out here?" she murmured against his lips. "We're going to get sand everywhere."

"Is that your subtle way of telling me no?" Unconcerned about

her answer, or the sand, he kissed his way down her throat, pausing at her pulse and licking the soft, satiny skin.

She laughed. It was a low, husky sound, and it warmed him
inside. "If I was going to tell you no, I wouldn't mess with being
subtle."

"So is that a yes?"

With gentle but insistent hands, she pushed against his shoulders. Reluctant, he pushed up onto his hands and knees and then
slowly settled back on his haunches, staring at her. A small smile
danced on her lips. Her hands went to the hem of her shirt, and
Cullen felt his mouth go dry as she stripped her shirt away. Under
it, she wore another plain bra of white cotton. The sight of that
simple white against the golden glow of her skin was damned
erotic. Her blue jeans shorts rode low on her hips. The bra and
the shorts did little to conceal the scars on her body: the puckered, faded scar from where she'd been shot; a thin, shallow scar
on the upper curve of her left breast. Her body was long, lean,
and strong, thinner than it should be, and the sight of her was
enough to lay him low. His sexy warrior. No, she wasn't just a
warrior, she was a warrior queen, and he felt like he should be on
his hands and knees in worship.

Hmmmm . . . not a bad idea. As she stood up in front of him,
he reached for the waistband of her shorts, but before he could
strip them away, she stiffened. From head to toe, her body tensed,
and she pulled away.

"Taige—"

Shaking her head, she flung up a hand and rasped, "Stay back.
Oh, God . . ." It was a harsh, tormented moan. Slowly, she sank
to her knees and doubled over, her arms wrapped around her
middle like she'd been punched right in the gut.

Frustrated, helpless, Cullen stood by watching until she fell over in the sand, and then he couldn't hold still anymore. A weak whimper escaped her throat as he scooped her into his arms and sat there, holding her in his lap. Stroking a hand up and down her back, he murmured to her and brooded. Prayed. He kissed her temple and rocked her back and forth, and all the while, she curled into him. She didn't speak. Occasionally, there was a soft little mewling sound, but that was it.

Cullen didn't know how much time passed. He lost count of the waves that crashed into the sand. The tide moved out, and water that had been lapping just inches away from his feet was a good five or six feet away. The clear, flawless blue sky slowly started to deepen and darken, the moon making its ascent while the sun still burned, sinking closer and closer to the horizon.

The setting sun had started to paint the sky with a palette of orange, gold, and pink when Taige finally moved. Deep in her throat, she made a harsh, guttural moan, and her spine bowed, her neck arching back. For the first time, he saw her face.

An icy chill ran through him when he saw her eyes. They were black. The pupil was so huge, it had all but eclipsed the iris, and he couldn't see the soft gray at all. In a matter of heartbeats, her icy skin started to warm, and by the time the sun had completely set, she was burning hot in his arms. Her skin was dry, although he had broken out into a sweat from the heat she was throwing off.

Terrified no longer described what he felt. There was only one time in his life he'd felt like this, and that had been in the hours after he'd learned that Jillian had been abducted. His fingers trembled minutely as he went to push her hair back. Fisting his hand in her soft thick curls, he said, "Taige. Come on, baby. Talk to me."

"It's him." Her lashes drooped low over her eyes. Her voice was dreamy and oddly disconnected. "He's there. Burning . . ."

Cullen didn't waste his breath asking *who*. He knew in his gut. The pad of his thumb stroked across her cheekbone. "Look at me, Taige."

It was as though she hadn't heard him. Lids hanging low over her eyes, she whispered, "There's gas. I smell it. Damn, it's hot."

A fine sweat broke out over her skin. For a second, the air stopped smelling of the heat, the sand, and the Gulf, and the sickly sweet stink of gasoline filled the air. A hot breeze kicked up over the water, and the smell faded. Or maybe he hadn't really smelled the gas to begin with. At that point, Cullen didn't know. She shivered, and Cullen rubbed a hand up and down her back, trying to warm her. Cuddling into him, Taige rubbed her cheek against his chest.

He kept talking to her, but nothing he said got through. Finally, he just wrapped his arms around her and held her as close as he could. One hand rubbed up and down her naked back. Her breasts were bare against his chest, but Cullen could honestly say he didn't have one lascivious thought. Amazing how terror could wipe out an all-consuming lust so easily.

It ended as suddenly as it came on. One moment, Taige was cuddling into him and holding on like he was some teddy bear warding off the boogeyman, and in the next, she was stiff in his arms and sucking in air like a drowning woman. Her body shuddered, and then she pushed against his arms. "You're going to crush me, Cullen."

He pressed a kiss to her forehead. "Damn it, you keep scaring me like that, I'm going to die of a heart attack before I turn forty." But he did let go, slowly, reluctantly. She tried to stand up, but her legs wobbled, and Cullen had a feeling she wouldn't make it ten feet without hitting the sand. Pushing to his feet, he gathered up her clothes. After tucking them into her arms, he lifted her. "You need to lie down," he said softly.

But Taige had other plans. "No. We need to leave. He's at the cabin, or he's going there." Her mouth twisted in a grimace. "At least what's left of the cabin—no telling how much of it Jones has torn down to get to the bodies."

The need for vengeance warred with the need to take care of Taige. Her hands shoved against his chest, but it was pitiful how weak she was. Under normal circumstances, if Taige wanted to be put down, he'd have a fight on his hands, and chances were, he could easily lose that fight. At the moment, she'd have a hard time holding her own against a kitten.

Physically.

The look in her eyes was one of sheer stubbornness, and Cullen knew that if he let her, she'd take off on her own and keep going until she collapsed. She was just that determined. If he wasn't so damned worried she'd end up passing out on him and scaring him to death, he'd go along with her just fine.

But . . .

Her eyes, once more that soft, misty gray, narrowed, and her pretty mouth flattened out into a tight, thin line. "Damn it, Cullen. You're wasting time. We don't have much as it is." Fisting a hand in his shirt, she gave him a fierce stare and said, "I am *fine*. Okay?"

"You're not fine," Cullen argued. The last rays of sunlight were fading fast, but he could still see how pale and wan she'd become. "You're almost as pale as I am. Hell, you probably can't even walk to the house on your own two feet."

Her lids flickered. "I don't need to walk to the cabin. And it's a good three hours north. By the time we get there, I'll be steady."

"And if you're not?"

"If we don't go *now*, it's not going to matter. Because he isn't going to be there."

Cullen gave in. He guessed there hadn't ever been doubt on that. Between the need for blood and the innate desire to do whatever Taige asked of him, Cullen didn't even have a fighting chance. They were out of the house before another twenty minutes had passed. She'd insisted on changing, and Cullen watched over her protectively, ready to catch her if she looked the least bit unsteady.

Never happened. Although he'd carried her to the house, by the time they walked out the front door, her color had improved, and she moved with that easy, confident grace that he remembered from years before.

Steady, she'd said.

Hell. She was going to be steadier than he was, that was for damn certain.

TEN

Too late.

They were still a good twenty miles away when the skin on Taige's spine went tight. Too late. He was gone. She couldn't explain how she knew, but by the time they got to the cabin, he would be long gone.

And there would probably be no trace left behind. Again. Somehow this guy managed to wipe the slate clean, psychically speaking, and she'd get nothing. None of those intangible little vibes that she couldn't see or feel, but which existed nonetheless.

Useless—

She blocked that out. If she started swimming in guilt or self-doubt, she'd be of no use to anybody. So, instead of dwelling on that old bullshit, she closed her eyes and reached out. It didn't come so easily this time.

Sometimes the gray came on her like a summer storm, quick, violent, and all-encompassing. Other times, it was like a heat mirage, wavering and unclear. Right now, it was like trying to push her way through quicksand. It came, but there was a reluctance to it, and the vision that had been so clear just a few hours ago was now murky.

There was nothing definitive this time. Reaching out, she tried to connect with her prey, and there was, for just a second, a brief connection. Tenuous at best and too weak to sustain contact. Even as she tried to strengthen the connection, it faltered and faded.

It left her with the impression of a deep rage and a conviction that could only come from the mind of the truly insane. Her mind tried to hold on to that little bit of knowledge. There was something important there—something very important. But she couldn't focus.

Couldn't see. Smoke obscured her vision, and heat stung her skin. She tried to take a breath, and it choked her. The underlying stink of gasoline filled her nostrils, and she gagged.

"Taige."

The sound of Cullen's voice was the sweetest damn thing, and she turned toward it, tried to reach out. Reached out—and he touched her. She felt his hand land on her shoulder, and he shook her. Feeling a little bewildered, Taige opened her eyes and rubbed them. Still the smoke burned.

Damn, am I still under? she thought. She breathed in and tasted the acrid bite of smoke in her throat.

But it wasn't the remnants of a vision. Smoke hung in the air, and the direction of the wind carried it to them as Cullen pulled to the side of the road. Off to the left was the pitted, sorry excuse for a road that led to the cabin. The road no longer looked abandoned, and Taige couldn't even begin to guess how many agents had been out here, how many forensics teams had gone over every inch of land.

Right now, though, it wasn't the FBI trekking over the rough road. It was a line of fire trucks, ambulances, and several black and tan county sheriff cruisers. Up on the mountain, just barely visible above the tree line, was a flickering orange glow.

Just as she'd seen in her vision, the bastard had set the cabin on fire.

He'd been here not long ago.

Part of her wanted to hope that maybe he'd been caught.

But Taige was a realist. He wasn't here.

Her Bureau ID got her and Cullen past the line of officials. There weren't a lot of gawkers, not this far out of the way. A few questions revealed that a father and son had been hunting and seen the flames. Dry as the summer had been, if they hadn't called it in when they did, the fire would have presented a serious hazard. Even now, it looked like the firefighters were going to have one hell of battle keeping the fire from spreading.

Sirens split the air again. As one, Taige and Cullen turned to watch another truck come screeching up. "We need to go," she said softly. "We're just in the way here."

"But . . ."

Taige glanced at Cullen and shook her head. "There's nothing here for me, Cullen. If there was, I'd know."

Somehow, her man had slid right past her, and just as before, he'd left behind nothing of himself.

Eyes burning from the smoke, Taige turned away. Cullen fell into step beside her. They wound their way through the mass of rescue personnel and law enforcement. A few people tried to intercept them, but Taige flashed her ID from the Bureau, and they grudgingly stepped out of her way, usually with a muttered warning, "Stay out of the way."

After the fifth time, Taige swore. "Damn, it ain't like I'm up here trying to throw a party."

And that earned her an irritated, territorial look. *Get the hell out,* was the general consensus. These people didn't want her here, but Taige honestly didn't give a damn. She wasn't too thrilled to be there, either. And then it got worse. Somebody recognized her.

Although she'd tried to avoid it, somebody had connected her to Jillian's rescue. Old pictures of her had been dug up and plastered across several major papers, and she'd had to dodge a couple of reporters back home. Word spread as fast as the fire was spreading, and she felt the change in the air, going from disgruntled territorial macho crap as the firefighters and cops thought the FBI was intruding, to curiosity, mixed with a little bit of outright hostile disbelief.

No thoughts were clear, but that wasn't unusual for her. Awful of her, but at that moment, she was glad the fire raged on, because it kept most of the people too damn busy to come up and pester her. It also kept them from staring at her. For the most part. She could see or feel several different gazes on her, measuring, evaluating.

It added to her already strained state of mind, and trying to block it out was getting harder and harder. Her control was always weaker when she was tired, and she had passed the point of tired a long way back.

Halfway to the car, the exhaustion snuck up on her, and she tripped, stumbled. Cullen caught her right arm and steadied her. Another hand closed around her left arm, and a concerned voice said, "Ma'am, are you okay?"

All conscious thought fled. She lifted her gaze and stared at the stranger without seeing his face. The gray dropped down on her like a lead weight, and she could feel it pressing on her, crushing her. Only Cullen's hand on her right arm and the stranger's on her left kept her from hitting the ground.

She saw faces.

Dozens of faces flashed before her eyes. Grief-stricken parents, lost children, infuriated, frustrated law enforcement officials. Their thoughts formed a collective voice, and it echoed inside her mind in a refrain: *Why?*

There was another question, just as loud, and it was one that Taige had asked more than once. *Who?* Until that moment, the answer had been unknown. But now there was a flicker of knowledge.

Elusive, it danced away before she could fully understand it. Reflexively, she reached up, grabbed hold of the stranger standing in front of her. The connection—it had come from him. Tenuous at best, and if she faltered for just a second, it would slip away again. Instinct almost had her forcing her way inside the man's thoughts, and she just barely managed to restrain herself, seeking instead to deepen that surface connection.

This isn't happening.

But it was. There was no denying it. From the corner of her eye, she could see the man who'd unknowingly brought this on. He was a paramedic, about her age, about her height, and when he'd been a kid, he'd lost his older sister. The girl had been in that stage where adolescence gave way to adulthood. They'd looked a lot alike.

The killer had seen the brother, seen him—and remembered the sister. Remembered killing her. The killer had relived those memories with a passion so intense it had left an imprint, like pressing his hand into fresh cement. And the cement, in this case, was the medic.

Son of a bitch. He'd wiped all traces of himself clean, then he'd run into this man who bore such a strong resemblance to one of his victims. This man didn't even realize he'd met his sister's killer, however briefly. And the killer probably didn't realize he'd left such a strong imprint, either.

The little memory flashes, the psychic imprints worked to fall into place within her mind. All the answers danced just below the surface, moving closer and closer, shifting, realigning, until the answer was there.

All but glaring at her. Taige moaned and sagged to her knees, jerking away from the two men trying to keep her upright. Tears burned in her eyes, and she buried her face in her hands. Warm hands came up and cupped her shoulders. Without looking, she knew who it was: Cullen. He knelt behind her, sliding his arms around her waist and pulling her back against him as her mind fought to accept the knowledge before her.

Cullen's warmth, his strength, surrounded her as she knelt on the ground and fought not to be sick. Fought not to cry. If she started, she wouldn't stop for a good long while. There'd be time for tears later. But not now.

Now she had to go. Had to find him and see if she'd really seen what she thought she'd seen.

Reaching up, she covered one of Cullen's hands with hers. "We need to go."

One hand smoothed across her shoulder to cup over her neck. "What's going on, Taige? Where are we going?"

"Back home. He's there."

* * *

Taige wouldn't speak to him.

It was damned eerie having her sitting in the car with him right then, because she seemed more dead than alive. Her skin had a grayish cast, her mouth had a tight, pinched look to it, and she gazed out the windshield with an unblinking stare. Cullen doubted she saw anything, not the scenery whipping by and not the cars they passed as they sped south down the I-65.

For the first hour, he'd tried to talking to her, but she hadn't answered anything he'd asked. She wouldn't speak at all. He shot the clock on the dashboard a glance. The damn thing hadn't ever moved so slow. He was driving nearly ninety miles an hour. On occasion, a snarl in the traffic had him pulling out on the shoulder to drive, and he only hoped that if they got pulled over, Taige's Bureau ID would get them out of trouble. Assuming she could focus enough.

The miles seemed to drag by, even though he was driving so fast the scenery sped by at a blur. Finally, he saw the exit he needed for Highway 59, and he took it at sixty-five miles an hour. The two-lane highway wasn't as busy in the middle of a Monday morning, but the cars were still moving too damn slow to satisfy him.

The silence got to him, and he glanced at Taige again. "Where are we going?"

Finally a response. "Just keep driving."

"Driving *where*, exactly?"

She didn't answer. The thick fringe of her lashes lowered, shielding her eyes. She looked—damn, Cullen didn't even have the words to describe how she looked. Shattered. Devastated. Shocked.

He wanted to hold her, wished he could pull the car off the road and say *screw it*. The need to do just that was strong.

Yet there was an equally strong need that kept him driving. A part of him that was hot with anticipation and the need to get where they were going, find who they were looking for, so Cullen could kill him. Slow. Nice and slow. Cullen hadn't ever pegged himself as a bloodthirsty type. He'd never admit it, but when he was in the delivery room the day Jillian was born, he'd gotten damn queasy when he saw the blood. His legs had gone all watery, and for a minute, he had been scared he was going to humiliate himself and pass out on the delivery room floor.

His dad loved to go hunting, but Cullen had gone with him exactly one time—one time, and he'd known that hunting was not his thing. The smell of blood, the sight of it, the feel of it. Hell, no.

But right now? He craved it. He didn't just want to find this man and kill him. He wanted to hurt him.

The bastard didn't know it, but he was already dead.

As they drew closer to Gulf Shores, the traffic from the tourists thickened until they were moving along at a snail's pace. At least it felt that way to Cullen. Blood roared in his ears so loud, he barely heard Taige's voice when she said, "Turn here." The narrow highway was just north of town, and it wasn't at all familiar to Cullen.

"Where are we going?" he asked as they started to head east.

"The church."

Cullen didn't want to ask which church. He had a feeling that he already knew the answer to that, just by that expression in her eyes: dazed disbelief and desolation. "What church? Why?" he asked shortly. She didn't answer. Just barely, he kept from growling at her. He took the turn onto that gravel road so sharply, the truck skidded, and the tires threw dust into the air. There was a sign set in a flower bed, surrounded by chaotic bursts of flowers.

Disciples of the Lamb, it read.

Under that, worship times. And under that . . . a name.

Leon Carson, Minister.

For just the briefest second, time seemed to stop. Cullen slammed on the brakes and read the name again, certain he'd misread it.

"Son of a *bitch*!" he roared. Shoving his foot down on the gas, he sped down the winding little drive, pulling in front of the church and stomping on the brake. Tires squealed.

"He's not here," Taige murmured. Cullen released his seat belt and paused, looking back at her. She moved slowly, as though each movement hurt.

"Did he take my daughter?" he demanded.

She swallowed. He could hear it, and it sounded as loud as a gunshot. "I think he did."

Taige wasn't sure if she'd be able to stand up just yet. In the entire time she'd known Cullen, he'd always been so self-contained. Even when she'd seen him after his mother died, he'd been contained. Holding his grief, his rage, everything he felt so tightly inside, only the echo of it could leak through to spill onto her.

But that restraint was shattered now.

She could feel his rage so strongly, her hands trembled in sympathy. Her gut was tangled into a million knots, and adrenaline pulsed through her. When she took a deep breath, the connection deepened, so strong and sudden that for a moment, she couldn't tell where she left off and he began. When she looked around, it was with his eyes.

When she moved, it felt wrong, felt off, and it was because her brain was still mired in his. It took three tries to get the door to open, and when she slid out, she had to brace a hand against the side of the truck just to stay upright. Closing her eyes, she forced herself to erect some sort of shield between them. It was shaky and thin, not strong enough to block him out, but it was better than nothing.

Just barely. Enough that she could open her eyes and look at the church and the rectory and know that she was seeing it with her eyes and not his. To her eyes, the church looked simple, plain, just a pretty country church with a white picket fence, flowers, and stained glass windows.

But the house—

"Shit." Taige swallowed the bile churning up through her belly. The house was new. Over the past ten years, the church had grown, more and more members joining, and five years ago, those members had built the rectory. Five years old. Most houses that new didn't have much psychic energy inside them, especially not a house where only one person lived.

But this house was screaming with it. Chilled to the bone, she crossed her arms over her chest and started toward the neat little brick house. She could sense Leon's energy, an echo of his personality. All people left it behind, almost like a scent. When she'd lived with her uncle, she had kept her shields up so that she couldn't pick up anything random from him. It had been an effort to avoid feeling his hatred of her and maybe, because she had always blocked him off, she'd missed the clues.

He'd been killing for a long time.

Those little memory flashes she'd picked up earlier from the paramedic told the story in vivid detail. She saw dozens and dozens of faces, all of them differing in physical appearance and age. There were hairstyles that had to date back to the seventies, girls wearing the big hair and stirrup pants of the eighties, blue eye shadow almost up to the eyebrow. A boy no more than ten wearing the red fake leather jacket made popular by Michael Jackson.

So many of them—rage churned inside her like bile, boiling up her throat, threatening to spill out onto everything around her, hot, potent, and deadly. She swallowed against it, struggled to breathe past the nausea. It wasn't time yet. She couldn't break down yet, couldn't get sick, couldn't scream in denial or let herself wallow in the storm of guilt that waited.

Not yet.

Because there was another child. When Leon had seen the paramedic earlier, he hadn't just thought of the man's sister, he'd also thought of another child. Blue-eyed, blonde-haired, her body just beginning to show signs of womanhood. A demon child with a demon gift, and the time to purify the child was drawing near.

"Please, God." Taige closed her eyes and prayed. "Don't let me be too late."

On the heels of that soft prayer came a rush of energy. Adrenaline-induced, she knew, and once it faded, she was going to crash, and crash hard. But for now, it gave her the strength she needed to pull the Glock 9 mm from the holster at her side and hold it steady as she crossed to the house.

"I thought you said he wasn't here," Cullen said, his voice neutral. Neutral, but it couldn't hide the rage blistering through him.

"He's not," she said quietly. But she'd been wrong before.

Terribly wrong. Bitter, futile rage burned inside her as she thought back to how many times she'd told Rose that Leon wasn't dangerous to anybody other than Taige. She couldn't have imagined him hurting somebody other than her, not in a thousand years. And she had been so very wrong.

Walking to the house, Cullen at her side, she took a few seconds to bolster her shields. Bad, bad things had happened inside that house, and it had left a nasty, stinking cloud of death hovering, all but coloring the air. If she walked into that unprepared, she'd never emerge with her sanity intact.

"So, if you know he's not here, you got a plan for getting inside? Or are we even going inside?" Cullen asked. His voice was calm, almost level, but it didn't quite mask the fury she sensed inside him.

"Oh, we're going inside." The adrenaline crashing through her still had her shaking minutely. "You feel like trying to break a door down? I've got some lock picks in the car, but I'm too shaky to use them." She held up her hand and stared at it, watching the fine tremors.

"You can't hocus-pocus it open?"

Taige shook her head. "No. Any telekinetic gift I have is limited to living things. I can't do jack with something inanimate." A door lock was about as inanimate as it got.

"In that case, I'd love to break the door down." He had a mean smile on his lips, and she suspected he'd like to break all sorts of things, a door being fairly far down on the list. But considering the real target of his rage wasn't handy, he'd make do with the door. For now.

A shiver raced through her on the tail end of that thought.

Cullen was going to kill Leon.

She understood his murderous rage all too well, and she couldn't blame him. She'd want to do the same thing, or worse, if she were in his place. Hell, she wasn't even *in* his place, and she wanted to kill Leon.

But Taige was also aware of the consequences of that. Dicey situation here. She couldn't blame Cullen, or rob him of his need to avenge his daughter and protect her, but she also wasn't about to let him do something that could end up with his ass in jail.

He deserved better than that. Jillian deserved better.

The sound of a door being busted off its hinges jerked her out of her reverie, and she looked up, staring at the front door. The door was half off its hinges, and the wood of the doorjamb was busted, little splinters and slivers of wood littering the pretty white tile inside the house and the wooden planks of the porch. Cullen glanced back at her and then pushed the door completely open. For a minute, they both stood there in the doorway, looking into the house.

The walls were painted a soft, pale blue, almost soothing. The hardwood floors gleamed a mellow gold, and there was a pretty blue throw rug with an abstract, geometric pattern. That very first glance was of a well cared for, pretty new home. There was a big cross hanging on the wall at the end of the hall, painted a pristine white. Under it was a table, and there was a huge Bible on it that lay open.

That sight bothered her, very deeply bothered her. As pretty and warm as the house looked, it stank with a miasma of death and pain. The sight of a holy book inside this house was so wrong. If she could bear touching something that Leon had touched, she'd grab the Bible and get it out of there.

Instead, she looked away from it and stepped inside the house, scanning and cataloging every sight, every sound, every little memory flash. There were a damn lot of those. Too many. Some of them even dating back to his childhood. The entire house was stained with them, although he'd only lived there five years. This place, it might never be clean again.

Three feet inside the doorway, the first memory flash assailed her: a girl, older than Jillian had been, but not quite on the cusp of womanhood, with big, pretty blue eyes and a sweet smile.

The girl saw things. Heard things. Believed in ghosts. Her mother thought she had a devil inside her, and she'd brought the girl to Leon. That had been the beginning. It hadn't happened here, but that girl, what he'd done to her, had left a mark on the man. She'd been his first, the first girl he'd tried to purify. The first girl he'd killed.

The first girl he'd raped. He'd killed her because of that rape, told her that she'd bewitched him, tempted him beyond what he could bear, and that her punishment for those sins was to die.

He hadn't raped every child he'd kidnapped. Most of them, he had grabbed with only the intent to purify them of their unclean thoughts, of the demons that controlled them. Demons—that was how Leon explained away the gift. It was something from Satan, and he was only doing his duty as a man of God by destroying that demon. But destroying the demon, in Leon's mind, required killing the infected soul.

It had been his own gift that led Leon to his victims. He'd considered it a sign from God, that sure and certain knowledge, but it had been a gift. An affinity for picking out the gifted people from the ungifted. He'd known when Taige was sent to live with him that she'd been gifted—another flash. Another. Another. They hit her like gunfire, one right after the other. Nights when he had gone into Taige's bedroom and stared at her while she slept, thought of killing her.

"Why didn't you?" she murmured, not even aware that she had spoken.

She drifted through the house, looking more like a ghost than anything, Cullen thought as he watched her. There was something eerie about the way she moved, more like gliding than walking. In the office, she stopped in front of the desk and held out a hand over it, her palm hovering just an inch away. She flinched. A harsh breath hissed out from between her teeth. "He knows that I found Jillian. He wants her back."

Cullen's blood turned to ice. "Is she . . ."

Taige shook her head. "She's safe. He knows she has people watching her. And there's another." Her fingers flexed. She swallowed. Then, taking a deep breath, she laid her palm flat against the surface of the desk. "Oh, God . . ." The words fell from her lips in a soft, tormented moan. She slumped forward, her hair falling down to shield her face. "Damn it, Cullen. He has some other girl. I can see her face."

"Is she okay?"

Taige started to shake. Her entire body trembled like a leaf, and a soft, keening moan escaped her lips. "I don't know—damn it, I don't know. Oh, shit. He's hurting her. Damn it, he's hurting her, and he loves it."

Outside, they both heard the sound of a car approaching, moving fast down the gravel driveway. Taige flinched, jerked hard back into awareness, and she moved with Cullen to stare out the window as the beat-up, ancient station wagon came roaring up the lane. Woodenly, she pulled the phone from her belt and punched in a number. Jones answered, and Taige said, "I'm going to need a team down here, Jones." She didn't elaborate, and she didn't mess with giving directions or an address. Her phone was GPS enabled, and he'd track her via the phone. Details were a waste of time and energy at this point.

After that short, terse message, she disconnected and then tucked the phone back into the holder at her waist. "It's not Leon," she said softly, although she didn't recognize the car.

"Do we need to get the hell out of here?"

Technically, they had no business being in this house. There was no physical proof inside these walls, and there was no endangered child there, either. The answers that Taige had weren't the kind that could be presented to a jury or a judge. By all means, she was violating Leon Carson's rights, and if she had any sense, or a little less compassion, then they should definitely get the hell out of Dodge.

But Taige didn't give a damn about Leon's rights. She didn't give a damn about technicalities, legalities, and the ins and outs of the justice system.

She cared about all the children who had died at her uncle's hands, and she cared about stopping him.

"No," she murmured in response to Cullen's question. Shivering, she folded her arms across her middle and then rubbed her palms up and down her upper arms, trying to warm herself. "We came for answers. We'll leave when we have them."

But it wouldn't take long.

Even from the distance, Taige could see the darkness that painted a dark, ugly void around the woman in the car. She stopped in front of the house and climbed out, paused to look at Cullen's big black truck, and then she looked back at the house. Taige felt the impact of her gaze from there, although a hundred feet easily separated them. Taige could feel *him*.

Leon had left a mark on this woman. She could feel it as clearly as she had when she looked into the paramedic's eyes earlier and realized who she was hunting. "It's Penny Harding," she said quietly. "My uncle's assistant."

Dragging in a deep breath, she closed her eyes and blocked the woman from her field of vision just long enough to ground herself. Leon had kept himself blocked from Taige, and she hadn't helped by keeping her own blocks in place, reinforcing them any time she came close to Leon. His hatred of her had been the initial reason she'd shielded against him, and over the years, her own dislike of him had added to the urge to keep him out.

But there had been no attempt on Leon's part to keep his

emotions contained around Penny. And damn, but he must spend a lot of time with this woman, because his psychic presence had all but eradicated Penny's personality. Muffled it, tamped it down, and kept it hidden under the force of his own.

It was a godsend.

Taige could follow a psychic imprint the same way a bloodhound could follow a scent. If Leon kept his presence muffled, there wouldn't be much of a trail for her to follow.

But Leon acted on instinct. His gift, strong as it probably was, was untrained. He probably didn't realize how much of himself he spilled into his home, onto people that spent a lot of time with him. He probably didn't realize that unless he kept himself shielded all the time, he was going to leak all over somebody like Penny, somebody who spent their days seeing to his needs and running his errands and buying his groceries.

Penny was like a homing beacon and a journal all wrapped into one.

At least for somebody like Taige, somebody who read a psychic imprint. When Penny entered the house, as she drew nearer to Taige, it was like she was working pieces of a puzzle into place, and by the time they met up in the hallway, Taige had the answers. It left a hell of a lot more questions though.

Yes, Leon had another child.

Yes, he was someplace with the child right now.

But that was when the answers stopped and new questions began. Because it was a child Penny knew somehow, a child Penny had put into Leon's hands, knowing what he'd do.

She's got evil inside her, Leon. Bad, nasty evil. You need to purify her.

And as she said it, she'd stared at Leon with the blind devotion of a madwoman.

"Taige . . ." Penny gave Taige a puzzled look and glanced back the busted front door. "Do you know what happened to the front door?"

"I did it. Where is my . . . uncle?" The word left a nasty taste in her mouth, just saying it. How could somebody that evil be her blood? It was sickening.

"He's out attending to the needs of his congregation," Penny said. She frowned and cocked her head, studying Taige's face. "You busted the door down?"

"Actually, that was me," Cullen said from over her shoulder. "Where exactly is he attending these needs at?"

"I'm afraid that's the business of Reverend Carson and his flock . . . Mr. . . . ?"

Cullen just grunted in response, giving her no answer.

"Hmmm. You do know that you'll need to pay for the damage, Taige. Honestly, what would your mother think? A civilized person simply comes back when there is somebody home."

"It's important, Penny." Taige didn't bother arguing with Penny about her civility or lack thereof. The woman clearly considered Leon a saint, so her judgment was definitely skewed.

"I see. Well, no. Not exactly." Penny's frowned deepened, and if her face dropped any more, she was going start resembling a hound dog, all mournful-eyed and sad-faced. "I just don't understand what could be so important that you'd break down a door. Did he even know you were coming?" As she spoke, she headed down the hall into the kitchen, leaving Taige and Cullen to follow behind.

The kitchen was painted a cheerful yellow. The floor was bright blue, and the appliances so clean, they could have come straight off the showroom floor. Yet, like every other room in the house, it looked dark to Taige, like she was seeing it through a black veil.

Penny stood at a bright white breakfast bar, rifling through mail and sorting it. The woman was nervous; Taige could sense it, the acrid scent of fear and nerves. Even if she hadn't had the memory flash just a few minutes ago, she would have realized there was something weird going on with Penny.

"Where is he?" she asked quietly, moving up behind Penny.

Penny, in the process of shuffling through the mail, looked at Taige over her shoulder, a confused smile. "I don't know, Taige. I'm his assistant, but he doesn't always feel the need to keep me informed of his daily schedule. The reverend is an important man. He doesn't answer to the likes of me."

"Then he can answer to me," Taige said, her voice flat. "Where the hell is he?"

Penny's mouth puckered up like Taige had just shoved a lemon into her face. "You really do need God's good grace in your life, Taige. Speaking so, swearing, displaying an utter lack of humility and compassion." She glanced at Cullen, and the look on her face probably wouldn't have been much different if she'd run into a john and his whore. "And the company you keep."

"Hmmm." Taige didn't bother asking again. Instead, she reached out and grabbed Penny's wrist. Pushing her way inside a person's mind left a bad taste in Taige's mouth. She wasn't a mind reader, and she was damn thankful of that. A person's thoughts were private, and they should remain that way.

Using her gift like this left her feeling dirty and upset, because it was wrong. It wasn't something she had to do much, thank God. Usually, she followed psychic imprints left in the environment. But while she couldn't read minds, she could read imprints;

fresh imprints were even clearer than a person's thoughts, and what she picked up from Penny was as clear and detailed as a blueprint.

Narrowing her eyes, Taige stared at Penny's face.

"He's at your house."

Penny gasped and jerked against Taige's hold, struggling to break free. "At your house—with your *granddaughter*."

Behind her, Cullen snarled, "Son of a *bitch*."

Sick, Taige let go of Penny's hand, and the woman folded her hands at her waist and gave Taige a pious smile. "Really, Taige. What kind of a language is that? No good, God-fearing soul speaks that way."

"No good, God-fearing soul lets a man like my uncle put his hands on a child," Taige said, her gut churning.

But Penny just smiled. "The girl has the devil inside her. Just like her mama. Just like you. I failed with my daughter, just like Leon failed with you. We're both stronger now. We'll save my grandchild."

There was another part of Taige's ability that really made her uncomfortable. Using it to cause physical harm left her riddled with guilt. But she doubted it would be much of an issue this time. She slammed into Penny's mind with all the strength she had in her, and when the woman collapsed to the ground, silent, Taige smiled in satisfaction.

She didn't have a chance too often to use her handcuffs, but she still carried them, just like she carried the Bureau ID and just like she carried the Glock. And she was just as competent with the cuffs as she was with the gun, crouching down beside Penny's unconscious body. "Help me sit her up," she said to Cullen. He braced Penny's body, while Taige cuffed her with her arms behind her back, looping them around the leg of the breakfast bar.

Taige didn't know how long Penny would be out. That little gift was unpredictable, and it wasn't one she practiced much. It wasn't one she could practice much, unless somebody volunteered to get psychically sucker punched. It could last a couple hours, a couple days, or, if Penny's will was really strong, a matter of minutes.

Thus the cuffs. It wouldn't do to have Penny wake up and call Leon, alerting him to the fact that Taige and Cullen were coming for him. "Can you check her purse, see if she's got a license or something? We need to find her house."

ELEVEN

IT was an older house, one that had withstood hurricanes, floods, and time. It sat by itself on a piece of land, and Taige's gut churned with nerves as they approached. Training had kicked in, making her think. They had to approach on foot. If Leon heard them coming, he could do God only knew what to the poor kid he had with him.

There was a chance that he'd know they were coming anyway, and not because of some warning from his Looney Tunes assistant, but because he'd sense Taige, the same way she could sense him. Hopefully, all the years of training and honing her gift would give her the advantage. She concentrated on muffling her presence, muffling Cullen's. Cullen's natural resistance to psychic energy was once more going to work in her favor. The anger inside him would normally alert any and every psychic within a mile range or more that he was coming, but his resistance muffled his emotions and his thoughts.

Combined with Taige's efforts, she thought they probably had him pretty much shut down.

Still, it was risky going in like this. The team was coming. On the drive over, Taige's phone had started to vibrate, and she read the message on the display. The team was en route with an ETA of thirty minutes. Jones must have had them on standby—hell, he had probably been following her with the damn GPS for days.

It wouldn't surprise her at all, and right now, she wasn't even that irritated by it.

The team would come in handy. Even if he managed to get past Taige and Cullen, there was no way Leon could evade some of Jones's psychic bloodhounds. He had a couple of psychics working for him who made Taige's abilities look like some hokey Gypsy fortune-teller at a county fair.

They kept to the tree line, and Taige thanked God that it had been getting late when they got back to Gulf Shores. Now it was full night, and they had the cover of darkness to help conceal them as they crossed the empty, exposed field between the trees and the old farmhouse.

It was quiet.

She couldn't hear any sign of life, but she could sense him. Closing her eyes, she focused on the trail Leon hadn't bothered wiping clean. When she opened her eyes again, she started circling around the house, searching for . . .

There.

The doors to the storm cellar were closed but unlocked. The hinges squeaked, and in the silence of the night, they sounded terribly loud. Logically, she knew they weren't all that loud, but still, she winced. Opening just one door, she ducked inside, and Cullen followed close on her heels.

At the bottom of the steps was a door. It looked out of place in the old storm cellar, clean, extremely modern, and very locked. Leaning against the door, she strained to hear something, but there was nothing. Either nobody was making any noise on the other side, or that door was damn good at muffling sound.

She had her lock picks on her this time, and she pulled them out and went to work, cursing the dim light that fell through the sole open door. Cullen had a flashlight, but she'd told him not to turn it on unless she said so, and she didn't want to use it now and risk alerting Leon to their presence.

Sweat dripped down her face as she worked. She'd done this in darker, worse conditions than this, and she could do it again.

There: a faint clicking sound. She turned the doorknob, and it moved, but still, the door wouldn't open. Damn it. Obviously somebody really wanted the door to stay closed. She stood and gave Cullen a look. He didn't even have to ask. She stood by as he kicked the door. Wood groaned, but it didn't give. He swore and then struck again, harder this time.

Wood splintered, and the door flew open with a crash. Light spilled into the stairwell and they both stood, frozen with shock, for a brief second.

Leon was in there, all right, his face wet with sweat, his eyes bright and mad—with a whip in his hand that came screaming through the air to land on the slender, naked back of a girl who looked to be all of thirteen or fourteen.

Her uncle wasn't aware of them. It was like nothing in the world existed, save for the helpless girl lying facedown in front of him. Blood streaked down her back and sides in rivulets, pooling on the table where she lay restrained. Thick leather straps held her in place at her waist, her thighs, each of her hands, each of her feet. Her head was turned so that she faced them, but there was no sense in her eyes. Nothing but terror and pain. As the whip landed, she made no sound.

It would have been hard to, because Leon had effectively gagged her with a piece of silvery gray duct tape. Above the strip of tape, her face was bruised and battered. Taige could see the imprint of a hand on her cheek, and the telltale bruising around her throat where somebody had wrapped their hands around her neck and squeezed. Both of her eyes were bruised and so swollen, it was amazing she could even open them.

It took less than a few seconds to take all of that in, but it seemed forever. Like a movie trapped in slow motion, Taige could see herself turn to look at Leon, each movement painstakingly slow. She was aware of each breath, each heartbeat. Fury knotted her muscles.

Still unaware of Taige, Leon lifted the whip, screaming out, "Will you repent?"

His own fury had blinded and deafened him, because he remained unaware of them until Taige pounced. Time sped back up as she leaped for him, using her weight to ride him to the floor, and there, she started to hit him.

Over and over. Pain shot up her arm, hands grabbed her and tried to pull her away, and still, she pummeled Leon. He screamed and swore, words that no decent preacher would ever speak. He struggled underneath her, and without thinking twice, Taige used her mind, blasting through his shields to hold him immobile with her gift. "You sick son of a bitch. You bastard," she screamed at him, seeking some outlet for the fury inside her.

But nothing helped. The anger grew, threatened to overwhelm her. Hands once more grabbed her arms, and Taige struggled against Cullen as he pulled her off and hauled her away from Leon, kicking and screaming.

Part of him wanted to turn around and finish the job as Cullen struggled to control Taige. She fought against him with the strength and fury of a tiger, snarling, practically growling. "Taige." He called her name over and over, but there was no response. Finally, he dragged her over to the table where the girl was still lying, breathing shallowly and staring into space with the blank gaze of a doll. "Taige, damn it, she needs your help. She needs us."

Leon lay in a pummeled, bloodied mess behind them. Taige fought a little more, squirming, but Cullen used his body to block Taige's view of her uncle, and that seemed to break through the rage, reaching the woman inside. Her breath wheezed in and out of her lungs. Slowly, cautiously, he reached up and cupped her face, forced her to look at the girl. "She needs us, Taige."

The girl. Taige blinked and stared at the girl. *Yeah, focus on the girl.* The girl's eyes stared at her, but Taige knew the girl saw nothing. She'd retreated into the safety of her mind. Whether or not she'd ever come out was something that only time would tell. *At least she's alive . . .* But Taige knew there could easily come a time when the girl didn't share that sentiment.

Taige had experienced brutality at the hands of her uncle before, but never anything like this. Not in her worst nightmares. "We need to get her up," she said, her voice hoarse. It hurt to speak, hell, it hurt to even breathe. She pulled the phone from her belt and punched in 911. After calling for an ambulance and the police, she disconnected and then called Jones.

The team would be there in another fifteen minutes, and after he told her that, Jones laid into her for going in alone. Just as before, she glanced at Cullen and told her boss, "I'm not alone."

"One of these days, you'll find yourself in a mess that we can't get you out of," Jones said. He had the same tone that a principal would have used on a recalcitrant student, and Taige cared for it about as much as that student would have.

"Kiss ass, Jones," she said sourly, and then she disconnected before he could start demanding some kind of status report.

The status is that my sorry, son-of-a-bitching uncle is still breathing. Fighting to control her rage, she glanced back at Leon again. He still lay on the ground, moaning, his breath whistling through his busted nose.

At the moment, he was unconscious. More than anything, she wanted to pull the Glock at her side, level it at his head, and pump him full of lead. She wanted it with an intensity that scared her.

Hatred—finally, Taige understood the hatred that had driven him, and it was that knowledge alone that kept her from pulling her gun. She wanted him dead too much to do it herself.

"Watch him."

Cullen smirked. "Great idea, baby. Like I don't want to finish him off myself."

Despite herself, she laughed. "Kind of like asking the wolf to guard the sheep," she murmured as she approached the girl, staying where she could see the girl's face. That way, the girl could see her—in theory. But she was lying there, still, motionless, her eyes not even tracking Taige's movements. "God help her," she whispered softly. "It's okay, sweetheart. He can't hurt you again. He can't hurt you . . ."

Nothing Taige did or said had any effect. The girl didn't so much as blink when Taige touched her, and if it wasn't for the warmth of her flesh and the blood still trickling from the open wounds on her back, Taige would have been checking for a pulse. Her pupils were mere pinpricks, and her breathing came in short, shallow pants. "She's in shock," she muttered grimly.

Damn it.

She didn't how what in the hell do for her other than free her. Rolling her onto her back would be best, so Taige could elevate the girl's feet, but her back looked like raw meat, crisscrossed with so many open, bleeding cuts. "Can you carry her out of here?" Taige asked quietly. The ambulance would be there soon, but Taige just couldn't let her remain on the table another second. She went to work on the thick leather straps, freeing the ones at her waist and thighs first. The blood on the straps and the tears in Taige's eyes made it slow going.

"Should we move her?" Cullen asked softly.

Her voice shook as she answered, "I don't know. But we can't leave her here." She finally got the first strap undone and went to work on another. Cullen moved around to the girl's feet and started working the ankle straps.

The girl finally made a sound, a soft, broken little moan. Taige wanted to touch her, reassure her somehow. But she had a feeling that anything she did would make it worse. So instead of touching her, she murmured, "It's okay, sugar. He can't hurt you."

She finished the wrist strap and looked up to see Cullen freeing the last ankle strap. Looking into his eyes was like looking clear into hell. There was rage there, something deep and fathomless. His eyes burned into Taige's, and she watched as he slowly turned his head, his eyes seeking out Leon's battered body.

Leon stirred.

A feral snarl twisted Cullen's features, and she watched as the air around him turned dark and red with rage. The power of his fury broke through his natural mental shields, and it pushed her back a step or two. Worse, it fueled her own rage. Her vision went red, blood roared in her ears, and nothing mattered more than getting her hands on Leon and tearing him apart.

Nothing but the girl behind her.

A second, pathetic whimper broke through her fury. It had little effect on Cullen. It was her turn now; he'd broken through her rage only seconds ago, and now she'd have to reach him. As much as she hated it, she reached out, laid a hand on his arm as he paced forward, intent on Leon. "Cullen, I can't carry her."

Her soft voice reached him, although Cullen wouldn't have thought anything could get through to him at that point. Not when he had a vicious, gut-wrenching need to maim and kill. In theory, he understood primal rage. He'd written about it in his books, and he thought he even understood it after what had happened to his mother. This went deeper than that, though. Deeper than anything he'd ever felt. He wanted to shrug Taige's hand aside and get to work, but instead, he turned his head and looked at her.

That one look, and then he could kill Leon.

But looking at her now, it was like time disappeared, and they once more stood in his room on the day she'd come to him after his mother had been killed. She'd tried to reach out to him. Tried to help him, and he in return had done something that had nearly destroyed them both.

His eyes closed. He felt his feet moving, and he looked up, found himself moving to the girl. Get her safe first. That had to come first.

Fate was a bitch. An ugly, nasty bitch. Sliding his arms under Leon's latest victim, he saw the movement out of the corner of his eye. He saw it but couldn't make sense of it until the cracking sound filled the room. He heard Taige's scream, turned his head, and watched as Leon stood, his whip in hand, an unholy light of evil joy in his eyes. He raised the whip again. Taige was on her hands and knees, still blinded by the shock of the pain. Cullen could *feel* that pain. It had knocked the breath out of her, and she was still reeling from it, couldn't see through it.

But Cullen could. Time slowed down to a crawl, and he could see the braided tail of the whip moving through the air. Instinct placed him between Taige's body and Leon, his forearm lifted. Adrenaline numbed the pain as the whip curled around his arm, twining like a snake. Leon tried to jerk the whip back, but Cullen reached up with his other hand and jerked, pulling with a savage strength. The whip flew out of Leon's hand, and Cullen caught the butt of it.

It was heavy, weighted. Closing his fist around one end, he used the other end as a club, striking Leon square in the temple. He fell like a stone, and Cullen moved to Taige. She still crouched on her hands and knees. Under the whip's lash, her shirt had torn, and he could see the long, ugly mark. The skin had split, and blood welled, trickling down her sides. Already the edges of the wound were swollen and bruised. "I'm going to kill him," Cullen swore.

Taige wheezed, fought to speak through the pain. Dear God, it was unreal. How had that girl lived through this? "Get . . . her . . . first."

Through the sheen of tears, she saw him look back at Leon. Taige shook her head. "Damn it, get her out!" Gritting her teeth, she shoved herself to her feet. Adrenaline had started to course through her body, and she could breathe through the pain now— barely. She swayed and had to lock her knees to remain upright. But she'd be damned if she went down again. Jaw clenched, she pulled her gun and looked Cullen square in the eye. His turquoise eyes bore into hers, burning with that bloodthirsty, frenzied rage. "The girl, first," she said hoarsely.

Then, if Cullen wanted to rip Leon apart limb from limb, she wouldn't give a hot damn. She'd even help hide the body.

She swayed on her feet, her hand clenched around the butt of her Glock. She clenched it so hard, the metal bit into her flesh. She focused on the gun, the weight of it, the solidity. Fantasized about lifting it, leveling it between Leon's eyes, and pulling the trigger.

Taige sensed the team's arrival before she heard them, and she made the deadly mistake of looking away from Leon. The old man's rage must have given him speed, because she hadn't ever seen him move like that, with venomous, deadly accuracy. She saw the gun in his hand, although where it had come from, she didn't know. The fiery injury on her back had slowed her reflexes, and she couldn't lift her own weapon in time.

She heard the shot echo through the basement, felt the pain explode through her.

Then everything else ceased to exist.

*   *   *

"No!" The word tore from Cullen as he watched Leon lift the gun. Yes. Fate was a serious bitch. Instinct had demanded he kill Leon, but the last time he'd let his rage dictate his every move, he'd shattered Taige. This time, he'd let her reach him, let her convince him to get the girl out, and because he hadn't listened to his own instincts, she was going . . .

No.

No.

He watched her fall, saw her eyes go wide.

Until he had his arm around Leon's neck, Cullen didn't even realize he'd moved. He jerked the older man off his feet with a savage strength brought on by rage. He felt bone crack, felt Leon go limp. Then he let go. Leon's gun had fallen from limp fingers, and Cullen, without thinking, stooped, grabbed it, and then turned, aimed between Leon's wide, unseeing eyes, and pulled the trigger.

There'd be no getting up this time.

Dropping the gun, he ran to Taige's side and fell to his knees. Her eyes were open, wide and glassy, her breathing coming in irregular, harsh gasps. Blood trickled from the corner of her mouth. Instinctively, Cullen covered the wound in her chest with his hand and pressed down against the flow of blood. The agony slicing through him was unlike anything he'd ever experienced. Cullen understood loss.

But this wasn't loss.

This was death, hers and his own. If she died, she was going to take the better part of his soul with him. "Don't die, baby," he whispered. "Please don't die."

As Taige's breathing slowed, as her heart faltered under his hands, he died a little inside. "God, please," he prayed, begging. "Don't take her now. Not now."

* * *

IT hadn't ever felt like this, Taige mused as the gray wrapped around her. Usually it was warm, almost comforting as it guided her along the paths she must follow. Even when it came on hard and strong, it wasn't ever cold. It wasn't painful. And always, she was filled with a certainty of what she had to do.

But now? Although there was a new path before her, there was nothing comforting about it. Somehow she knew some ugly piece of hell didn't await her at the end of this journey, but she didn't want to go.

It was cold, and as she drifted along, it grew colder. Darker. Behind her, she felt something warm. Then she heard a voice. His voice—the warmth of him, the strength of him. Cullen—

He called her name, and she could feel him trying to reach her. If a person's will alone could anchor somebody, his would do it.

But then, right when she found the strength to reach for him, he was pulled away. Something intruded. Others came. She heard their voices, felt their presence. Chaotic confusion. More voices. God, the pain. It ate at her. Tore at her, ripped into her with jagged teeth and claws. The gray, as cold as it was, was better than this pain, and she retreated back into it, even though she could faintly hear Cullen's voice, even though she could feel the presence of friends crowding around and reaching out to her.

She drifted. It was cold, but it wasn't that bad. Better than the pain. Much better.

* * *

"WE'RE losing her!"

Cullen heard the paramedic's grim voice, and he fought his way through the medics and the federal agents. When Jones's team had shown up, the agents had been forced to tear Cullen away so the medics could get to her.

But now, nothing in hell was going to keep him away. He fought free, and when one of the men tried to grab him, he struck out. Pain flared up his arm, but he never noticed as he ran to Taige. Falling to his knees by her head, he cupped her face, bent down, and kissed her.

They tried to pull him again, but he wouldn't leave. "Come on, baby. Don't do this to me," he pleaded, pressing a desperate kiss to her cold lips.

"Sir, you have to get away. Let us . . ."

"No." The woman's voice was strong and certain. "Damn it, give him a minute. I can feel her."

Cullen didn't even have the time to be grateful. The medics

argued, but when the woman refused to back down, the rest of the agents gathered around, keeping them from Cullen.

"Taige, you're stronger than this," he whispered, cradling her face. Dipping his head, he buried his face in her hair. Through the stink of blood and sweat, he could still smell her, soft and sweet. Her skin was cold, frighteningly so. She was . . . *No. Don't think it*. He couldn't think it.

"Don't leave me, Taige. God, I love you so much."

* * *

CULLEN had gotten used to the incessant noise of the hospital equipment. He even took comfort in the high-pitched little beep. It was strong, it was regular. Taige's heart continued to beat. The trip to the hospital was one that was going to live on in his nightmares. Twice, they'd lost her.

Twice, they had been forced to shock her heart back into beating, and each time it had happened when one of the medics tried to force Cullen to give them a little room. The second time they'd been forced to revive her, Cullen had looked at one of the medics and said, "You want me to move again, you're going to have to kill me to do it."

That had been three days ago. Although the medical staff hadn't been forced to revive her since arriving at the hospital, she continued to linger in a coma.

Cullen and four of the agents on the scene had donated blood. She hovered between life and death, and Cullen was right there with her.

"Daddy?"

He heard that soft, hesitant little voice, and he looked up, felt his heart squeeze in his chest as Jillian peered into the room. Cullen's dad stood behind her. They both heard the nurse's quiet voice, and Robert went to intercept the nurse as the woman said, "Sir, there are no children allowed in here."

Cullen tuned out the sound of his father's cajoling voice and reached out a hand to Jillian. "Hey, baby."

She glanced at Taige, her eyes huge and round in her face. "She looks different."

Yeah, she did. Taige's skin had a strange grayish cast, but she looked better today than she had yesterday. At least that was what he told himself. "She's just sick, darlin'. She's going to be just fine." Silently, he added, *She has to be.*

Jillian nodded. She glanced back at her grandfather and then at Cullen. "Granpa didn't want to bring me up here. But I had to see you."

"I'm glad you came, Jilly." He forced himself to smile. "You want to say something to her?"

"Will she hear me?"

Blowing out a sigh, he murmured, "I think she does. I hope she does." Managing a faint grin, he murmured, "I sure do hope she hears me, because I've been talking to her a lot."

Jillian eye's widened. "You never talk a lot." Nervous, she edged a little closer to the bed and then reached up, brushed her fingers over Taige's arm. It was the only part of her visible that wasn't covered with tubes, bandages, or wires. "She helped you find the bad man, didn't she?"

"Yeah." His throat went tight, and his voice was barely more than a whisper. "Yeah, she did."

With a solemn nod, Jillian said, "Now he can't hurt anybody again, right?" Without waiting for an answer, she shimmied a little closer to Taige's head. Cullen reached out for her to pull her away from the machines, but she didn't bump into either of them, and she carefully sidestepped all the tubes and wires. "Thank you, Taige."

* * *

TAIGE heard that soft little whisper. It brushed across her subconscious like a soft breeze, warm and comforting.

She thought she recognized the voice, but it was so damn hard to think. So hard to feel, so hard to even force herself into some state of semiawareness. She'd been fighting to wake for what seemed like ages, and she just couldn't do it.

Taige couldn't open her eyes, couldn't even move. She wanted to, but any time she gained the strength to reach out, exhaustion rose up and pulled her away before she could make contact. The weight of that exhaustion killed her purpose, and she'd have to rest before she had the energy to try again.

There were people all around her, but the only one she was really aware of was Cullen. He'd been there since the beginning. When she'd felt herself fading away, it had been Cullen who pulled her back. A few times, something or somebody had tried to take him away, and she'd felt her hold on reality slip again, felt herself falling away.

He'd forced himself back to her side each time, and she knew if it wasn't for him, she would have drifted away altogether, off into the gray, until she grew smaller and smaller and then just faded entirely. Cullen wouldn't let her, though. All around her, she could feel his strength, smell his skin, hear his voice.

She needed to touch him, though. Needed to . . .

* * *

EVER since Taige had been brought to the hospital, bleeding and hovering near death, he had lived on catnaps, vending machine coffee, and stale sandwiches. It had been exactly seven days since he had stood by, helpless, as her uncle shot her. Seven days since Cullen had killed a man with his bare hands.

His eyes were gritty with exhaustion, his entire body clumsy with fatigue, and his stomach was so knotted up that he doubted he could keep a meal down should he try something beyond the stale sandwiches the hospital cafeteria specialized in.

Tired as he was, he wouldn't let himself sleep. He couldn't really sleep. Not until Taige woke up. He was terrified to leave her side for more than a couple of minutes. Couldn't do it. Although logically he knew that the danger was mostly over, he still couldn't tear himself away for longer than it took to go to the bathroom or take a quick shower.

He ate by her bed, he slept next to her, and when the nurses came in to care for her, he stood at her side and watched them like a hawk to make sure they didn't hurt her. After the first day, they'd given up trying to get him to give them some privacy. They'd argued and threatened to call security, but in the end, none of them pushed it beyond a lost argument.

One or two of the smarter nurses had started waiting until they knew he was either grabbing a sandwich or using the phone in the family lounge to call home so he could check on Jilly. While he was gone, they'd slip in, do their work in speed and silence, and when Cullen returned, Taige would be sleeping in fresh sheets with her bandages changed.

"You really should lie down."

Cullen, foggy and half out of it, didn't process what the nurse said until nearly a minute after she had said his name. She was young, pretty, and he suspected she was fresh out of college. Muffling a yawn, he just shrugged.

"What if I had a cot brought in?" she offered.

It wasn't the first time he'd been offered a cot. He started to make his normal refusal, but then he realized he was drifting off, even in the middle of trying to form some sort of coherent response. Shit, he did need a nap. A nap of the horizontal variety and not in that torture device of a chair. "Yeah." Before he could change his mind, he nodded again, "Yeah, I'll take a cot so long as they can put it in here. I'm not leaving her."

The nurse smiled. Her teeth flashed white against the darkness of her skin, and her eyes were bright with amusement. "You haven't left her side since they brought her up here. I didn't figure you were going to leave now."

A nap.

A real nap.

He leaned forward and closed his hand around Taige's. "You need to come on back now, Taige." It was early in the afternoon yet, but he figured he had less than an hour before Jones or one of the other jerk offs in the Bureau showed up. Jones was persistent. He showed up like clockwork every day at four, only moments after Jilly and Robert came by to bring him clothes. Cullen half suspected that Jones was following Jilly and her grandfather. Cullen knew damn well how persistent Jones had been getting with Jilly, and when he saw the bastard today, he was going to make sure Jones understood that it had to stop.

Just a quick nap, and he'd be ready to face all of it: the well-meaning, intrusive nurses, the impersonal doctors, the agents who came by singly or in small groups of two or three, not to mention Jilly and her grandfather. Ready to face another day that didn't really include Taige. The only contact he'd had with her was holding her hand or brushing her hair back from her face.

The nurses wouldn't let him help with anything. If he tried to so much as change her blanket, they showed up. He was starting to think the linen closet was bugged, and that's how they always knew when he was trying to either change a blanket or give her a pillow. Hell, even move the bed around a little. Granted, he didn't really need to do any damn thing, because the nurses were taking good care of her. Even Cullen couldn't fault their care. But just sitting there was driving him nuts.

The lack of sleep wasn't helping. The worry and lingering fear over seeing her go down, blood blossoming on the front of her shirt like a vicious rose—that was really driving him nuts. Every time he closed his eyes, he saw it again, but it was getting harder . . . and harder . . .

It dropped down on him like a meteor crashing to earth, fast and unstoppable. One minute he was thinking about that quick nap and how much good it might do him, and the next, he was under. Arms folded across his chest, legs stretched out and crossed at his ankles, his chin tucked against his chest, Cullen slept.

Out in the hallway, the nurse paused at the door, the supplies she needed for rebandaging her patient's various injuries already out and ready on the treatment cart she pushed in front of her. The sight of the man, though, sound asleep in that damned uncomfortable chair had her stopping in her tracks. She heard the squeak of wheels behind her and looked up to see one of the housekeeping staff pushing a folded-up cot down the hallway. She held up a hand, and he stopped. "Just leave it there," she said, keeping her voice low.

The guy finally crashes, there was no way she was going to wake him up just yet. Wasn't like the cot would be much more comfortable than the chair, anyway. She glanced at her chart, gauged the time. Ms. Branch's wounds were healing well enough, and she could hold off an hour before she changed the bandages.

That hour wasn't much. This man looked like he needed a

week horizontal. During shift changes, the nurses had talked about their unusual ICU patient. They didn't get too many patients come in with a collapsed lung, an injury from a whip, and an escort that consisted of federal agents and a best-selling fantasy author.

A bestselling author who hadn't left the patient's side for more than ten minutes at a stretch, and then only to get food or call and check on his daughter. A bestselling author who was currently sleeping by the patient's bed and, to her knowledge, this was the first time he'd done more than catnap for five or ten minutes.

This was no catnap. Already his chest was moving in the slow, steady rhythm of deep sleep. Since he hadn't woken up at the sound of the cot's squeaky arrival, she figured he wasn't going to wake up for a little while, not until he rested some or she woke him up.

No, an hour wasn't much, but it was the best she could do right now. Too bad he hadn't waited until after she'd changed the dressings on Ms. Branch's wounds. He could have managed two or three hours before shift change.

* * *

EVEN before Cullen opened his eyes, he knew he was dreaming.

Instead of the steady beep of hospital machinery, he heard the crash of waves into the sand. Instead of the cool air that smelled faintly of antiseptic, he could smell the ocean and the scents of summer: hot sand and sunscreen.

Yeah, he knew he was dreaming, but still he panicked. The sound of the heart monitors was the only thing that kept him sane right then, and not hearing them was enough to have his own heart speeding up in panic.

Body braced, he opened his eyes.

And then he sagged.

Taige.

She stood staring out over the blue green waters of the Gulf, her arms crossed over her chest, her hair blowing back from her face. Incongruously, she still wore one of those ugly, utilitarian hospital gowns. It flapped around her body, a body that was too thin and battered.

The sight of her was the most beautiful thing he'd ever seen, and once more, the panic inside him welled up.

Shit—she wasn't . . .

Stop it! She hadn't survived those first hours only to die now. Still, when he finally opened his mouth to speak, he had to clear his throat twice, and his voice cracked on him. "Taige?"

For a second, she didn't respond, and then she turned her head and looked at him over her shoulder. "Hey." A faint grin curled her lips. "You look like hell."

"You look beautiful." And he meant it. It didn't matter that her hair was tangled, that she still had that dull, grayish cast to her skin, or that she looked like she needed a month's worth of decent, home-cooked meals. She looked absolutely beautiful to him.

Her grin spread into a full-out smirk, and she laughed. Plucking her hospital gown away from her chest, she gave it a disgusted look. "Yeah, I bet. I look ready to walk down a runway, don't I?"

That wry, self-deprecating humor finally managed to break through the ice surrounding him. He crossed the sand in four long strides and grabbed her, not thinking about the injuries that had put her in the hospital bed. These were dreams—sort of. Whatever was physically hurting her didn't really exist here.

Pain of the nonphysical variety was different, though. Cullen knew it for a fact, because he had a very real, very huge ache centered square in his chest, taking up the void that had been his heart ever since she'd gotten shot. "My God," he muttered, burying his face in her hair. "I've been so damn scared . . ."

He wouldn't say it, though. Saying it made it real. Until she actually woke up and talked to him, that was more reality than he could handle. Even after she woke up, he suspected that would be too much.

She cuddled into him, her hands curling into his T-shirt. "I'm okay."

"You're in a damn coma. That's pretty damn far from okay," Cullen gritted out. Finally able to touch her, even in a dream, he hadn't thought he'd pull away from her so quick, but he did, leaning back just enough so he could see her face. "You died on us three damn times."

"I know." That plain, simple statement froze him clear to down to his feet. "Close to four, I think." She reached up, touched her fingers to his mouth. "But I heard you. You kept calling me, and you just wouldn't let go."

Wrapping his arms around her, he said, "I'm not going to, either. Ever. So you might as well wake up."

He pressed his forehead against hers and whispered, "Come on, Taige. You need to wake up, baby."

"I'm trying . . ." She grimaced as she spoke, and then she started to fade away.

In his arms. As he was holding her. She faded, growing more and more insubstantial until he couldn't see her, feel her, smell her—although he did hear her.

I love you . . .

*   *   *

AT first, when Cullen woke up, he wasn't certain what it was that had disturbed him. His head had that muffled, disconnected thing going on that came from far too little rest, and he knew however long he'd been out, it hadn't been long enough.

But then he heard it again. Something soft.

Something faint.

Something he'd been praying for, pretty much nonstop, for the past four days.

A sound. From Taige.

Her lips were moving. Her lids were still closed, but her lips were moving. He couldn't understand what she was saying at first, and the words had no real sound to them. At least no coherent sound.

He was out of the chair so damn fast, he tripped over his feet and ended up on his knees beside the bed. Apt enough, since she'd been knocking him to his knees on a regular basis for a good, long time. He reached out, folding her cold hand between his. She wasn't as cold . . . was she?

She whispered again, her lips forming the same words, and finally, he understood what she was saying: "I love you."

"Taige?"

Her lids flickered. A faint smile curved her lips. And between his hands, hers moved, her fingers sliding between his. She squeezed, oh so faintly. And then, a soft sigh escaped. She fell silent, as though that simple movement had drained her.

But for the first time since she'd been hurt, Cullen breathed just a little easier.

TWELVE

A WEEK after that, seven days after she'd roused from her coma and smiled at Cullen, they finally let her leave the hospital. She didn't remember smiling at him, talking to him or the doctors, the nurses, Dez. Nothing, not until a day or two later when she fully woke up.

Taige did remember the dream, though. Just like most of her dreams with Cullen, it had been almost painfully real. But it hadn't been bittersweet. No, that dream had been different.

It had left her hopeful.

Hope wasn't something she had wasted a lot of time on over the past few years, and letting herself feel it now was more than a little bit terrifying. Fortunately, the drugs clouding her brain, the pain that managed to bleed through those painkillers, and her very overpowering desire to put some miles between herself and the hospital all combined to keep her from dwelling on much of anything else for too long.

Right now, the only thing Taige really needed to dwell on was the art of breathing. Since waking in agony to find tubes shoved in her chest, she realized that breathing was a lot more complicated than the typical person realized.

The window was down. It was hotter than hell outside, but she needed the feel of the air on her face, the wind moving through her hair. Cullen sat next to her, speeding down Highway 180. It didn't seem like he could go more than a minute without glancing over at her. "Are you okay?" he asked. It was only the tenth time he'd asked since they'd pulled out of the hospital parking lot. And that was a huge improvement over the first day or two after she woke up. Then she hadn't been able to take a breath or blink without him asking.

But she didn't mind.

She was awake for him to ask, right?

But Taige did sincerely hope that he wouldn't still be asking her that every ten minutes or so for too much longer. Of course, it would be easier to lie to him if she could move without hurting, if she could breathe without hurting. She'd always healed pretty fast, but she'd never been hurt this badly before.

With all her heart, Taige hoped she wasn't ever hurt this badly again. The stitches in her chest itched, her muscles hurt, her bones, breathing. Just breathing took some effort right now. She had to concentrate and make sure she didn't breathe too deeply, because if she took regular breaths, it hurt. Yeah, it was an art, trying to breathe just deeply enough that she managed to get enough air, but not so deeply that she made those abused muscles and healing tissues and bones ache.

Logically, she knew she shouldn't have left the hospital yet. They'd only been able to take the chest tubes out a few days ago, and the lung specialist wasn't too thrilled with her lung function either. The fact that they had let her leave the hospital was nothing short of a miracle.

The doctors hadn't wanted to let her go, but she'd made up her mind that she wasn't going to stay in that damn hospital another day. Even if she had to walk out on her own two feet. So what if she collapsed before she made it to the parking lot?

Fortunately, Cullen had offered a compromise. She could leave the hospital, go home, and a private duty nurse would visit her twice a day for the first few days. Cullen had said he'd be staying with her. It wasn't like she'd be alone, and she'd be a hell of a lot more comfortable if she was some place—okay, any place—other than the hospital.

She wanted to go home, and if that meant promising to eat three square meals a day that included lots of leafy green stuff, chugging down sixty-four ounces of water, and popping vitamins, then she'd do it. So long as she got to go home.

Then Cullen drove right past her house. She glanced at the gravel drive that disappeared into the trees and then back at him. "Cullen . . ."

But before she could ask where they were going, he did turn.

Her heart skipped a beat or two and, forgetting herself, she gasped. Once she'd recovered from the pain that caused, she blinked through her tears and stared at the house in front of her.

It had been on the market for nearly two years. It was beautiful, custom-built from the ground up, and the price tag was a little high. But the For Sale sign was missing from the little patch of grass by the mailbox. "What are we doing here?"

He glanced at her. "I bought it."

"You bought it."

He slid her another glance and then looked away. Nervous. Cullen was nervous. There was no mistaking that look. "You bought it."

No response.

"Why?"

His eyes narrowed. "Because your house doesn't have room for me and Jillian, and I don't plan on letting you out of my sight for a while. If you don't like it, too bad."

"Exactly how long is a while?"

For a minute, he didn't answer, and she started to think he was ignoring her . . . or maybe he hadn't heard her. But then, in a quiet voice, he said, "The rest of my life sounds pretty good to me."

The sheer, intense emotion in his voice was enough to have her eyes start to burn from tears, her throat go all tight, and her heart swell. Unsure of how to respond to that, Taige didn't respond at all.

They pulled to a stop in front of the house, and for a minute, they just sat there staring at it. The walls were stone, giving it an old-world look, and there were a lot of windows—really big windows—sparkling in the early morning sun. The door was painted a bright red, and as they watched, it opened, and a small girl came barreling through, running down the steps with a huge smile on her pretty little face.

For a second, Taige almost didn't recognize her.

She hadn't ever seen that girl with a smile on her face. Not once. In reality, Taige knew she'd only physically seen the girl twice. Once when they'd found her in the cabin and then once in the hospital while the girl was in a drug-induced sleep. In all the dreams, all of the weird little visions that had come to Taige over the past twelve years, Jillian Morgan never smiled in them. Not even once. Of course, Jillian hadn't had many reasons to smile during those visions. In truth, no reason.

There was no logic to life, Taige knew. There was no logical way Taige could have dreamed about this girl before she even existed. No way she could have spent so many years searching for a girl who hadn't needed Taige until less than a month ago. Logic had no place in this mess because, as improbable as it all was, it was real. It had all happened.

Cullen glanced at Taige, and she forced a smile. "Go on. I'm fine." God knows, he'd spent so much time at Taige's side over the past few weeks, and that pretty little girl must have missed him something awful. He climbed out of the car and caught up with Jillian just as she reached the driveway. Taige watched as Cullen threw Jillian up into the air and then caught her close in a hug. Tears misted her eyes as she saw the two of them together.

Jillian smiled down at her dad and brought her hands up, cupping his face between them and then leaning down to kiss him. There were no words between them, but there was a love so deep, so strong that Taige guessed the father and daughter really didn't need words.

Then Jilly turned her head and looked into the truck. Her eyes landed on Taige's face, and her smile faded away.

A fist wrapped around Taige's heart. The poor baby. She'd gone through ten different kinds of hell, and seeing Taige was going to remind her of that. This wasn't going to work. Yeah, she needed somebody with her for a few days because she wasn't sure she could walk from a bed to a toilet without help, but she'd call Dez. Dez would come and probably be grateful for a break.

Jillian squirmed in Cullen's arms, and he put the girl down. Taige figured Jillian wanted to go inside, get away from her and all the memories that Taige's presence had to bring back. But instead, she walked up and climbed through Cullen's open door, onto the leather seat, until she could crouch on the console like a little cat. "You still look sick," Jillian said with the brutal, frank honesty of a child.

Forcing herself to smile, Taige said, "I'll be fine." An awkward silence started to spread between them, and desperate to keep that from happening, Taige asked softly, "How are you doing?"

Jillian grinned. "I'm great. We got a beach. A real beach. And it's *ours*." She cocked her head, and the fat, inky curls fell over one thin shoulder. "You like the beach?"

"I love the beach. I live on the beach, too." Her gaze slid to the huge, sprawling house, and she added wryly, "But I doubt it's as big as your beach is."

"Can you swim?"

"Like a fish."

"Can you teach me?"

Taige glanced at Cullen as he approached, staring at Jillian and Taige with intense eyes. Her heart pounded in her throat as she forced the words out. "We'll have to see." She was a little floored that Jillian even wanted to speak with her.

That thought had barely formed in her head when Jillian leaned a little closer and whispered, "Of course I wanna talk to you. You're my friend." She smiled sweetly and reached up, laid a hand on Taige's face. "I'd miss not talking to you."

Now Taige couldn't speak. She couldn't force the words, and it took several tries and a couple of deep breaths before she managed it. "You remember talking to me?"

Jillian rolled her eyes, and for a minute she looked exactly like what she should be: a child just hovering on the stage of prepubescence, convinced she knew every bit as much as any adult ever could. "Of course I remember talking to you." Then she glanced back at her dad. "I think you're going to have to make her get out of the car. She's scared."

With that, she pulled back and took off running back up the driveway.

Hardly able to speak around the knot in her throat, Taige murmured, "She shouldn't have to see me, Cullen. It can't be good for her."

He didn't respond at first as he circled the truck and opened the door for her. He slid a hand under her legs, helping her shift her lower body around, and then he cupped his hands on her hips. But instead of helping her slide to the ground, he stood there, holding her just like that as he said, "You're wrong." He glanced at the house and murmured, "Jillian's a serious kid. She always has been. She almost never smiles, and she hardly ever talks to anybody unless they talk to her first. She smiled at you; she talked to you. She said you're her friend."

Taige shook her head. "She doesn't even know me, Cullen. Hell, she's just a kid."

"Yeah, but she's my kid, and I know her." He dipped his head, putting his face on a level with hers. "You know why I brought you here. You know why I bought this house. You know what I want, and I don't even have to explain it. I will, because we need to put things out on the table and talk them through. But if you're nervous about that, don't use Jilly as a reason to pull away from me."

The smile wobbled on her lips, and she just barely managed a whisper as she said, "You're awful damn cocky."

"No." He shook his head, still staring at her with intense, serious eyes. "I'm just determined. There's a difference." He glanced at the house once more and then back at her. "You know what I want, Taige. I'm not giving up on us. But if you want distance, this is your one chance. You come in that house with me, and it's settled as far as I'm concerned. You're mine. I won't let you go. Not ever."

Amused despite herself, she grinned at him. "Is this what you call laying it out on the table?"

He grinned back and brushed her hair away from her face. "Well, I'd planned on waiting awhile, seeing as you're supposed to be resting and recovering, but then you started looking skittish on me."

She lifted a brow. "I got skittish?"

His hands smoothed down her hips. Through the loose cotton of her pants, she could feel the heat of his hands. An answering heat flickered inside, and she dropped her gaze to stare at his mouth. It felt like it had been ages since he'd kissed her. Ages since he'd held her.

A groan rumbled out of him, and the hands on her hips went tight. "Don't look at me like that, baby. We can't even think about it for a while yet."

"Thinking doesn't hurt me," she said hoarsely.

"Maybe not. But it will hurt me, especially if you decide you're not ready to walk into that house with me."

She started to lean forward, but the pain radiating through her chest froze her in place. So instead, she lifted a finger and hooked it in the neck of his shirt, tugging him closer. Pressing her lips to his, she murmured, "I've been ready for that for years, Cullen. I just didn't think it would ever happen."

She was talking about a lot more than just going into his house with him, but he knew that. There would be plenty of time to talk it out later.

EPILOGUE

"You look gorgeous," Dez said from the doorway.

Taige looked up and met her friend's gaze in the mirror. Then she looked back at her own reflection. She didn't look bad, she guessed. In the month since she'd been discharged from the hospital, she'd put on some of the weight she'd lost over the years, and she actually saw something beside skin, muscle, and bone when she looked in the mirror. She still had all her scars, but Taige was trying hard not to pay them any attention.

The most obvious scar was the one on the right side of her chest, a fairly neat little wound that was still red and puckered. The thin scars from the drainage tubes were a lot less noticeable, and she knew they'd fade even more with time.

The dress she'd chosen covered those scars and still managed to be sexy and feminine. Everything a bride's dress should be. The longer, thinner scar on her back wasn't completely hidden, but

Taige had no plans of hiding away every scar she'd acquired in her lifetime. It wasn't like Cullen would let her, anyway.

"I can't believe this is real," she said, more to herself than anyone else.

Stepping into the room, Dez closed the door behind her and then crossed over to stand at Taige's shoulder. "It's real, sugar. And you deserve it one hundred percent." She grinned, a wide, wicked grin, and winked. "But if you wanna take off running, I'll stand in for you. That man of yours is something else. Those eyes of his . . ." She rolled her eyes and pressed a hand to her chest. "Talk about intense."

Narrowing her eyes, Taige said, "Whatever you're thinking . . . just stop. I'd hate to kill my only bridesmaid right before the wedding."

Dez laughed. "Girl, you are so gone over on this guy." There was a knock at the door, and Dez went to answer, stepping aside to let Jillian come in.

Jillian had on a blue dress she'd picked out, and she already had her white basket looped over her arm. Faintly, Taige could smell the fragrant, sweet flower petals held inside the white wicker.

Taige hadn't really wanted a formal wedding or anything, but somebody had mentioned *flower girl*, and Jillian's eyes had widened. Unable to deny the girl something she obviously wanted, Taige had decided against trying to talk Cullen into a simple civil ceremony at the courthouse.

It hadn't taken any time to fall in love with Jillian. It might have taken years to find her, but Taige knew in her heart that Jillian was hers—her daughter. Every bit as much as hers as she would have been if Taige had been the one to carry Jillian inside her and give birth to her. "You look beautiful, angel," Taige said with a smile, turning on her stool to look at Jillian as Robert escorted the child inside.

Jillian grinned, her nose crinkling. "You, too."

Taige glanced down at her dress, still feeling a little self-conscious. Okay, a lot self-conscious. She could probably count on one hand how many times she'd worn a dress in the past ten years. And still have fingers left over. So the strapless, sarong confection made of silk and scattered with small, delicate pearls and sequins was definitely not something she was used to.

Jillian peered down at Taige's feet. "You really aren't wearing any shoes, are you?"

Taige shrugged. "I don't like to, anyway."

Cocking her head, Jillian stuck out her foot, studying the white straps of her sandals. "Can I go barefoot, too?"

"I wouldn't mind a bit."

While Jillian went to work on her sandals, Taige looked up at the man who was about to become her father-in-law. Robert hadn't aged as much as she would have thought, considering how much hell he'd been through the past twelve years. That many years could change people a lot, and the violent death of his wife, the kidnapping of his granddaughter—well, some people would have broken under it.

Robert hadn't, though. The lines around his eyes were deeper, and his blond hair had gone mostly silver, but he was still a handsome guy. He smiled at her, and she felt her heart melt a little. There was a lot of Cullen in that smile—or maybe it was more that Cullen had a lot of Robert inside him. They looked alike, and Taige figured if Cullen looked as good pushing sixty as Robert did, Taige was going to be beating the women away from her husband with a stick in thirty years.

"Jillian's right. You do look beautiful." He glanced around

and then nodded to the doorway that opened to a huge balcony. "Mind if we step outside for a few minutes?"

She followed him outside and moved over to the railing as Robert shut the door.

"Are you nervous?"

Taige grimaced. "Nervous? No. I don't know if nervous describes it."

"Any doubts?"

A smile spread across her face until she knew she was grinning like a fool. "Doubts? Not a one."

Robert nodded. "Good." He leaned his elbows on the wrought iron balcony railing and stared out over the beach.

Taige hadn't done much of anything for the wedding other than pick out her dress and tell Cullen she'd like to go to Europe for a honeymoon. Cullen had hired somebody to take care of the details, and right now, those people were attending to chores like setting up some chairs out on the beach and tables that scattered across the huge backyard.

"You know, the first time I saw you with Cullen, I knew you were the one for him," Robert said abruptly. He gave a faint smile and shrugged. "There was just something about the way he looked at you. Reminded me of how I felt when I looked at his mama back when we first got together. I knew he loved you; he never told me that, but he didn't have to."

Taige swallowed the knot in her throat and looked away so he wouldn't see her blinking back tears. Damn it, she'd gone and put makeup on and everything.

"After his mama died . . ." Robert's voice trailed, and he blew out a rough sigh. "It was a hard time for both of us, but I guess I don't need to tell you that. I know he did something or said something to hurt you. I saw you when you left, and I knew you were upset. I tried to catch you, but you were moving too quick, and you never even heard me."

He paused, and in the weighted silence, she knew he was waiting for some kind of response. She glanced at him, one quick sidelong glance, as she tried to figure out what he wanted her to say. "That was a long time ago, Robert," was all she could manage, and it sounded completely lame. Even if it was true—so what if it sometimes felt like yesterday?

"Yeah. It was a long time ago, but time doesn't undo harsh words or actions, now does it?"

Forgetting about her dress, her carefully done hair, and the makeup she'd worked on for nearly thirty-five minutes, Taige turned around and leaned against the iron balcony. She ran a hand back over her hair and then crossed her arms in front of her. "It's over, and it's done. Cullen wasn't in a good place right then. He needed somebody to lash out at, and I was there. Hell, he wasn't much more than a kid at the time, a kid who had just lost his mom in a very bad way. I'm not going to hold that kid's mistakes against the man he is now."

With a sad smile, Robert shook his head. "Cullen stopped being a kid the day we found out what had been done to his mama, Taige. But that isn't really what I wanted to talk to you about."

Perplexed, she stared at him. "If that's not it, then what?"

"Jillian." Robert slid his eyes back toward the French doors. Through the transparent, filmy gray curtains, they could see Jillian as she talked with Dez. Her face was animated, and showed a happy smile. "Have you . . . I don't know how to ask this. But have you been doing anything with her?"

Wary, Taige asked, "Anything like what?"

Robert laughed. "Honey, you and me are about to become family. Considering how you saved Jillian, what you did for her

with Cullen, as far as I'm concerned, you are family. Stop looking like you expect me to take a swing at you and start accusing
you of something awful." Then he shrugged. "Anything like—
hell, I don't really know how to explain. She's just different. Happier."

He glanced back at Taige, sadness creeping into his voice as
he murmured, "All her life, she's been different. It's made her so
unhappy." Looking back at Taige, Robert said quietly, "You know
what she can do."

"Yes."

"It's always interfered with her life. Kept her from being the
kid she should be. Even when that gift, or whatever you call it,
was quiet for months on end, she wasn't like other kids. But now
I see her laughing. I see her making friends around here, and I
see her talking to people like she's talking to your friend in
there." Robert glanced at her, and there was a world of emotion
in his eyes, emotions she suspected he couldn't even begin to
voice. "Jillian's never really had a childhood—not the kind she
should have had. And then, right when she should have been a
mess inside and still trying to cope with what happened, you
show up. The day Cullen brought you home from the hospital,
she was different."

Taige started to lie. Discussing her abilities with people wasn't
ever something she enjoyed doing. It was like breathing to her. A
person didn't go around explaining how they managed to take in
oxygen and blow out CO_2, did they? But Robert was right. They
were about to become family, and hiding what she'd been trying
to do with Jillian wasn't the way to start off any kind of relationship. "Jillian has next to no natural shields," she finally said.
"None. With her gift, she needs them. Otherwise, contact with
others can be overwhelming. It's almost like attention deficit—she

has too much stimulation coming in, and her way of dealing with it is to lock down, to shy away from others."

Pushing off the railing, she moved to the French doors, staring through the curtains at Jillian and Dez. "Without those shields, she's vulnerable. It's probably his thick head, but Cullen's not an easy psychic read. That might be why she never had to learn the intuitive skills a lot of kids like her—and me, I guess—had to learn."

Understanding dawned even before she started the actual explanation part. "You're shielding her. Or teaching her how?"

Shaking her head, Taige said, "Jillian isn't ready for that. What happened when . . ." She couldn't bring herself to say Leon's name, or even mention him. "What happened this summer did a lot more trauma than we can see, but she's hiding from that. I know Cullen's told you about the visits to the therapist. Right now, she's got herself in a mental cocoon over the kidnapping. Once she's handling this better, I can start working with her on shielding, but she's had enough stress for a while." With a bitter laugh, she added, "That girl has had enough stress to last her entire life."

Turning away, she stared back down at the beach. "I'm shielding her as best as I can. Part of her brain, I think, is trying to back away from her ability, anyway. Almost like some kind of cancer going into remission on its own. That's the only way I can think to explain. So it's making the shielding part pretty easy for me. As long as nothing tries to force it out, it's going to keep hiding until she's more ready to deal with it."

"And when will that be?"

Glancing at him, she said, "My personal opinion . . . never. She shouldn't have to deal with it." She heard one of the caterers call out, and suddenly, she panicked. Remembering her dress, her hair, her makeup, she craned her neck around, trying to see if she'd gotten anything on her butt. "Damn it!"

Robert laughed and moved around, checking the back of her dress. "Relax, honey, you're fine. You look beautiful." He moved around, inspecting her hair, and then he gave a wry smile. "Admittedly, I don't know much about a lady's hair other than my opinion on how it looks, but your hair looks fine."

He cupped her face in his hands, and Taige felt a familiar nervousness move through her. She hated to have people touching her. But Cullen's natural reticence must have come from Robert, because she didn't pick up anything from him. "Make him happy, Taige. And don't be afraid to let him make you happy. You both deserve it."

Her throat knotted. "Now, you keep going on like that, you're going to get me all weepy."

Robert laughed. Then he kissed her forehead. He started to say something else, but something happened before he could. Terror. Harsh and unrelenting. She recognized the source before her brain had even started to process it. Automatically, her hand went to her side, but she wasn't wearing her weapon.

Taige hadn't worn the Glock in more than a month, and she could remembering thinking she'd be perfectly content to never wear it again. Except in that instant.

Snarling, she moved away from Robert and strode inside. Taylor Jones was crouched in front of Jillian, a familiar look on his face. "Leave her alone, Jones," she said, her voice harsh and cold.

Taylor gave her a smile. "I'm not doing anything more than asking how she's been."

Not aloud, maybe. But Taylor knew how Jillian's gift worked. Taige knew the man too well to believe otherwise. The little mental pokes and prods were one of his training tools, tools that Taige remembered all too well. And the bastard was using them on a child.

"Don't hand me that, slick. Get the hell away from her."

Robert stood behind them, staring into the room with confusion. He hadn't heard the shrill yet silent cry for help that Taige had heard. Jillian stood frozen in front of Taylor, and she hadn't said a word. Off to the side, Dez stood glaring at Taylor with furious eyes. Feeling Taige's gaze, Dez glanced at her with apologetic eyes. "Sorry, Taige. I forgot he had such lousy manners. I never would have thought he'd bother a kid as young as Jillian."

Shaking her head, Taige said, "It's not your fault." Grimly, she added, "It's mine. I never thought he couldn't pretend to behave at my wedding."

"What's going on?" Robert demanded, moving between his granddaughter and Jones.

"I'm taking care of it," Taige said, her voice flat. Every protective instinct she had rushed to the fore, and when Taylor turned his charming, empty smile to Robert and Jillian, she could see the wheels spinning inside his head, knew he had plans to just bide his time.

Like hell, she thought. He reached out to pat Jillian on the head, some false, trite apology falling from his mouth, and Taige reacted without thinking.

"Don't touch her," she said. To back up her words, she touched him. But not with her hands. Her darker power, that gift that was akin to telekinesis except it only worked on living things, like people and animals, and right now, Taige had classified Taylor somewhere along the class of hyena or jackal. She was content to treat him as such. Using her mind, she wrapped a "hand" around his throat and cut off any attempt he made to speak. Without looking away from him, she said to Robert, "Why don't you and Jillian go on downstairs and wait for me?"

"Taige?"

She shook her head. "I'll be right along."

Dez left without asking, and without once meeting Jones's wide, shocked eyes. He clutched at his throat, trying to speak, but he didn't have the air. His face was rapidly turning a fascinating shade of red. "You'll leave her alone," Taige said clearly. "You will not speak to her. You will not project thoughts to her—and don't hand me the line that you're not psychic. You don't have to be psychic to think very loudly. You're not recruiting her, Jones. She's just a kid."

His eyes bulged in his face, and with a sulk, Taige let go and watched as he sucked in harsh, desperate gasps of air. "She won't always be a child, Taige."

"Maybe not, but for as long as she can, she's going to stay that way. And even when she's not a child, you're not coming after her the way you came after me."

Smoothing a hand down his dark gray suit, Taylor gave her an arrogant grin. He'd recovered fast enough, but that was Taylor Jones for you. The man was a born politician, even if he hadn't made those forays yet; he landed on his feet like a damn cat. "And if she decides she wants what I can offer?"

"A stressful, heartbreaking job?" she asked sarcastically. "Oh, however could she pass that up?"

Jones looked at her. For once, he dropped his company face, and she saw the intensity that she'd always suspected lurked under his surface. "The chance to use that gift to help mankind. Like you've done." He reached into his pocket and pulled out a piece of paper. Without even seeing it, she already knew what it was. The letter she'd sent to him telling him that she no longer wished to work for him in any way, formal or informal. "I don't care what this letter says, Taige. It's a compulsion, my dear. You can't help it; you *need* to help. She won't be any different."

Taige wasn't making any bets on that one way or the other, because she suspected he just might be right. "Regardless, it will be her choice."

"She's going to need help with her gift."

"Nothing that I can't handle." She heard a knock at the door, and when the door opened, and the wedding coordinator peeked inside, Taige breathed out a sigh of relief. A good reason to get the hell away from Jones before she punched him.

"It's time!" The woman—Taige had forgotten her name—bustled inside and circled around Taige, oblivious to the tension in the air.

Taige's gaze cut back to Taylor's face. "You pull a stunt like that around Jillian again, Jones, and you and me are going to go a couple rounds." With a mean smile, she said, "You've been riding a desk awhile now. You really don't want to go one on one with me." Lowering her voice, she leaned in and whispered, "I do fight dirty . . ." She reiterated her words with one hard, psychic surge that closed ever so briefly around Jones's throat.

Pulling back, she gave the wedding coordinator a wide smile. The woman had finally picked up on the tension between Taige and Jones, and her smile slipped a notch or two. "Is everything all right, dear?"

Glancing over her shoulder, she saw Jones reach up, rub his throat. He eyed her with just a little bit of wariness. Looking back at the wedding coordinator with a smug smile, she said, "It is now."

Watching as the two women left the room, Jones swallowed, and the resulting pain was enough to have him swearing in fury.

He bit it back, though, and just sighed, rocking on his heels and staring after Taige consideringly until she disappeared around a corner. She'd meant every word she said. Jones would have to be blind not to see the fierce protectiveness that had darkened her eyes.

He should have known she'd already comfortably settled into mama mode.

It was all right, though. Jillian's gift was strong. No, he wasn't a psychic, but he knew power. Jillian's mind was trying to protect her, trying to shut the gift down. It wouldn't work, though. And as long as Taige was around to control things if the girl's control wasn't up to snuff, he could wait.

He had plenty of time.

*   *   *

"I can't believe we just left without saying anything," Taige said.

Cullen grinned at her. "I can't believe I didn't get you out of there sooner."

The boat was docked at a private marina just a mile down the highway from Cullen's house. Just like the wedding, he'd handled the details of the wedding night on his own. Taige hadn't much cared what they did, as long as she was with him, but she'd expected a hotel or some private little cabin.

Not this slick, sweet little number that had been decorated with flowers, rose petals, and huge swathes of some gauzy, wispy fabric. Discreet little lights cast a faint golden glow, and overhead, the stars sparkled like a thousand diamonds in the sky.

"We going anywhere, Captain?" she asked brightly. All of a sudden, she felt really nervous—and shy. Now how stupid was that? It wasn't like they'd never been alone before. It wasn't like they'd never had sex before—although they hadn't ever done it on a boat.

They hadn't been together at all since before Taige had gotten shot and Cullen had killed her uncle. The few weeks that followed, she'd been healing up from her injuries. Then when she'd tried to start anything between them, he'd pulled back. The first time, he had laughingly said that she had to make an honest man out of him.

She hadn't taken him seriously and thought he was still worrying she wasn't up to it. But then he'd presented her with an engagement ring that next night over a romantic little picnic on the beach. Well, it had been intended to be romantic, but then Jillian had shown up, Robert trailing after her with an apologetic smile.

Cullen had proposed to her with his daughter playing in the sand ten feet away and his father crouched in the surf hunting for shells. She'd said yes without hesitating, and then she'd leaned in with a suggestive whisper. But he'd told her no.

Now, she was damn nervous, and the longer he waited, the worse it was going to get. Romance, nice as it was, just wasn't something she was comfortable with. But obviously Cullen didn't have a problem with it, she mused as he closed the distance between them and pulled her into his arms.

He moved her around to some unheard music, staring down at her like she was the only thing in his world. "You look nervous," he said.

"Wow. You're observant," she said sarcastically and then she winced. "Sorry. I sound like such a bitch. I'm just . . ."

Cullen laughed and said, "Nervous?" He didn't wait for an answer before he kissed her.

"Hmmmm . . . nervous about what?" she asked when he

lifted his head a few minutes later. Not nervous at all, just very, very hungry. Lowering her gaze to his lips, she wiggled her hips a little and said, "You must be good for my state of mind. I feel a lot better now."

He trailed a hand up her side, finding the hidden zipper in the side seam of her dress. "You're getting ready to feel even better than that, I promise."

"Better than this?" As he lowered his head to kiss her bare shoulder, she sighed dreamily. "Damn, does it get better than this?"

He tugged the zipper down and leaned back, watching as her dress fell to her waist, lingered on her hips for a second, and then fell the rest of the way to the deck. Under it, she wore nothing but a thong of ivory silk. The strapless bra the seamstress had tried to force her into had been sheer hell on her healing wounds, so she had gone without. The dress had been designed to work without a bra as well as with one, and Taige was much in favor of not wearing it.

His eyes slid down her face, fastening on her naked breasts. "A lot better," he muttered hoarsely. "It just got a lot better for me, at least." Bending his knees, he dipped down and slid an arm around her waist. When he straightened, her body weight was supported by the arm at her waist, and the hard length of him pressed against her front.

"You're wearing too many clothes," she whispered against his lips.

With a pained groan, he said, "Self-preservation. A wedding night should be romantic, right?"

Taige looked around at the flowers, the soft lights, the privacy of the beautiful little yacht. "I think you already hit the romance quota, Cullen. Besides . . . I don't need romance. I only need you."

His eyes flashed hot—so hot her skin seemed to sizzle.

Cullen stared down at her beautiful face and felt his heart clench. The sincerity in her eyes, the need that shook her voice, it was enough to lay a strong man low—and he wasn't feeling particularly strong in that moment.

"I love you," he muttered, sliding a hand up her naked back, over her neck, and then fisting it in her hair. His mouth covered hers as he carried her across the deck. He didn't make it far, though. His hands in her hair, his tongue in her mouth, it wasn't enough; he needed to be inside her body, inside her soul. Sinking to the deck, he took her with him. He lay down on his back and stared up at her. In the faint, golden light her skin gleamed. Her eyes met his, and a small, feline smile curled her lips as she straddled his hips and braced her weight with her hands on his chest.

The most perfect sight he'd ever seen in his life, Cullen knew. Until she reached up and pushed her hands through the sexy, tousled curls. Her breasts lifted with the movement, and Cullen's mouth went dry. "I need you," he whispered, sliding his hands up her torso, one stopping to cup her breast, the other curving over her neck and pulling her down to meet his lips.

"Then have me," she sighed against his mouth.

It only took seconds to free his cock, seconds to lift her up and then push inside her, and it was still too long. She was soft, silky wet, and strong, wrapping around his cock like a silken glove, and he needed it to last. Forever.

With his hands on her hips, he rocked up into her. Her lips clung to his, but neither of them closed their eyes. This moment—they'd been waiting for it for years, their entire lives, it seemed. Closing their eyes meant missing out on something, a sigh, a flutter of lashes—anything. Nothing could be missed, not then.

So they watched each other as they made love, Taige riding

him while he filled his hands with the sweet curve of her ass, her hips, her breasts. Everything that he could touch, he touched. Every part of her that he could taste without breaking contact, he tasted.

Like any perfect moment in life, the ending came rushing up way too soon, and Cullen gritted his teeth, tried to hold back. He could feel how close she was to coming, but still, he didn't want this first time over with so fast. His body, though, and his heart, they had other plans.

Sliding his hand between her thighs, Cullen touched her, traced the skin of her pussy where she was stretched so tight around him, then her clit. At the first touch on that hard little bud, she moaned. "Come for me, baby—I don't want come alone," he whispered, staring at her face, even though the sight of her hovering on the brink was almost more than he could handle.

She screamed out his name and came, hard, fast—once—then, as he bucked under her and started to drive upward, shuttling his cock in and out in hard, rapid succession, she came again. That time, they fell together.

And when it ended, they remained sprawled on the deck in the cooling night air, wrapped in each other's arms, together. A faint smile curved his lips as he stared up at the night sky.

Turning his head, he kissed her temple. "I've been waiting for just this. Seems like I've been waiting for it my whole life."

"Hmmmm . . . me, too." She lifted her head just an inch and gave him a smile that damn near stopped his heart. Happiness and satisfaction gleamed in her eyes, and she whispered in a teasing voice, "It's a good thing I'm a patient woman."

Cullen laughed. "Patient, my ass."

"Okay. Maybe not." Then she squirmed a little, pulling an

arm free. Cullen groaned in disappointment, but she reached up, touching her finger to his lips. "Maybe I'm not patient. But you were worth waiting for. You made me whole again, Cullen."

Kissing her finger, he whispered, "No. We made each other whole."